COURT OF HEATHENS

COURTS AND KINGS BOOK FOUR

K.A KNIGHT

Court of Heathens (Court and Kings).

Written by K.A. Knight:

Edited By Jess from Elemental Editing and Proofreading.

Proofreading by Norma's Nook.

Formatted by The Nutty Formatter.

Cover by Jay at Simply Defined Art.

Art by Dily Iola Designs

READER CONSIDERATIONS

This book contains explicit violence, explicit sexual violence, dubious consent, murder, gore, torture, kidnapping, and more.

PROLOGUE

freya

"Now, little witch," the dark voice calls, the husky timbre making me shake.

For a god, he truly is a patient man, being held in my trap for so long. When I set it and cast a summoning spell, I didn't expect this, but I had nowhere else to turn. The magic in me called something dark, and I need help or it will be the downfall of my coven, my court, and this world as we know it.

"From the beginning once more," he urges, sitting cross-legged.

He disappeared a few days ago, and I panicked, but he returned, which begs the question—if he can leave, then why hasn't he?

"I told you," I say as I pace. "I don't know how I called it, and neither does the demon that feeds on our magic. When you left, I was trying to rid my coven of it. I thought if I could show them I could banish the demon, we would be okay, but I called something much worse." I peer at him. "I called something wrong, something dark . . . something dead. Please, Phrixius, please help me."

I feel the demon I speak of pushing from the shadows as if the world takes a pause when such evil emerges. A cold chill goes over me as the demon's heat meets my back. The god stands then, anger furrowing his brow as he meets the demon's eyes—the eyes of the demon I've been haunted by my entire life, the demon I tried to rid myself of before I got all of us into this mess.

"He cannot, but I can. I told you, little witch, just make one pesky little deal and I'm yours," he purrs in my ear. His voice is smooth and relaxing, making me sway into him, wanting to give in to the bargain he has been peddling since I turned eighteen.

One I can never agree to, but for a moment, I falter.

"No," Phrixius snaps, his fury breaking me from the spell the demon weaves around me, and with a furious look at the chuckling demon, Phrixius steps from the spell circle, righting his suit, and he doesn't stop until he stands before me.

Their powers surge through me, leaving me breathless.

"I will help you. You called and trapped me, after all," he counters.

"What could a god know of such dark, evil things?" the demon retorts.

"More than a lowly ground crawler," the god replies, leaving me swaying between them, my head aching from their power.

Something dark, evil, cold, and dead grasps my ankle and yanks me down, and with a scream, I reach for the demon and the god, but it's too late.

The thing I called forth rips me from my cave and into its grasp.

CHAPTER 1

Six Months Ago. . .

I hate this fucking demon.

I really do.

Not only do I not know his name so I can curse him, since that would give me power over him, but he is such a creepy stalker. I don't know if the others simply don't see him or don't want to, but he won't stop following me around, whispering in my ear at inappropriate times, like now.

"Don't you think Hagatha"—his name for Agatha, the head witch—"looks particularly ugly today?"

"Shut up," I hiss to him, and a witch close to me frowns in my direction then moves away.

Great, another person who thinks I'm crazy, hence the no friends thing, just the demon chuckling in my ear.

Being a witch isn't easy. The more powerful we are, the more we are praised and revered. It's a hierarchy without men, but don't get us wrong, we aren't nuns. No, there are local warlock covens who are visited often, not to mention the nearby town, but our village is a sanctuary for women and magic. It always has been, with lineages tracing back to the witch trials hundreds of years ago and blood so deep in magic, you cannot separate it.

Family is important, or at least that's what I hear often, and it's another reason I am mostly ignored.

I have none.

I am completely alone. Add that to the fact that I have been haunted by a demon since before I could remember, and most think I am strange or odd and choose to ignore me as much as they can. They don't shun me or kick me out since I'm useful. I'm not super powerful, but I'm not weak either. I make spells and charms no one else can. Usually, they are the darker kind, which worries them, but beggars can't be choosers. It's why they keep me here, under the protection of the blood circle and within our magical village.

Most would assume it resembles something from the fifth century, and although there are buildings that look like some of the historical shops and homes, the rest are influenced architecturally by the modern era. It's a mix of what shouldn't work but does. It is also a paradise where you are free to be as you wish without persecution.

Unless, like me, you have a demon taunting you, telling you to do bad things, which you may or may not sometimes give into when he dares you so he will stop calling you his ridiculous, little nicknames.

Like now, facing down Hagatha—Agatha, oh my goddess!

I duck my head in shame but also to hide my moving lips. "Go away right now or I'll never speak to you again."

"Liar." He chuckles in my ear. "You'd be lonely without me. Admit it, little witch, you like my company and my naughty whispers, daring you to do things you want without repercussions on your soul."

"Well?" Agatha demands for the third time, her impatience evident in her voice.

I lift my head, my veil of black hair falling over my shoulders with the movement. Usually, it's tied back since it's so long and thick, but my hairbands keep magically disappearing. It's the demon, I think, since he seems to love playing with my hair. More than once, I've woken up to my locks in braids so intricate, I cannot unravel them.

Once, he even made them into horns on my head, and I had to hide for days as I worked to undo them.

"What do you have to say for yourself, child?" Agatha booms, tired of waiting for me to repent.

She leads our coven as the matriarch. She is the strongest witch within our ranks and also the oldest. You do not cross her unless you want to be turned into a toad or worse.

Rest in peace, Toad Angelina.

"I'm sorry," I murmur through the magic weaving around the room. We are inside her shop, one that sells some of the most powerful spells in the entire world, and I can taste the raw magic and talent. It calls to me, overpowering my senses like a fragrance.

As always, my eyes catch on the mask locked in the glass in the back. I swear I have heard it sing to me once or twice, so I quickly look away. Objects hold power and memories, and some can be filled with evil that can possess you. I have my theories on the mask, but Agatha will never tell.

"Sorry? Child, you blew up the water plant!" She sighs, rubbing her tired face. "I cannot keep protecting you, Freya. You have to stop making mistakes. Just because you lost your family, it does not give you the right to act out. You know better than this. You could be such a good witch if you tried, but it's like you are determined to sink into the darkness you wear like a cloak." Her eyes see too much. They always have.

When I was born, Agatha told anyone who would listen that I had a forked path before me.

Good and evil.

It was up to me to choose.

Most didn't know what she meant, but I did, since evil is my companion in the form of a demon. One day, I will either give into him and go completely mad, being as bad as any witch can, or I will free myself from him.

My hands move behind my back, weaving a spell as I twist my fingers, and then I fling it at the demon only I can see. I hear his grunt as he's tossed through the door and the wall. The glowing gold net will pin him beyond our borders, but not for long. It used to last months, weeks, then days, but now it only takes hours for him to free himself from my magic.

Hours of peace without him is not worth the cost of my magic, but sometimes, like now, I'm desperate.

"I am sorry, Guardian Mother," I tell her respectfully, lowering my head once more.

Her sigh fills the air, and spells breathe to life with it. Where I am darkness, Agatha is light. She is happiness and love and nature. I wish I had that ability. Instead, I am drawn to the dark and mystical things that hide within. Most witches land somewhere on the scale, but me? I'm off the other end, and I hate it.

I also hate that I gave into the demon's taunts that I couldn't summon a troll and accidentally blew up the water plant when I sent it back. He laughed his ass off, holding popcorn the entire time.

Evil bastard.

"You are always sorry. I thought you would have outgrown this by now. You are not a teenager anymore, Freya. You must do better. This coven relies on every member."

"If one cog is broken, then the whole system is broken," I repeat. It's something I have heard since before I could speak. "I know, and I truly am sorry. I will do better."

"I hope you will. The coven is getting restless. They grow tired of your mistakes." My head rises at that, my eyes widening in fear.

Being exiled and cast aside by your coven is a death sentence.

No witch can live alone; it drives you mad.

"Guardian Mother," I whisper.

She waves me on. "Think on it. Now go, I have some guests arriving soon who ought not see you."

I frown at that but nod, grateful she hasn't exiled me or worse, and then I hurry from the shop. The looks I receive once I'm out on the cobbled street have my cheeks heating, so I pull my hood up to hide my face. It won't do much, since I am recognisable even here. My raven-coloured hair is as black as night, while most others' locks are bright, and my lips are as red as blood.

It seems I was born to be bad, but I fight it every single day.

I hurry through the streets before Agatha changes her mind. She is fickle like that. I keep my head down as much as I can, knowing the roads like the back of my hand. The streets in our town are a woven tapestry of madness with dead ends, tunnels, and alleys that seem to lead nowhere. Houses and shops tower into the sky and down into the earth, representing each witch perfectly. They appear when you are of age. Some have mansions and palaces high up on the hills behind me, the sun gleaming through their stained-glass windows. Some have cute, little cottages out through the trees by the bubbling brooks, close to nature.

Not me.

I'm not that lucky.

I live on the outskirts of the village, as far as you can before you hit the blood circle, and mine is buried in the earth, filled with darkness. Most thought it was an omen, and at first, so did I, but I found I like my solitude out here. I can be who I am without tempering myself, and others won't hear me cussing out a demon who doesn't exist to them.

Maybe I am mad.

I scream and fall back when the demon appears before me with a macabre grin.

"Miss me, little witch?"

CHAPTER 2

Whistling happily, I skip by my little witch's side as she does her best to ignore me, but I got a reaction. She screamed, drawing eyes, and I can't help but laugh. Sometimes her will is so strong, even I cannot bend it—me, a higher demon. I am one of the most powerful of my kind, but sometimes, when I whisper in her ear enough, she gives in out of frustration and anger.

Right now, we are back to her ignoring me, as if that will make me go away. She should have learned after twenty years that it won't work.

We are bound together, my witch and I, and one day, her soul will be mine.

"Good morn." She nods respectfully at a passing couple. Men are allowed to visit for the night but must be gone by morning. The walk of shame they do is hilarious.

Leaning in, I whisper wickedly, enjoying her shiver at my closeness, "Did you know he's fucking her brother? Quite scandalous. I watched them going at it the other night under the moon."

"You are a pervert," she hisses, and a passing child's eyes widen.

She sighs as she runs away and tugs her hood closer, doing her best to ignore me, but I've already cracked her, and she knows it. My little witch hates not having the last word, and more than that, she hates having me at her side.

It's a fun little game we play.

"You're just jealous I wasn't watching you play with yourself." Her magic smacks into me, throwing me well past her barrier. I laugh as I cut through it. She's getting stronger. Most others wouldn't dare strike me, but they also couldn't succeed in doing so. It is only because I allow her to.

I pop back to her side, and she sighs.

"Look, who am I going to tell that you get yourself off to manga? Or that you have a tentacle dildo?" She waves her hand, and my lips are suddenly sewn shut. Laughing, I snake my tongue through the magic, the forked muscle drawing her gaze as it cuts through the spell woven into my skin. My body heats at the sudden lust in her gaze, and I move closer, letting her feel the warmth flowing from me as my tongue flicks in the air, tasting her. This is a new game we play. It started recently, but it's quickly becoming my favourite.

She swallows and turns away with a swish of her cloak as I smirk.

The little witch wants me, and it will be her undoing.

Sauntering by her side, I wave and jump at the passing witches, not that they can see me, only she can. It's another perk of the deal I made.

"Can you stop?" she mutters under her breath.

I sigh. "They cannot see me."

"But they can feel you," she points out as a green, big-breasted witch looks around after I spank her ass. Her eyes land on my little witch and narrow, and she hurries along, making me laugh.

"She was cute. Maybe you should break your vow with her," I press. "You've had women before. It was hot to watch."

"Which is exactly why I made the vow. I was sick of you popping up while I was mi—"

"Eating pussy? Sucking dick? Getting fucked into oblivion? Doing the horizontal mambo?" I supply helpfully. Though I've watched, I've never gotten to touch. I've grown stronger over the years, but sometimes I ache for more.

I ache to feel her skin pressed against mine.

I yearn to taste the darkness and evil that hides within her.

She is very beautiful for a human.

It's something I realised as she grew up. That fact became hard to ignore, and my own desire for her made it that much harder not to take what I want. Demons are not patient creatures, but for her, I am, so instead, I resigned myself to watching her pleasure and feasting on it with others, until she took that away from me too.

Cruel little witch.

She turns her gaze to me, and as usual, I am lost in her beauty.

Her heart-shaped face screams of innocence, and her dark eyes, almost bordering on black with flecks of purple within, are captivating. Her long black hair always smells of wet earth in the best way, and those thick locks are my new obsession. There are natural purple streaks throughout, which I love. Her cheeks dimple with every smile, and I ache to lick the creases within her cheeks. Her lips are plump and always painted black, and her eyes are sharp and lined with makeup. She's small, even for a witch, barely five feet, but her curves make my mouth water—delicious plump breasts, thick waist, and round hips.

She is the epitome of nights well spent, sweaty and fucked.

Her skin is as pale as the moonlight, something she constantly moans about and tries to change with her magic, but if she knew how she would glow while I fucked her under a blood moon, she would never complain again.

It is the darkness in her gaze, however, that draws me, speaking of death and decay. It is the taste of her magic, of blood and ruin, that makes me obsessed.

My little witch does not know the truth, but she will soon enough, and I cannot wait to watch.

She will be magnificent.

Gods, save me.

CHAPTER 3

freya

I'm ignoring him. I will ignore him. I'm ignoring him—

I reel back as the demon appears on my workbench, forcing himself between the carved wooden edge and my body. Sitting back heavily, I glare at him. It's hard, it really is. I narrow my eyes and try to look annoyed, but as they trace over his grinning face, I have to acknowledge that he is pretty.

He has curved black horns, fangs that hang over plump, gold-dusted lips, and a wicked tail, which is currently sweeping across my ingredients, but under those differences, he's fucking beautiful, and his attributes only add to the otherness that is the demon. He looks obscenely wicked.

His hair is a mixture of blacks and browns, hanging to his shoulders. I swear I sometimes see hints of red within his locks, but maybe that's a trick of the light. It's thick and slightly wavy at the ends, and he usually wears it pushed back. The top is tied in a braid that reaches his shoulders. Wisps escape, curling in front of his pointed ears adorned with bones. His eyebrows are the same colour as darkness, slanting over his pitch-black eyes. There are no irises or sclera. They are just black, slightly upturned, and pointed. I swear they are lined with gold since they seem to shine with it. His nose is thick and regal, and his cheekbones are high and would look feminine if it wasn't for his rugged jawline which sports a black, carefully maintained beard. Hell, I once caught him conditioning it with my expensive herbal shampoo made from pixie blood.

Despite the weather, he's wearing his usual fur coat. It drapes down to his thick thighs, the worn leather scarred. The white-tipped fur surrounds his neck and falls open, exposing his massive, bare chest. Muscle is stacked upon muscle there, creating the image of perfection in the form of a wicked demon.

His leather trousers cling to his thick thighs, which are as wide as tree trunks, and I once asked if he had to cut a hole for his tail to fit through. His hands are strong as he grabs the wooden carving I was playing with, and he throws it around without looking as his nipple bar catches the light. I swear gold dusts his muscles too, catching my eyes.

I remind myself he's evil.

He's a psychopath, a walking red flag, but red is my favourite colour, and I'm noticing just how attractive the demon who never leaves me alone truly is.

Evil, I hiss in my head.

Evilly hot, a wicked voice whispers back.

"Stop," I mutter, knowing it's him. Stupid fucking demon.

"Stop what, little witch?" he murmurs, tilting his head in a human fashion, but there's a wicked smirk dancing over his lips that tells me he knows exactly what he's doing. He realised I liked his muscles and decided shirts were no longer necessary.

Asshole.

"Want to see my new piercing?" he teases as he leans forward, the wooden sculpture floating mid-air as if he hasn't realised he froze it there. I snatch it away before his evil power infects it and carefully lay it down. He doesn't look away from me the whole time.

His black eyes observe the world around me as my house seems to darken despite the fire burning and the candles shining brightly.

"New piercing?" I ask curiously, which is exactly why he

mentioned it. One day, he turned up with a nipple bar, and I figured he'd got bored. He doesn't go to a piercer, that's for sure.

"I saw something I thought you might like." He slides from the table, and before I can protest, he shoves his trousers down.

I jerk my gaze away, but curiosity gets the better of me, and my eyes go back to him despite my conviction.

I mean, I'm only so strong.

His hairy thighs lead up to his cock, and I cannot look away. He's huge, and the tip of his cock appears to be dusted in the same gold as his body. He's so thick I wouldn't even be able to fit both hands around him. The veins bulge along its hard length, but that's not what I stare at, nor the spikes that seem to run underneath.

It's the eight black piercings running down the length of his cock that have my attention. I know he didn't have them before.

My mouth goes dry as his fist strokes his length, exposing the piercings for me.

"You like them, little witch? I got them for you." He smiles. "I noticed you liked that clit piercing the girl had, and I found out there is a male version. It makes pleasure so much sweeter . . . and pain. You want to taste them for me and find out? I haven't had the chance to try them yet."

"Did it hurt?" My hand drifts up, and before I can stop myself, I trace the piercings. He groans, and I snatch my hand away as he chuckles darkly.

"In the best way," he replies without an ounce of shame. "But feel free to lick it better."

"I'm working. Go away," I mutter, even as I feel my cheeks heat. I curl my hand into a fist to stop myself from touching him. I shouldn't want to as much as I do, but it's like he draws me to him. He doesn't seem disappointed, even as he tugs his trousers up and disappears, suddenly appearing on a chair at my side—one that was not there since I don't want to invite him to stay any longer than he already does. It's bad enough that I wake up and find him hovering in the air above me, watching me sleep.

Creep.

"So what are we working on today?" he asks happily.

I swallow, not looking at him in case he sees the dirty thoughts in my head. Maybe he's right. Maybe it's been too long since the desire inside me was let out.

"Little witch, are you wondering how I would feel inside your sweet pussy?" he whispers in my ear as his tail wraps around my front and slides across my throat. "How about you bend over and find out?"

I snap my hand out, and he leans back, chuckling. Muttering to myself, I move closer to the workbench. I have orders waiting to be fulfilled. Most are from outside the coven, since it's how us witches make money. It's not the kind of money humans use, but the kind us creatures use in this world. Sometimes I will set up a stall at the local market for supes, and I'm due there tomorrow, where my orders will be picked up. One is for a pixie who wants a love spell, despite my warnings, and another is to heal a fae's illness. There's even a spell bag to deflect evil for a siren. I have finished most of them, but not all, and the demon isn't helping.

"If you're distracted, I can help fill orders. I'm bored," he whines, reaching for my spells, but I swat his hand away.

"We both know what happens when you try. They end up dead or cursed. Your magic has a way of morphing the intention." I sigh. I've had to give money back to a customer or apologize to a loved one after they died more than once.

"I just want to help."

I glance over to see him pouting.

A bored demon is a dangerous thing.

"There's a new present for you in the trunk." I nod at the trunk at the end of my bed, and he perks up. He and his chair vanish, and then he appears surrounded by smoke before tearing the trunk open in excitement.

He pulls out the wrapped parcel and appears cross-legged on my bed as he tears into it like a kid, not a seven-foot demon with smoking horns.

Paper goes flying into the air, and I sigh at the mess. He clicks without looking, and it burns to a crisp. Fucking demons. Next, he tugs the box out, his eyes wide. "Is this the new version?" he asks happily.

I nod, and he appears before me, wrapping his entire frame around me before materialising before the TV I bought a while ago. I tell myself it was for me, not him. Sitting cross-legged on the rug, he plugs in the new game and loads it.

I watch as he coos, creating a class and beginning the shooter game. When he puts his headphones on, I cover my eyes. He has been banned for cursing people out more than once. They don't realise it's an actual curse, thank the gods.

"Screw you, kid. I will eat your mum alive."

"Demon," I warn.

He grins at me over his shoulder. "Oops." He turns forward, stabbing the button as he shoots.

I turn my head to hide my smile.

Dangerous demon indeed.

The market is bustling today. It's busier than I've seen it for a while. It can take days to get here, but I don't travel as most would. I simply open a portal and appear with my goods. It takes me an hour or so to set up. The black tent hangs above me with some floating lights, my wooden sign is out front, and my wares are spread across the table.

Other stallholders line the way on every level of the underground market. It's called Conventus Market, which quite literally means meeting point—a meeting of all supernatural creatures.

If you dream it, you can buy it here.

There is everything, including curses, monster parts, the brothel, and eateries catering to darker elements. Nothing is taboo here, so everything goes. The towering market goes all the way to the sky and changes where it appears all the time, yet it's always the same, made of red stone and packed dirt as if nature built it herself.

The stall to my left boasts fae elixirs, and it has everything from hair growth to impotence cures. On my right is a blacksmith with cursed blades.

I relax when I am here, since no one cares who I am. Here, I am not weird, and I blend right in—apart from the demon hanging in my stall that no one can see. Demons aren't welcome, but he doesn't care.

He whistles as he plays with the troll-made toy I bought to occupy him so he doesn't spook or curse my customers, which has happened in the past.

Music floats through the market, no doubt from the bars just above us. I wave at familiar customers, and a nice troll giggles next to a dragon shifter. Here, I'm not a freak, and I love it.

Hours later, I sell out of my wares, so I close up early and send everything back through the portal before hesitating. Usually, I would go back through, but I remember my thoughts from yesterday, and despite the demon's eyes on me, I turn away and head towards the bar a level up.

It's a dark haven with alcohol that can get us supes drunk. The bright light flashes with the music, and I ignore the dance floor in favour of the bar. I'm not here to drink or dance. I scan the patrons as the demon murmurs in my ear.

"Feeling needy, little witch?" I ignore him, and he licks my ear. "I could take care of it for you."

When I ignore him, he chuckles darkly, but I can almost taste his glee at me finally giving in. "Who will it be tonight? How about a nice fae? I like the way they glisten below you. No? How about a vamp? You do like blood play, and I love watching it trickle down your skin."

He always watches.

It shouldn't excite me, it shouldn't make my core clench, but it does. Knowing he will watch me fuck whoever I bring back helps me choose my target for the night. He loves to watch, and tonight, I'll give him a show. Weaving through the crowd, I head to my mark.

Supes are so much more open than humans with their sexual habits, and I'm no different. I love to explore and push boundaries, and tonight, I'm going to give the demon the show he so desperately wants.

The gargoyle is bent over the wooden table, making it look dainty.

He's the colour of stone, with stone wings tucked into his back. His face is chiselled and handsome, though made of rock, and I can't wait to feel his hard lips.

He lifts his head, his brown eyes widening as I approach, and when I reach him, I flutter my eyelashes. I might be small, but I like them big. I like to feel their strength.

"I've never had stone," I remark as I watch him. "Is it as hard as it seems?"

He blinks, and I realise stone can blush, but it's a deeper grey colour. "Why don't you find out?" he asks in a deep voice.

Good boy. He'll do.

Smirking, I turn and walk away, feeling his disappointment until I turn back. "Follow me."

He downs his drink and pushes from his chair. He's easily double my height and width, but I lick my lips in anticipation. When he's behind me, I wind through the bar and out, leading him where I want.

"What's your name, little witch?"

My demon hisses at that.

"Freya. Call me that or anything other than little witch." If I'm to get what I want, then the demon cannot be angry and murder him, and he doesn't like it when someone else calls me little witch.

That's reserved for him.

"Freya," he repeats, rock crashing in his voice. "Beautiful."

"Thank you." I grab his hand and back under the curtain to the dwelling cut into the side of this level. We all use them. They are spread out, and this one is free. There's a bed and not much else, which is all I need.

"My name is—" I cover his mouth, climbing him to do so.

"I don't need it. No words, just fucking," I murmur, tracing my tongue over his stone lips. A shiver goes through me at the idea of grinding my pussy against them and feeling that hard stone against my clit.

"Fine by me." He grabs me, and I fly through the air, hitting the bed hard, and then he's on me.

My head tips back as he rips off my clothes, his wings spanning the width of the room as he grips me firmly, denting my curves. His stone lips slide down my chest, rubbing against my hard nipples, and I open my eyes, my gaze clashing with the glittering demon's as he leans back against the wall in the corner of the room.

He wears a hungry smirk on his lips as he watches me, ready to feast on my desire.

CHAPTER 4

Freya

Narrowing my eyes, I grab the man's stone head and pull him up, kissing him while I hold the demon's gaze. I conjure my magic and send the gargoyle sprawling back to the bed. His eyes widen in surprise as I climb above him, slinging my now bare leg over his wide chest as I click and dissolve the last of my clothes.

There's a groan from my demon, but I ignore it.

Sliding higher, I press my hands to the wall so my pussy is above the stone monster's face. "I want to grind against your lips," I tell him. It's all I've thought about since I saw him. "I want to get nice and wet so I can take you." I glance over my shoulder at the huge, stone cock standing to attention. If I'm not careful, it will split me in two.

His wings flap against the bed where he's pinned, his jaw grinding. "Then use me, Freya, and ride my face until you're wet enough to take me."

Smirking, I press all my weight against his face, knowing he can take it. I grind down, forcing him to feel my pussy on his stone features.

"Stones, you smell delicious. Can I—"

I shush him as I grind my hips. "Don't talk. Eat my cunt until I come or I'll find someone who can."

In response, his stone lips part, and I groan as they hit my clit and hole. My head falls back as I use his face shamelessly. I grind my hips until it hurts, my clit throbbing. I feel my demon's dark magic slide across my curves, and I would usually smack it away, but right now, I let him touch, his magic tweaking my nipples as I cry out.

I come with a cry, gushing on the gargoyle's face, but he does not utter a word. I slump then move down his body, circling his stone length with my fingers as he groans.

"You're big." I lick my lips, feeling my own wetness coating my thighs.

I lean down and taste him. He tastes like earth and rock, but as I squeeze, liquid beads at the tip of his length, making me grin. His head thrashes on the bed as I sling my leg over his hip and press his cock to my entrance, and then I sink down on him without warning.

He groans, rolling his hips and forcing himself deeper as my cunt stretches around his massive length. My knees barely touch the bed, so I push harder, needing leverage to take him.

"Most cannot take all of me. It's okay," he begins, but I narrow my eyes.

That sounds like a challenge.

I lift and slide down his length. It hurts, stretching me brutally to the point of pain, but I keep going, forcing him deeper and deeper until I take every hard inch.

His back bows as he yells, and I groan at the feeling. He's so deep, I can feel him in my stomach. I press my hand against it as I start to roll my hips and grind on his stone cock. It's unbending and so hard and cold, it hurts in the best fucking way.

He pushes up, fucking me from below, and I bounce with the force, so I hold on as he snarls and fights my pussy. The pain melds with pleasure, but I need something else to come.

I pull off his length, ignoring his questions as I turn and force my pussy back onto his slick stone cock. My eyes lock on my demon, and that lust turns into an inferno inside me. My core clenches around stone as I meet his hungry gaze.

Obsession and fire burns within the depths of his eyes, and flames ignite between his horns as he watches me fuck the monster, his hands fisting his own throbbing length.

When his words float to me, they are pure sin, pure darkness, and for me alone.

"You love monster cock, don't you, little witch?"

I groan as he pumps his cock.

"You love fucking creatures, love their big cocks." His voice wraps around me, casting its own spell.

My heart races as I ride the stone man harder, his grunts fading into nothing as I focus on the demon.

"You love making me watch you fuck someone else, love making me watch what I want and can't have. Don't you, little witch?"

I nod, speeding up my hips as I watch his hand stroke his cock so firmly, it has to hurt.

"You love the way it feels to get fucked by an inhuman creature. Most shy away from the darkness, that's why they are always so surprised when someone so beautiful wants them, but you revel in it. The weirder the better, and the harder you come."

My core clenches at his filthy accusations, as I know he's right.

I love monsters, and the more fucked up, the better.

I also love to taunt the demon with what he will never have.

I flash him my glistening cunt, my hole stretched around the stone cock. The gargoyle pounds into me from below, my pussy fluttering around him. I'm drawing closer. The demon's words push me towards the edge, no matter who I am with.

"Come, little witch," he whispers in my ear, and I can't do anything but.

I scream my release as I clench around stone, wishing for a moment it were fire.

The gargoyle bellows, bringing me back to the present, and I gasp as he shoots his release inside me. It flows over me, and my eyes find my demon to see him tucking his hard cock away without release.

I slump back, and stone arms wrap around me. "Beautiful, Freya. Thank you, thank you."

My demon is right, they are always thankful, and I am always wanting what I cannot have.

Maybe it's wrong to use them, but I don't care, not with bliss running through my veins and fire in my heart.

CHAPTER 5

Whenever my little witch gives into her desires and lets me watch, she hides from me after. I allow her the space, knowing she will only freak out if I push. She has gotten better, but not to that degree, so I disappear into the forest surrounding the village while she makes her way home.

I can feel her anxiety from here, knowing she is spiralling, but tonight was different. She watched me with something akin to understanding in her eyes.

Has she finally realised how much she wants me?

Will she give into the darkness, make a deal for me, and ensure her soul burns for eternity with me?

Maybe, and it certainly seemed that way from the look she gave me before I left—one I've never seen in her eyes.

I wonder if she remembers that she is the only being in this world that I have ever told my true name to.

I gave it to her upon her birth, and every night since, I whisper it in her ear, hoping she will speak it one day.

Even knowing what it will mean, I hope to hear it, even once.

I'm swinging from a tree, debating that, when I feel her magic.

It's strong and dark as it blasts through this world and into the others, causing me to stagger back and gasp. My eyes go to her house hidden within the village.

"No!" I bellow. "Little witch, what have you done?"

I appear at her house, rushing inside, my black heart racing with fear. She stands with her arms outstretched, her lips working a summoning spell. A trap is before me on the floor, and so much magic fills the room I have to fight through it to get to her.

It peels the skin from my bones, but when I reach her, I tackle her. She gasps and opens her eyes, the spell stopped.

"What have you done?" I roar into her face.

She blinks, swallowing nervously. Red fades from her eyes, a colour I don't think she even realises they turn when she works dark magic. "I-I thought I could trap you inside the spell. Why?"

"That was not a trapping spell, Freya," I snarl, and she flinches at her name. "It was a summoning spell, a fucking strong one."

"Summoning . . ." She stumbles over the word, her eyes widening.

We both turn when we hear a loud groan, and my eyes widen when I see the man inside the trap meant for me.

No, not a man.

A god.

CHAPTER 6

Phrixius

I always thought being a god would bring me purpose and happiness, and for a long time, it did. As the god of magic and the moon, I don't have much to do. The moon has a new goddess —if you consider new as the last thousand years—and I leave the wolves and such to her, so magic is my companion, and magic is everywhere and uncontrollable. It is a wild entity, with no law unto itself.

There have been no issues, which I know I should not wish for, since issues would be bad.

But I am . . . restless.

Even the mundane meetings we hold no longer capture my attention. I ignore the discussion, just nodding and agreeing until they are over, and then I wander around my island, alone and restless.

I dream of a little chaos, not that I would ever tell anyone else that.

I am the god of goodness, and I am known as being helpful, kind, and law-abiding. I believe in the laws, in helping others, but as I stare at the sky around my island, I cannot help but wonder what it would feel like to be excited again.

That could possibly be why I do not ignore the call I feel as I usually would. This one is so strong, it reaches into my chest and grabs me.

Summoning . . . Someone is summoning me.

I blink and make a split-second decision. I could fight it and stay, but for one single moment, I give in, and magic wraps around me, yanking me from my island and the realm of gods and onto Earth.

I sit up and blink. I'm inside an entrapment spell, more confused and slightly worried. Whoever called me was very strong and a little dark—no, a lot dark.

Gods, I answered the summoning of a dark witch.

I should have known better than to wish for excitement, because this world has a sick sense of humour when it delivers what you want.

I curse myself, about to leave, when my eyes land on the witch who summoned me. I'm speechless and lost in the darkness of her eyes.

I don't even see the demon pinning her at first—all I see is her.

She is stunningly beautiful, with long dark hair and bright magical eyes. Her pale skin looks like moonlight, and she is all delicious, deep curves despite her small stature. My eyes clash with the black gaze of the demon pinning her, and then I understand.

"I see you are in trouble. Demon, be gone," I snap.

She is a witch, so I am her god. It must be why I am here.

"You can see him?" she asks, looking at the demon and then me.

"I can," I say slowly, hesitantly, wondering if she will speak again.

Her voice sounds like magic and has an odd effect on my usually calm heart.

"He should be able to, since he's a god and all," the demon hisses, glaring at me. "Fucking idiot witch, you summoned a god."

"I did what?" she screams shrilly and glances from him to me. "No, I didn't."

"Did." He nods emphatically.

"Didn't," she hisses, getting in his face.

"Did," he hisses right back, standing toe-to-toe with her, which surprises me since you tend to end up as ash or some sick, twisted animal if you annoy a demon, yet this witch narrows her eyes on him, totally unafraid.

"No, you," she snaps.

"You did it!" he roars.

I'm getting a headache. I knew I didn't want excitement. I have a feeling that if I do not intervene, they will carry on like this for hours.

"He's right, which I never would have thought I'd say about a demon," I interrupt. I rise gracefully, standing in her trap to keep them both calm, making them believe I cannot leave. They both snap their gazes to me, and I grin, holding my hands up. "Sorry for interrupting. Now, little witch, why did you summon me?"

"Oh, you have got to be kidding me. First a fucking demon, and now a god." She drops her head back and just screams.

The demon watches her with one eyebrow arched, and we exchange a look. He nods at the worry he must see in my eyes. "She's dramatic sometimes. Just give her a minute to let it out or she'll be grumpy all day."

"Interesting," I reply as we wait.

When she stops screaming, her chest is heaving and she looks at me again as if hoping I will disappear.

"Well, fuck," she grumbles.

"Pretty much." The demon sighs. "Welcome to the family, I guess."

CHAPTER 7

freya

When I'm done screaming, I breathe through the panic. I'm such an idiot. I should have known better than to try the trapping spell, but I was desperate. I spiralled into terror when I got back because this thing between the demon and me is getting stronger. He's getting harder to resist, and I was worried about what would happen when I finally gave in.

I realized tonight that I would, hence the trapping spell while he was gone. I thought if I could trap him, it would give me time to figure out how to escape him and undo whatever causes him to be tethered to me. I never thought it would go so wrong, and as I eye the man casually standing in the trapping spell meant for the demon sighing next to me, I can't help but gulp.

A god.

I summoned a god, and not just any god, but a very attractive god. My eyes rove over him like I'm seeing the sun for the first time. Where I am darkness, he is light. Golden spun hair hangs down past his shoulders, some of it braided back to reveal shapely ears. His face should look stern or even feminine, but he has a square jawline devoid of any hair or stubble, a straight nose, and high cheekbones that, quite frankly,

I'm jealous of. His dark eyebrows are furrowed over his vivid eyes, which are as bright as the sun before they seem to shift to an even brighter icy grey. He only wears loose trousers that look like they belong in a different century, so his chest and arms are completely bare and stacked with muscle. There isn't an ounce of fat on him, and I count the number of indents on his abs. He could be a cover model for those dirty books Agatha writes in her spare time.

Or an angel.

The guy looks like he should have angel wings—wait, is this where all the references for angels came from? This guy? It wouldn't surprise me. He's all golden sunlight and godliness.

He watches me patiently, his expression showing he's slightly worried. I almost giggle out loud at that. I mean, I would be worried as well if some crazy witch with a demon sidekick summoned and then trapped me.

Oh gods, what has my life come to?

Groaning, I cover my face as the demon chuckles. "Can't say I expected our night to end like this, but you always keep me on my toes, little witch." For a demon facing down a god, he doesn't seem so worried.

"I'm sorry, okay?" I throw my hands in the air and look at the god. "Erm, to you too, nice god. Don't smite me. I didn't mean to summon you."

"I do not smite people." His head tilts, a flirty smile teasing on his plump lips. "Not ones as pretty as you anyway."

"Nope. My witch. Back off, god," the demon sneers.

Light and darkness.

I would look good trapped between them—*shit, stop right there!* They are both watching me, and I feel my cheeks heat.

My demon snickers. "What were you thinking about, little witch?"

"Nothing," I blurt, stumbling over the word.

He appears behind me, his smoky voice filling my ear. "Pretty liar."

I jerk away, pointing in his face. "Do not make me build you a trapping spell too," I warn.

"Maybe I'd like to be tied up by you," he flirts.

I glare at him, he smiles at me, and we only stop when the god clears his throat. We both whirl around to see the god with his eyebrow raised.

"Right." I turn back to him. "I'll just, erm, let you go, but here's the thing—I don't actually know how. I was never good with trapping spells," I admit. "I can ask one of the others, but then they will know I summoned and trapped a god, and I'm already an outcast, and being stalked by a demon doesn't help. Maybe there's a book I can use?" He just watches me babble, his eyebrows getting higher and higher with each confession and a smile growing on his lips. "A book, yes, a book. I'll have to break in, though, because Agatha is still mad about the troll thing." My voice is high as I run out of air.

"Breathe, little witch," my demon orders with a smile.

I take a deep breath and nod, bowing all the way over. "I'm sorry for summoning and trapping you. I will go steal the book and figure out how to free you, and then you cannot smite me, and everything can go back to normal. Be right back." I almost sprint away—well, I walk fast because the only way I would be running is if something were chasing me. I've never understood people who run for fun.

My demon's mocking laughter follows after me.

Asshole, this is all his fault.

DEMON

I watch Freya go with a shake of my head. Was she really going to trap me? She's tried to get rid of me over the years in a lot of different ways, but I thought we were past that. I thought she understood I'm here to stay.

Apparently not. My feelings might even be hurt if I had any.

"A demon hanging around a witch," Phrixius murmurs. Yes, I know who he is. There aren't that many gods left, nor any with such golden hair and eyes. This is the god of magic, and my little witch called him. He has the power to ruin this, so I need to be careful. I need to give him enough answers for him to lose interest. Gods are like demons that way. They don't care after they get bored.

They want excitement after so many years of living.

"She has good snacks." I perch on top of her table. "We both know you could break that binding spell and leave, so why don't you?"

"Maybe I'm curious why she called me, or maybe I'm curious about why a demon is so determined to stay at my witch's side."

"Not yours," I hiss before I can stop myself.

Phrixius's eyebrow simply rises as he gracefully sinks to his knees. "Very well. So tell me the truth, demon. Give me a reason to leave, and I will allow you to stay at the side of one of mine. She is magic, after all."

"Dark magic," I point out, since he already knows.

"Dark or not, she is mine," he counters. "So tell me why I shouldn't intervene."

I stare at the god, realising he isn't going to leave, not just like that.

"If you help rid her of me, she will die," I admit honestly, something that's not easy for a demon. We thrive on lies and deception, but I see no other way out. I am uncharacteristically serious as I move to the edge of the binding spell meant for me. "You would be killing her, and that is the truth."

"Sadly for her, I think it is," he murmurs as he watches me.

My smirk grows as I step back. "Good, then off with you. I have some very ungodly things to say to the little witch, and our fights tend to get . . . physical." I wiggle my eyebrows, but he simply watches me.

"Fine, but I think I'll stay a while and see how this plays out. Plus, it's been a long time since I was in this world. It's about time I checked on my people."

"Now listen here—" We both stop at the sound of a scream. It's an internal one, but one I'd know anywhere.

Sighing, I point at him. "She is trapped in the potions room again. Be gone when I get back." I evaporate to find my little, troublesome witch before she ends up destroying her own village by mistake.

My job truly is a hard one.

"Freya, hells," I snap as I appear. "What are you doing up there?"

She's hanging from the top of a bookshelf in Agatha's house, one hand on a book, the other holding her up as ladders clatter to the floor where she can't reach them.

"Oh, you know, just felt like hanging for a spell," she hisses. "Help me."

"No. Say sorry for trying to make me leave," I demand.

"Never."

"Fine." I hop up on a bookshelf next to her, swinging my legs as I wait. I can see her fingers and arm straining to hold her up. She was never very good at physical exercise, and she says the only time you should run is if someone is chasing you—I put that to the test more than once and wound up being turned into a lizard for three days.

My little witch can be terrifying when she needs to be.

"It's dusty up here. You'd think Agatha would use a spell to clean," I comment idly as I watch her face turn red from exertion, her legs kicking at the shelves loud enough that I'm surprised the old hag hasn't come down to find out what's going on.

"I'll make a note to tell her." She puffs, her cheeks blowing wide with air as she tries to drag herself up but falls with a groan. "I've got this. I'm totally fine."

"You don't seem to be. Say you're sorry and I'll help," I tell her as I lean in, my forked tongue flicking across her ear. "Or better yet, let's make a deal, little witch."

"Never. You'll want terrible things from me." One finger slips from the top, but my stubborn Freya doesn't ask.

"The only thing I want from you, little witch, is the thing you'll eventually give me, and we both know it, but keep fighting because it will only make your surrender that much sweeter," I say as I lean back.

Her hand finally gives and she plummets, heading right for the floor far below. My girl might be a witch, but she's still breakable.

I evaporate then reappear midair, catching her as I stop us so we simply touch the floor, the book clutched to her chest. "Stubborn little witch," I murmur as I check her over for injuries.

"Pesky, annoying demon," she responds, but her lips tilt in a smile —one I can't help but return.

No, it's not so bad at all.

CHAPTER 8

freya

The demon doesn't put me down until we are back inside my house. I'm mildly surprised to see the god sitting there patiently, and I huff, struggling from the demon's arms and slamming the huge tome down on my workbench.

"Okay, one freeing spell, coming right up," I mutter as I glance at the god. "Do you, like, want a drink or something?" There's a sputter, and I point at my demon without looking. "It's called being a good host."

"I once asked for a blanket and you sewed my mouth shut," he retorts.

"You enjoyed that, and what do you call that?" I gesture towards the huge entertainment system bought just for him, and he quiets down. "That's what I thought. Now be a good boy and fetch the god a drink. What's your name? I can't keep calling you god, or does it have power like the demons and you can't tell a lowly mortal like me?"

"She talks when she's nervous," my demon adds helpfully, but he manages to duck to avoid the vase I chuck at him.

"My name is Phrixius," the god says confidently, and I just stare.

"Phrixius?" I repeat, and he nods proudly, as if it should mean something to me. As if I should worship the ground he walks on.

"What kind of name is Phrixius?" I snap.

"A godly one, passed down by the heavens—"

"It's dumb. They clearly hated you, and I'm not calling you that. How about . . . Bob?" I respond.

The chortling that comes from my demon makes me grin. "You wish to call me Bob?" the god repeats, and I worry I offended him, but honestly, he said he wouldn't smite me, so what do I have to lose? I gamble my life every day picking on the demon.

"Or Fred?" I suggest, and he blinks. "How about Faro? No, wow, you are hard to please. I mean, Phrixius, really."

"It is a name given to me by the universe and fitting of my station as the ruler of all magical beings," he mutters.

"Yeah, it's a mouthful. So, Todd, what were you doing when I summoned you?" I ask as I open the tome, a cloud of dust hitting me in the face as I cough and wave it away. "Let me guess, ruling over existence—"

"I was watching the horizon." His voice is quiet, and I turn to see him, his eyes far away. "I was debating my existence and what it meant."

"Ah, the casual Tuesday existential dread. Nice to know gods feel that too." I nod before clapping my hands. "Well, Rodger, let's find this spell and free you."

"He looks more like a Richard, you know, because then we can call him Dick," my demon chimes in.

"Demons can be banished, you know," Phrixius offers casually.

I jerk around, but my demon covers my eyes. "Ignore him. He's lying. Free the bastard so he's gone, and we can get back to what we were doing."

I elbow him, ignoring the scent of sulphur wrapping around me as I focus on the book, but my eyes go back to Phrixius. Is he right? Could I banish the demon? I need to get him alone and find out before I free him. Otherwise, he's not likely to help me, but it seems my demon knows my thoughts and is determined to stick by my side at all times and not give us a moment of peace.

I spend the next few hours researching the spell and hoping my demon will get bored and wander away like he usually does, but he sits right next to me, glaring at the god as if he personally offended him. It's distracting, and I sit back, rubbing my head.

"Why are binding spells easier than freeing spells?" I mutter.

"Usually, you bind something you intend to kill or use. Not much use for a freeing spell," Phrixius calls, his voice matter-of-fact.

"Wait, you're the god of magic. Don't you know how to break the spell?"

He watches me for a long moment. "This is your magic. I cannot intervene in another's magic."

I frown, watching him. "But you're a god—"

"And he's a demon. Your point, witch?"

"My name is Freya," I mutter, and he smiles.

"Freya," he explains, "magic is linked to the user and the intention. You know this, since you intended to trap a powerful being and it worked. You look tired. Maybe you should rest and try again tomorrow. I understand mortals need to sleep more frequently than creatures such as us and hellspawn there."

"Did the god just make a joke?" My demon gapes. "I didn't know they could do that."

"Met many gods, have you?" I ask.

"One or two." He shrugs. "They are quite boring and so into themselves and obsessed with rules—apart from Mors, the god of death. He's pretty fun, if angry."

Phrixius sighs. "He is not angry. He has been given the hardest duty of all time—"

"Sure, sure." The demon nods. "Anyway, demons and gods don't mix, but since we are immortal, we cross paths every now and again."

I frown. "Wait, how are demons made? I never really even asked. Like, I know you exist and the types, but are you just another supernatural creature or more like Teddy over there?"

"Sticking with the Ts, I see. Well, when two demons love each other very much, their bodies come together—you know, why don't I show you instead?" I narrow my eyes, and my demon sighs. "You can't blame a guy. You never asked before."

"I guess I didn't think about it," I admit as I sit back. "Well?"

My demon sighs and settles back. "Technically, we are part god." I blink, and he smirks. "A small, corrupted part. There was once a god called Luellen—it's where your people got Lucifer from, though I heard he changed his name when he fell."

"Fell?" I ask, sitting up.

"From grace. If we do not follow the rules and laws set forth by our roles we are destined for, then we fall from our world and into yours," Phrixius adds helpfully.

"Exactly. Well, he fell, and he was pissed. He'd fallen in love with a mortal, you see, and as a master of reincarnation as well as many other things, he brought her back when she died. It broke his rules, and he fell. His mortal was taken away, her soul imprisoned to stop her from reincarnating again as part of his punishment. It drove him a little mad, and all that power corrupted. We were born from his hatred and his need to settle the score and defy the universe."

"You were quite literally made to be a nuisance." I grin, and he chuckles.

"Pretty much."

"What happened to him?" I murmur.

"No one knows. There are rumours even amongst our kind that he is hidden, trying to free his mortal's soul. Even now, thousands of years later, he still loves her."

"How sad," I say. "All because of love."

"Love is the most dangerous thing in this universe," my demon says, sounding serious for once, his eyes on me. "It makes even the strongest creatures do things they ordinarily would not. It is unpredictable and wild, like magic. Love is the most dangerous thing this universe has ever created. Even more than hatred."

"Good thing you'll never have that issue." I chuckle, looking at the book, but he's quiet. When I glance at him, he's staring at me, his face devoid of any amusement.

"Indeed," he murmurs before he blinks, and then he evaporates, leaving me alone, but I have a horrible feeling in my chest that I have upset the demon.

"Demons are capable of love." I jerk back to see Phrixius. "Just in case you were curious. Most think they are creatures born from hatred, but hate is close to love. They are capable of feeling the same emotions as their creator—a man who loved someone so deeply he scours this Earth looking for her, even now."

I feel like I'm being reprimanded or am not quite in on the joke in the room, but then he smiles. "Rest, witch. Tomorrow will be a new day for you to find the freeing spell."

"And you?"

"Gods do not need as much rest as mortals."

With nothing else to do, I slump into my bed, and despite having his eyes on me, I fall fast asleep.

"Gods don't need as much rest my ass," I mutter, staring at the god. He's sprawled across the circle, his mouth open as he snores loudly. He almost looks normal. He sighs and rolls over, and I swear he's drooling as the snores start back up.

I grab a blanket and throw it over him as I look around.

My demon is nowhere in sight, which is strange in itself. He never leaves me alone this long. Did I hurt him? I should take the time to grill Phrixius for information, but I find myself heading out into the village to find him, leaving the god to his dreams.

I avoid Agatha's shop and house in case she realises I broke in last night. Technically, all knowledge within the coven is to be shared, but that doesn't mean I want anyone to know why I was looking for a freeing spell. I'm already in enough trouble, and I cannot afford another mistake.

My dress swishes over the cobbled steps as I walk through the village. It is early, the sun barely up, so most are still asleep, meaning the streets are empty. I wander aimlessly up and down winding paths, past Victorian mansions and the cute cottages, but my demon is nowhere in sight.

There are a lot of places for him to go, but as I step into the village square and turn, I wonder if he left for good. All my worries would be over. I could be a normal witch with a normal life, so then why aren't I happier with the idea?

Why do I feel almost hollow? Like I'm missing something?

Sitting heavily on the edge of the pentagram-shaped fountain, I look around, wondering where he could be, when there's a pop and his grinning face appears before me.

"Looking for me?"

I scream and fall back, all while flinging my magic. I splash into the red water, sinking under with a sputter. When I break the surface, his eyes are narrowed, and he has a cage around him.

"Really?" he sighs.

"You scared me!" I yell as I look down at myself and groan. My hair and dress are soaked. I point at him. "Look what you did."

"I like you all wet." He smirks, and my eyes narrow. My hand moves quickly, and he laughs as he disappears from the cage just as I fling my magic at him again. I search around, looking for him.

"Get out here, demon," I warn, magic waiting in my hand.

"I'm right here," he whispers in my ear, and then I'm plunged under the water again.

I come up sputtering to find him laughing, and then he's gone once more. Suddenly, a tidal wave of water hits me, and he laughs. I kick water back at him, and he howls as it hits him.

I race around the fountain with him hot on my heels, both of us flinging water at each other with hands and magic until we are drenched and laughing loudly.

Panting and grinning, I lift my head and find two coven members there, their mouths agape as they watch me have a water fight with myself and talk to thin air.

"Morning." I wear a guilty grin, water dripping down my face.

"She's getting crazier," one murmurs before waving, and then they hurry away.

I kick out the demon's legs, and he yelps as he hits the water and goes under as I climb from the fountain. Waving my hand, I dry myself off.

When he leaps from it, he pouts at me. "Do me."

"You have your own demon magic," I snap.

"Not what I meant." He winks.

"Demon," I warn, but he reappears dry, blinking innocently at me.

"Yes, little witch?" He backs me up. "Did you miss me?"

"Nope."

"No, you weren't looking all over for me?" he replies as I hit the edge of the cage I made. Swallowing, I meet his eyes. "I think you were. I think you were worried I left you, little witch. Keep denying it all you want, but we both know you like having me around."

"Keep telling yourself that," I mutter as I push past him. "I better get back and carry on with the spell."

He follows me, and I hide my smile at the rightness of him being at my side just as a yell comes from the square. "Why in the heavens is there a cage here?"

Oops.

CHAPTER 9

freya

"I found it!" I shout, and the demon falls from where he was napping on top of my workbench. Lifting the book, I grin over at Phrixius. "This spell will counter the binding and free you."

"Good witch." He grins, and something bubbles up inside me at the praise.

I deflate, though, the more I read. "It's going to take a while. Some of these ingredients . . . I don't even know where you would get them anymore."

"A few days or weeks is nothing to a god," he says. He's been the perfect house guest, unlike the demon. Well, he is picky about his food, and he and the demon fight about what film they are watching while I work, but he hasn't smotten—smitten—smited me? I don't know. Regardless, he's not done it, and he's being surprisingly patient considering I basically kidnapped him.

"The sooner the better," my demon snaps. "This idiot wants to watch some weird shows."

"Because I do not want to watch porn all the time?" Phrixius retorts, and I sigh. They bicker like this all the time, and it's annoying.

"Enough, Perry and Demon," I warn. I don't know why, but I've taken to calling the god every name under the sun. He seems to find it amusing, and I admit it's funny watching his reaction to each one.

"I preferred Picasso," he says as I grin.

"Okay, I'll start on this spell now and collect the ingredients as we go. Some of it takes at least ten days to brew anyway." I clap my hands and get to work, but part of me is reluctant.

I might have even become accustomed to Phrixius being here. He's a god, not a pet, but he's fun to be around. He tells good stories, and he seems to fit. It's foolish, I know, so I shake off those feelings and warm the cauldron. I pinch some oak root into the base, adding moon juice and some of the herbs along with volcanic ash since they will take the longest to brew. I leave it there as I scan the list and groan.

"Demon." I smile sweetly.

"No." He points at me, no doubt reading my expression.

I pout. "I need a branch from the oldest tree in the world. It will take me forever to go get it."

"Oh, so now you want my help," he sneers.

"The quicker we make this, the quicker he's gone," I croon, and he waves.

"If you want my help, then you make a deal like everyone else."

"What do you want?" I sigh, knowing he won't give in. Demons are stubborn like that.

"A kiss." He jerks his chin up, grinning. "One kiss and I'll go and get your stupid branch."

I stare, grinding my jaw. It could be worse. We've never crossed that line, but something about it feels . . . inevitable. I need that branch. "Fine, no tongue," I reply.

"Oh, sweet witch, you'll beg for tongue." He waits, eyebrow arching. "Well?"

Muttering under my breath, I step over, grab his horns, and yank him down, covering his lips with mine. For a moment, he's unmoving, and I go to pull away when he groans, gripping my ass and hauling me closer, his lips moving against mine harshly.

He tries to pry mine open, and when I gasp for a breath, his tongue slips in, tangling with mine. He tastes of fire and sulphur as his warm hand slides up and across my shoulders. I shudder as he swallows my moan. When I realise I'm leaning into it, I rip away, wiping my mouth on the back of my hand and stepping backward.

The demon looks dazed, his chest heaving as he stares at me.

"Branch," I remind him, my voice hoarse.

"Branch," he repeats, staring at me, and then suddenly, he's gone—no cocky remarks or teasing.

I'm left with my mouth tasting like flames as desire licks at every inch of me.

That was foolish. I should know better than to make a deal with a demon.

Never again.

I'm busy working on the ingredients when something passes my barrier—something strong, otherworldly, and dark.

It has more power than I've ever tasted, and the feeling of the grave comes along with it.

"Well, isn't this homey?" a deep, evil-sounding voice remarks.

I spin, my eyes widening at the being casually leaning against the entrance to my home. My magic automatically reacts, flying towards him for invading my territory. It hits him, and he seems to absorb it, which is impossible. He's really tall, but there's something about the glowing man that gives me pause.

A voice tells me this one is very dangerous.

He seems to dismiss me with a look and glances at Phrixius, who's on his feet now, his fists clenched at his sides. "The others sent me. Shall I kill her and free you?"

My eyes swing between them as I conjure more magic to protect myself in case Phrixius turns on me with this guy—or god, as I'm starting to believe.

Judging by the skulls decorating his arms, I have a truly bad feeling I know which one.

The god of death.

"No!" Phrixius's sharp voice cuts through my panic as he jumps to his feet before hesitating. "I mean, no, I am fine."

I panic. Okay, I'm not proud of it, but the god of death is in my home, threatening to kill me. I pick up a ladle and throw it, and then a bowl.

"You have been kidnapped," he says calmly despite the things I'm tossing at him.

"I have not been kidnapped. Okay, I was, but it's fine. I have this under control," Phrixius protests way too calmly.

"I'm sure you do." The man grins, ducking as I fling a cauldron at his head. "But the other gods are worried."

"Lie to them. Tell them I am free and will return."

That gives me pause. Why would Phrixius want him to lie to the other gods? Does he not want this god to free him? Or is he just worried how he would do it? He's already admitted he has dominion over magical creatures, so maybe he's just doing his duty as a god.

I fling a knife, and he catches it midair with a growl that makes my soul wither and die. "Don't tempt me, witch. If one more item is tossed my way that could affect my ability to please my . . . Well, you will be in trouble. Understood?"

Okay, so throwing things is not working, but I understand what it's like to be surrounded by beings more powerful than I am, and I know the first rule is not to show fear, so I cross my arms as I meet his gaze defiantly. "You do not scare me."

"I should. I could kill you without even touching you." He says it casually, like one would voice a greeting. I have no doubt he could. I can feel his power.

"You will do no such thing!" Phrixius's booming yell makes me gape and turn to him to see him glaring at his fellow god.

He's angrier than I've ever seen him.

"You are doing this for her? A witch?" the god of death asks slowly, his brows furrowed in confusion. He's not the only one. Phrixius is protecting me from his own people. Why?

"I would not expect you to understand," he hisses at the other god, shooting me a worried look. "Now leave, serpent, I have this under control." I see the god flinch slightly at the name, but he stands taller.

"Fine." He shrugs. "You can deal with their wrath later. I do like to cause chaos, though, so I will lie for now. Don't get stupid, not over a pesky, little, mortal witch, and not even a very powerful one."

He disappears, and I feel my barriers reform. I slump back, my wide eyes going to Phrixius. "Was that—"

"Mors, the god of death," Phrixius murmurs. "You're lucky to be alive."

"Why did you protect me from him?" I ask softly. "I trapped you. He could have helped, and yet you protected me. Why?"

He watches me carefully. "It is my job to protect those born with magic."

I nod. At least I have an answer. Turning away with a shaking hand, I freeze at his voice.

"And I want to protect you more than I have anyone else. I don't know why, but when he threatened to kill you, something within me snapped. I have never denied another god before. Read into that what you will."

My heart hammers at the confused confession.

That makes two of us who are confused.

I know one thing for sure, Phrixius doesn't belong here, and I could die if I'm not careful. You cannot keep a god at your side without facing the consequences. They are not made for this world.

CHAPTER 10

Grumbling under my breath, I appear at the very edge of this world. It's a place even the humans do not know about—a mystical place born from every fibre of magic. It stays protected from those without magic and acts as a haven for those born from it. True magical beings reside here, some even older than the gods themselves or the ancient beasts of the forest. It would do me well to be quiet and get in and out quickly. I might be a demon, but if one of those decides I am its mid-morning snack, then I'm screwed, and not in a good way.

I stand here, pressing my fingers to my lips where they still burn from her touch. She tasted like sin and death, and it was so addictive, I'm almost begging for another kiss.

That was my first.

Demons are immortal beings, and although I am one, I am not as old as some. Besides, the sins of the flesh never bothered me before her. I made deals for death and fun until her. When she started to explore pleasure, it felt like I was as well, as if she unlocked something within me—something she controls, even if she doesn't know it. Maybe the deal we made is why, but my little witch controls that part of me.

I have dreamed about tasting her, feeling her, and claiming her for years, yet with one little kiss, I am undone, lingering in a place no foul beast like me should, darkening the lands of ancient magic that fights to reject me.

Shaking my head, I glance around for what I came for. The quicker I get it, the quicker I can return, get rid of that pesky god, and deal with this addiction once and for all. It's time my little witch made her final deal—to become mine.

Luckily, my magic allowed me to home in on the tree, even if it is hard to focus on. They often say it erupted here, taking root as soon as this world came into existence, as if it's the beating heart of this world.

I'm about to strip it for my little witch. I almost smirk, glad to be doing something so evil.

I suppose she does let me have some fun, even if she won't let me eat Hagatha.

The old broad would go down in one bite, and I bet that pure, self-righteous soul would be delicious. No matter how good my little witch tries to be, she's just as dark as I, and I cannot wait for her to give in, which means getting rid of the god first. My lips still burn like the pits of hell as I focus on the tree before me.

There is a river of pure, glistening magic guarding it like a moat. The tree stands tall and proud, reaching into the clouds upon a granite island. Easy-peasy. Taking a few steps back, I get a running start and leap over the moat, landing on the granite island. I feel the magic reaching for me, so I skip to the tree and slap my hand onto the rough bark, knowing it won't touch me now.

"I taste delicious, but only one witch can eat me." I waggle my finger at the magic before glancing back at the deep brown tree. The branches are small down here. Will she need a bigger one? The god is a big bastard, and I don't want any delays.

Gripping the bark, I fling myself up, quickly climbing to the very top of the tree. I'll get her the biggest branch there is so there are no errors or mistakes, that way the god can fuck off and I can play with my witch again.

The tree is big, and by the time I get to the large branches, I'm exhausted, knowing I might not be able to carry one bigger. I climb onto the one I want and then reach above me. I hold onto a branch and slam my feet down over and over again until it starts to crack. I dare not use my magic here. I have a feeling it would not go well. After several jumps, the branch finally falls, and I ride it down to the ground where it crashes. I hop off and roll at the last minute and then grab it, dragging it over the river and disappearing once more.

I reappear back in my witch's house.

"I present to you the branch from the oldest tree in the world, also one of the biggest." I snap my fingers as it floats through the cave and place it on the table. It's so long, it hangs over either end, and I grin happily, waiting for my reward. My smile soon fades when Freya and the god just stare at me.

"What? I know I'm handsome, but there is no need to gawk. Actually, little witch, look all you want. In fact, feel free to test out how handsome I am." I slap my cheek with a wink. "Why don't you ride it and see?"

She just sighs, shakes her head, and turns back to her potions, but her back is tight, and her shoulders are tense. My eyes narrow on her, then I glance at the god. If that son of a bitch did anything to hurt her—

He must sense my thoughts because one perfect eyebrow arches. "Mors, the god of death, popped by."

My body freezes, my eternal fire dousing as pure fear fills me unlike anything I have ever felt. It must be fear, right? I have heard humans speak of it, but I have never felt it before. I pop into existence at her side, gripping her and turning her roughly. My hands trace every inch of her, even as she tries to slap me away. I look for any wound or grievance.

I was gone, and he was here.

She could have been killed with nothing but a look.

She could have been lost to me forever.

The organ inside my chest squeezes so tightly, I can't even breathe, and it's only when her hands cover mine on her chest that I inhale. "I'm okay," she whispers softly. "Bob protected me."

I swallow hard around the lump in my throat.

Fear tastes like acid in my mouth, my gut churns, and my skin feels too tight, too hot, and too cold at the same time. My chest hurts, and my fingers are shaking.

No wonder humans are so weak.

"He could have killed you."

"But he didn't." She grins softly. "Besides, I wouldn't have gone out so easily."

"Do not even joke about that." My hiss fills the air, and she blinks, her eyes widening as I step back.

She's okay, she's alive, and she's here.

She watches me carefully, looking confused, so I turn away, only for my eyes to clash with the god's. A knowing look fills his gaze as his lips tilt down. He sees too much.

"I just can't believe I missed all the fun," I joke flatly, but the silence after is long. "I will go check on the blood border." I disappear before they can say anything else.

I showed my hand.

No demon cares for another being, not in the way I do for my little witch.

The idea of her being gone . . .

No.

I would end up like the god in Phrixius's story, our creator, searching for her soul for the rest of my immortal life. She will never know or understand why. None of them can, but that terror that took root at almost losing her chases me even as I run away from the feelings inside me.

The blood border is intact, not that it would stop the god of death. It was simply an excuse to escape, and once I calm down, I pop back into our home, but my little witch isn't there. The god is stretched out, his eyes on the TV. He doesn't even spare me a look. "She went to fetch some herbs of some kind. She didn't go far."

"I didn't ask," I retort as I throw myself on my seat, my head tilted back to stare at the ceiling.

"You know, I have been trying to figure out what you meant about her dying if I broke the deal. At first, I thought you meant you would kill her or the deal would. I thought you were simply here to collect on that deal or for fun, but you are not here for any deal or fun, are you, demon?"

"I don't know what you mean, god," I hiss. "You beings always read too much into things. Us lowly demons do shit just because we can. Don't overthink it."

"That act may work on Freya, but I have been around a long time, demon—"

"No shit. You're so ancient, your bones are practically dust. I bet you spunk cobwebs." I smirk, lifting my head to meet his gaze.

He simply sighs. "You cannot distract me, demon. Freya is one of mine, and now I want to know."

I don't like him claiming her like that, but arguing that point would only prove him right. It's a bad precedent to let a god think he's right.

"Know what?" I sit up, knowing he is not going to stop talking. That's the problem with these gods: they love the sound of their own voices. Nobody ever dares to tell them they are annoying, so they never learn to shut up.

"The truth, like why you two cannot be separated and what deal was made. Why will she die?"

"Oh, so not much. At least take me out to dinner before you try to fuck me."

Rising elegantly, he steps from the circle. I fall back with a fake gasp, my hand over my mouth as I point at him. "Liar! Traitor! I'm going to tell little witch you are faking it to stay here."

He ignores my threat and doesn't stop until he is before me. "Now, demon, the truth. No half lies or games. What have you done to her?"

For a moment, I stare into his narrowed eyes, and I don't know why, but some of the truth slips out—maybe because I'm worried he will try to take her from me if I don't. "I saved her."

He's quiet for a moment. "From what?"

Luckily, I am saved by our little witch. He hears her too and appears back within the trapping spell just as she enters. She blinks at us before hurrying to her cauldron, talking to herself as she brews, and I can't pull my eyes away from her.

If she knew . . .

No, she can never know, even if it means she hates me.

I have a deal to keep.

Even a lowly, evil demon like me will not break that—not the kind made in blood and death.

I feel his eyes on me, but I ignore them. He can never know—no one can.

It would ruin everything.

CHAPTER 11

I have ten days to figure out what the demon meant.

I should go back if Mors and the others are looking for me. It could spell trouble, but for the first time in many, many years, I have a purpose.

This little witch was born from my magic, from people like me. She is one of mine, and it's my duty to protect her. I know it's a lie though. Something about her compels me to stay and protect her, even from my kind. Mors could have killed me for standing before her. I was lucky he was in a good mood, but the demon, on the other hand . . .

Demons only do things for two reasons.

The first is a deal.

The second is because it's entertaining.

Which is it for him? Since it's been so many years since he appeared, it has to be a deal. Someone made a deal to save her. My brow furrows as I glance between them. They work seamlessly together, even if neither notice, communicating without words. He helps her brew the spell I do not need, reaching up for a vial when she cannot and handing it over without a word. When she steps back, he moves with instinct to block her from tripping. It is like a dance between them. Both are so very aware of the other.

Do they even realise it?

Why does the thought irritate me?

Has anyone ever been that aware of me? Have I ever trusted someone so much that I can rely on them without even thinking?

No. I have never let someone in that much. They trust each other, which makes this a lot harder. If I am to save her and free her from the deal with the demon like she so clearly wants, then it will hurt them both, maybe even kill her.

Does she truly want to be free of the deal, or has she spent so long fighting his presence, she doesn't even realise what she wants anymore?

I need to know more before I make a move. This could be a dangerous situation for them, and I do not wish to hurt the little witch. She is kind and funny. I blink at my thoughts, and when she glances over her shoulder at me and grins, I find myself smiling back.

For the first time in a few millennium, I smile at another, unable to help it.

The demon was right. This little witch is far more dangerous than I thought.

"Freya, get out here right now!" someone hollers from outside the cave.

Both Freya and the demon turn, frowning, and then they share a look. The demon disappears and reappears a moment later. "It's Hagatha."

"Why?" Freya's frown deepens, but she hurries to the entrance. I discreetly follow, shielding myself so neither of them sees me. Freya is half bowed before an older lady who has her arms crossed, an irritated expression on her face.

"Tell me it was not you, child," Hagatha demands. What a strange name.

"Erm, see, usually I would be feigning innocence, but for once, I'm lost. What was not me?" Freya asks with confusion. She has been in her home with us for the last few days, brewing the spell, not up to trouble, and from the look of this white witch's face, this is the usual for her.

Hagatha sighs, scrubbing at her face. "Freya." Her voice fills with power, and it lashes out, wrapping around Freya, who gasps, dropping to her knees. I grab the demon before he can react. "Wait," I hiss at him.

The glowing white bindings wrap tighter around Freya's throat. "I want the truth, and this spell will ensure that. I am sorry, child, but I cannot trust your words otherwise. Did you steal the mask of origins from my shop?"

"What mask? I have stolen nothing," Freya rasps as the threads dig into her throat. It won't hurt her, just feel uncomfortable and allow her to speak nothing but the truth. It's not harmful, but even I do not like the sight of my little witch on her knees, being forced to speak.

Hagatha frowns. "What have you been up to, Freya? You have been quiet, and then the mask disappeared."

The demon stills—we both do. If she speaks the truth now, it will not be good for her. No coven would be happy that a member summoned and trapped a god to break a deal with a demon.

They could cast her aside.

"I have been trying to contain my magic so I do not make any more mistakes." Despite the spell, one of the strongest I have ever felt outside of my realm, Freya manages to lie.

She lies through a truth spell.

Just how powerful is this little witch?

The spell suddenly unwinds, and Freya gasps, falling forward. "I'm sorry, child, but I had to be sure." Hagatha sighs, crouching down and offering her hand.

Freya climbs to her feet, ignoring the proffered hand, and glares at Hagatha. "And you cannot trust my word? You trust me that little?"

"You have never given me a reason for it." Hagatha sounds tired.

"Am I not a member of this coven? Do I not deserve the same respect? You have all looked down on me since I was a child, and now you use magic on me as if I were a traitor?" Freya hisses, and black smoke seems to wrap around her.

Hagatha notices, glancing at it worriedly, but she doesn't appear surprised. "Child, calm down. I had to know it was not you—"

"Yes, it was not, yet here we are," Freya hisses, and the sound raises the hair on the back of my neck.

It is chilling.

It is cold.

It is death.

I stare at Freya. Just what magic does she possess? She doesn't even seem to notice she is doing it, as if it's outside of her control, which is even more worrisome.

"Child." Hagatha spreads her hands wide, watching her magic. "That mask, you know it, the one that sings to you." Freya stills, as does the smoke. "It is the origin of the necromancers, and it is one of the most cursed objects in this world. It's filled with so much evil and pain, it can corrupt even the purest soul. It is missing, and I am questioning everyone like this. Follow me if you do not believe me."

The smoke slowly retracts. "Who would steal something like that?"

"Nobody with good intentions," Hagatha admits, her face almost collapsing. "I swear, child, I am not singling you out. We have to get to the bottom of this swiftly. That mask . . . it could cause the end of this world."

"Necromancers are all gone," Freya murmurs.

Hagatha eyes her. "Or they want us to think they are." She waves her hand. "I will continue to search, but if you see or hear anything, let me know, okay?"

Freya nods and watches Hagatha go with a frown on her face. She looks all soft and innocent, but I cannot forget what I just saw—the darkness leaking from her soul.

When the demon glances at me, he is not surprised.

He knows what she is.

We both do.

The question is, does she?

CHAPTER 12

I should be sleeping, but all I can think about is what Agatha said.

Someone stole the mask, the creepy one. How did she know it sang to me?

What does it mean that such a cursed object called to me?

Nothing good, that's for sure, and the panic in her tone when she saw me arguing had me questioning everything. I feel like my whole world is spiralling as I lie in my bed and stare at the ceiling, trying to put it back into order so my feelings don't overwhelm me. I have always kept careful control over them to keep order, but they seem to be squeezing through more often, and I don't like who I am when they do.

As usual, the demon crawls up onto my bed, wrapping his arms and legs around me. It is usually too tight. "Breathe through it," he murmurs softly in my ear. "I'm right here. In and out slowly."

I try, I really do. I do the breathing exercises he taught me after many nights like this—after fights with other coven members, a bad day, or one too many drinks . . . .

How many nights has the demon spent breathing with me until all those pieces inside me go back where they should be?

Too many to count.

I don't know why, but that only makes those pieces scatter more, leaving me frayed and vulnerable. My hands curl into the sheets as I breathe in his scent, and the thing inside me surges forward as if sensing my weakness. The tight fist of control I always keep loosens.

He senses it, as he always does.

"Enough, control it." His nails dig into my cheeks, and the sharp sting of pain makes desire flare inside me. I drop my eyes to his lips, which are inches away, remembering the taste of him.

I try to roll away, deciding I'll go seek out a partner for the night.

I'll paint these worries across their skin, and in the morning, everything will be back to normal.

I'll use them like I always do.

"No." Arms drag me back, flipping me, and suddenly, the demon is above me, his eyes glowing. "Not tonight, little witch. If you are going to use anyone to fight the war, it will be me. You are too out of control, and you can feel it. They cannot handle that, but I can take it." His lips slide across my cheek to my ear, leaving me trembling. "So use me, little witch. I can take it all. I can take everything inside you. Nothing there scares me."

"It scares me," I admit softly.

"I know." He kisses over my jumping pulse. "Fight, little witch. Fight with me."

He lifts his head, just a few inches above me. His hands are on either side of me, and he's pinning my legs down. I see the determination on his face. He's not letting me go, not tonight, and despite the fact that there is no deal, I reach for him.

I drag him down and press my lips to his, and I lose myself in him. I pour my darkness into him, and I let him drink it down.

I use him just like he said.

He moans against my lips and falls into my body, every hard inch of him pressing me to the furs on my bed. The weight should be suffocating, but I tear at his back with my nails, needing him closer. He hisses in pleasure, and my hands wrap around his horns, yanking him off. I throw him across the bed and then lunge, pinning him down as my lips meet his once more.

I rip at his clothes, feeling them tear, but I need to get closer. My nails cut him, and I taste his blood as our teeth clash. His moans mix with my groans as I take out the darkness on his skin.

My hands slip lower, sliding into his trousers, and he gasps, his back arching as I wrap my fingers around his huge cock. It should stop me, and I shouldn't do this, but I do.

It's beyond me now, beyond us. This is out of control.

This is life or death, and I cannot stop or I'll shatter, and I do not know what will be left.

He moans as I pump his length. "Little witch."

I tease him, feeling every inch of the cock I've only ever seen, never touched. He's so big, I can't even close my hand all the way around him. He's larger than any I've ever had and so hot it nearly burns my hand. Fire, he feels like fire in my grip. It's the underside of his cock, though, that has me mewling and grinding into his thigh, pleasure filling me.

Spikes run down the underside of his cock, and when I stroke down to the base, they bend, tickling my palm. How would they feel inside me? They could dig in like barbs, but the thought only makes me hotter, and my lips find his again as his cock jerks in my grip.

I want all his noises. I want his surrender despite what and who he is.

He gives it to me, knowing I need it.

He lets me use his body like a toy, the feelings inside me flowing from me to him as he groans, lifting his hips to slide his cock into my hand until I grind against his thigh, hitting my clit with each movement.

I cry out into his mouth as I come. His hand grips the back of my head, keeping me there as he thrusts into my fist and swallows my cry of pleasure. When he groans, I feel him jerk in my hand before red-hot fire coats my palm, and I know he came.

I slump forward, all those emotions suddenly just gone, leaving me feeling alone, confused, and guilty.

I pant against his neck, tasting the sweat on his skin. My hand is still in his pants as he lies there, twitching, but when I lift my head, I see a blissful look on his face. It's almost peaceful, his eyes closed and lips slack.

Suddenly, what we just did hits me, and I yank my hand free, wiping it on his jeans. He just grumbles.

I lift my head and look down. My lips are bleeding and swollen, my nails are broken and jagged, and my skin is bruised. The demon lies below me, his eyes dark and lustful, his skin and muscles on display.

He looks every inch the sinner he is, tempting and filthy, and he's all mine.

Shit, what am I thinking? What did I do?

I crossed the line I never should have.

Sliding as far over on the bed as I can, I give the demon my back.

My cheeks heat even in the dark. I dare not turn to see if Phrixius is awake and watching us, yet some part of me likes the idea of the god watching me use this demon to control this thing inside me.

The thing that scares me.

CHAPTER 13

I should be horrified by what I saw last night.

Did Freya even realise what she was doing? She poured that dark magic of death and decay into the demon. Any other being would be dead from how much she gave him, and the demon knew it. That's why he did what he did . . . or at least I think so.

Little bits of that magic would have been fine for anyone, and they would just feel weak the next day, but that amount would kill any other.

I could see the darkness between their lips, pouring into him.

Did she even know what she was doing?

I should feel guilty for watching them, and it's clear she's embarrassed as she hurries to the bathroom upon waking. No doubt her magic was in control more than she was, but despite all that, I feel hunger.

I want to see her that desperate atop me, using my body. I want her hands touching me like that.

Fuck, the sound she made when she came is burned into my brain. I want to swallow it, to memorise it. I have never hungered for something as much. It is as if she's calling to the primal side of me, and after watching her find her pleasure last night, I've been hard and aching for the little witch in a way an immortal being should not be.

Of course I noticed her beauty, but last night in the dark, it was as if she cast a spell upon us all until our darkest desires unravelled, and now we are all left in the aftermath. Can we go back?

Do I even want to?

Not too long later, Freya returns, dressed and ready for the day. Her hair is plaited down both sides of her face, with dark wisps escaping even as she blows them from her eyes. Her curvy body is encased in flowing dark pants and a blouse, and she seems totally oblivious to the effect it has on us both. The demon and I track her movements with lustful, hungry gazes as she moves over to the brewing potion and checks on it. When she bends over to reach for something, the demon actually groans, looking at me as if to check if I'm seeing this.

I nod solemnly, and we share a pained, almost brotherly look in solidarity.

"Okay, I added the next ingredient. It just needs to boil down now, so we have time. What?" She blinks as she turns to find us both staring at her. Pulling my legs up, I rest my chin on the top of them to hide my arousal. The demon makes no such moves. In fact, he presses his hands to his hips as if to present his very obvious erection to her.

"You look very good today." His eyes run down her body appreciatively. "Very fucking good."

Her lashes flutter as she stares and then peers at me. "And why are you being weird?"

"Very good." I nod, unable to say any other words since my eyes keep drifting to her body, much like the demon's.

I am supposed to be a god, good and ancient—I wonder if she would let me bite that plump flesh.

"Men. God or demon, it doesn't matter what kind, you are all the same," she mutters as she grabs a coat and pulls it on, causing us both to lament as it covers her chest.

"Men or women. If you go around looking like that, we are bound to stare," the demon remarks seriously. "Where are we going?"

She glares at him. "I am going to walk around. I want to know what's been going on with the mask that was stolen."

He and I share a knowing look. "Maybe that isn't such a good idea," I say. If they know what or suspect what she could be like Agatha, then they will be looking to blame her, and things like this can spiral quickly. I would hate for her to get hurt by her own people, especially since she is oblivious as to why.

She glares at us. "Now let's get one thing clear, this is my life, my house, and my coven. Do not try to tell me what to do. Demon or god, I don't care. If you start pulling that shit, I will turn you into dildos and pass you out to the coven." She flips a braid over her shoulder and marches out of the cave while we both gawk.

"She wouldn't, would she?" I ask incredulously.

The demon nods, glancing back at me. "She once turned me into a flagpole during one of their celebrations. I have never felt so violated. It was amazing."

"I would have different feelings," I mutter.

Grinning, he pops out of existence, and I sigh, left alone once more. I could follow them, but I don't want her to suspect me of lying to her with how hard she's working to free me. Instead, I turn to the TV with a frown. "Demon, where's the remote?" He doesn't answer, so with a sigh, I click my fingers and send magic to the TV. I watch it fizzle before it starts to smoke. I turn away with a wince. I'll just blame the demon.

Freya will believe me.

CHAPTER 14

freya

While the potion is brewing, I decide to kill some time. I've been locked away for days, which isn't unusual, but with everything going on, I feel the need to check in on everyone and see what's happening. Agatha said the mask was stolen, and I was angry at first, but now I'm just curious.

How and why?

Entering the coven's blood circle would take more power than I've ever sensed, unless they are a god or dead or something. That's what keeps circling my brain as I head into town to listen in on rumours.

It's unusually quiet today, and the few members I do pass seem to give me a wide berth, their eyes downcast or accusingly staring at me. "They probably heard Hagatha came to ask you about the mask. You know how fast rumours travel and change. I bet they think it's you," the demon supplies helpfully as he skips by my side.

"Gee, thanks, now they all think I'm a thief as well as weird," I mutter, ducking my head as more pass, outright glaring at me.

Just fucking great.

I don't protest though, and I stop at Agatha's shop, peering through the window to see the case where the mask was sitting open and empty, just like she said. I don't know why, but seeing it makes it real, and I shiver. I remember the call of that mask. It didn't feel good. Why would someone steal it?

"She's a dark witch, after all," comes a whisper, and when I turn, a gaggle of young witches freezes, their eyes snapping to me and widening before they take off giggling.

"Want me to stalk them and scare them?" my demon offers helpfully.

"No, that's mean. Okay, maybe a little." I grin, and he vanishes as I laugh.

"Freya?" The voice is hesitant. I whirl around to see Agatha standing in the doorway, watching me carefully. We didn't end our conversation on such good terms the other day.

"Have you found anything?" I ask.

She shakes her head, her mouth opening before someone passes. She waits for them to go and opens the door wider. "Come in, child. Let us speak in private."

I hesitate before ducking past her. Despite everything, she is still the leader of this coven and a good woman. She was just doing her job, even if it stung. My gaze cuts to the empty shelf before I turn to her.

"Nothing at all. No connection or trace within the coven whatsoever," Agatha admits worriedly.

"You think someone broke the blood barrier from the outside and came in and stole it and none of the elders felt it?" I frown.

"Not even a slight change in the barrier," she says, and it's clear she's concerned. They don't feel my demon, and they clearly didn't feel Mors, but they are ancient beings. Do I mention it? If they can get through the barrier, whoever stole the mask obviously can too, meaning they have great power. "What is weirder . . ." She trails off, and I wait.

"Weirder?" I repeat when she just stares.

"There are no traces of any magic or power around the sector at all, and when we asked Lilly, she said she couldn't see anything." Shit, they asked Lilly? She's a recluse who's even worse than I am. Being born with powers of prophecy and foresight isn't easy, and she once told me she sees every world and every possibility all at the same time. That shit must be exhausting.

Lilly is never wrong, ever, and for her not to see it?

"You think somehow someone was able to block her?" I ask. I didn't even know that was possible.

"They must know about it, know she was searching. I don't know. That or they are simply that powerful, which is all the more cause for concern." She lays her hand on my shoulder. "Ignore the whispers, Freya. You are good at that. We know you did not do this. I am very sorry for our doubts causing you harm."

"I get it." I shrug and step back. Her hand feels almost patronising now after everything that happened. "I'm different, and differences are always questioned."

That makes her frown sadly. "Be careful, Freya," she cautions, not denying what I said since we both know it's true. "I worry about what this means for you."

"Why?" I ask.

Her lips purse as she stares at me, and it seems she is about to divulge something when the door opens. We both turn and frown at the empty doorway, then we share a glance. Was it the demon? If so, where is he?

"Anyway, I should let you get back to your day." Agatha shakes herself, smiling at me. "We will update the coven when we know more, so for now, do not worry."

I nod despite my confusion, but I see the fear in her eyes as she turns away. She's telling us not to worry, but Agatha is terrified, and if something is scaring the most powerful witch on this Earth, then you can damn well bet I'm shitting my pants.

I wander the coven for hours, but it seems everyone can sense our head witch's mood. The place feels subdued, as everyone is either working or hiding. Fear is thick in the air, like they are waiting for something else to happen, and the whispers as I show my face have only gotten worse. I can't stand them anymore and decide to head home. The demon is quiet at my side for once, which also worries me.

"Do you know who stole it?" I ask once we are out of earshot.

He startles when I speak, which means he was lost in his own thoughts. "No, little witch, I do not."

"You didn't feel or sense anything?" I ask, frowning at him as I quicken my steps, feeling eyes on my back—not a threat but just watching.

"Nothing, though I could have been distracted," he admits, winking at me. "You are worried about this."

"Aren't you? If someone can just waltz into the coven—"

"Like me, Phrixius, and the god of death?" he jokes.

"Then they can do anything. They might be suspicious of me and mean sometimes, but this is my home, demon. These people are my family. I cannot let them suffer or be bound by fear. They blame me already, which makes me worry they are not really looking for who did this," I explain out loud.

"You want to track whoever it is down, don't you?" he grumbles. "That's stupid, even for a demon."

"I do, and you're going to help me." I turn to him. "Find out what you can. Check the barrier or ask your demon friends. Whoever it was has power and lots of it. Please."

"And why would I help with this without a deal?"

I roll my eyes and step closer. Grabbing him by the horns, I yank him down and kiss him hard. "Please," I murmur against his lips.

His eyes are wide and unfocused as he nods rapidly in my hands. "Sure, yep, totally. I will be right back." He disappears.

Shaking my head, I turn to head home when he suddenly appears before me again, winding his arms around me as I yelp when he drags me closer. Dipping me deeply, he kisses me. "Fair is fair," he whispers before he's gone again, and I nearly fall on my ass, his laughter chasing after me.

"Asshole," I mutter, even as a smile curves my lips.

When I get back home, Phrixius is studiously sitting in the circle, facing the door.

"Everything okay?" I ask as I take off my cape and drape it over the chair before heading over to check on the spell. My nose twitches at a burning smell. Shit, did I burn it?

I hurry over, breathing a sigh of relief when I see it bubbling away. Turning with a frown, I sniff deeper and head around my home until I stop at the smoking TV. "Fucking demon!" I roar. "This is the third one this year! It's coming out of your pocket money."

"You give the demon pocket money?" Phrixius asks.

"Is that important right now, Rodger?" I ask, my hands on my hips before I point at the TV. "This was the latest model. I'm going to tan that demon's ass."

His cheeks heat, and I wince. "Sorry, language. You're a god."

He huffs, rubbing his neck. "It's fine. Demons are known for mischief. Why don't I help you?"

"Huh?" I ask, and he rises gracefully to his feet and closes his eyes.

Within seconds, the TV is gone, replaced by a huge, brand-new one. "Oh, Willy, you didn't have to do that. It wasn't your fault. Trust me, the demon has broken enough things."

"Erm, still," he says with a small smile. "Is that okay?"

"Thank you. At least one of you is kind." The smile on his face tightens. I bet gods are used to flattery, but Phrixius doesn't seem to be. How odd. That reminds me, I know hardly anything about him. With nothing to do but kill time, I brew some tea and make a plate of snacks, which I push to the circle and then sit before him as he sits with a confused frown.

He lifts the cup and sniffs it. "This isn't poison, is it? Will it turn me into a flagpole?"

"What? Why? I only do that when the demon pisses me off," I mutter as I sip the tea. "It's chamomile."

He nods but eyes the tea worriedly. "Yes, well, I have done nothing, nothing at all."

"Right." I watch him in confusion as he sips the tea and seems to relax. "So, tell me about you, Sammy."

His eyebrows rise. "You wish to . . . know me?"

"Well, we are stuck together for now, and despite you being a great house guest and seemingly able to piss my demon off by just breathing, we don't know much about each other. So tell me."

"You could simply look me up," he points out.

"Where's the fun in that?" I sigh. "Besides, I don't believe everything people say or write. They have a tendency to portray their own feelings and not the truth. I've found it's best to go straight to the source."

"That is quite profound of you," he comments, settling back. "What would you like to know?"

"How old are you?" I grin, and he laughs.

"I began existing not long after this world." My eyes widen, and he chuckles, his expression shining with mirth. "Yes, I am that old."

"So you're not like a daddy, you're like a great-great-great-great-granddaddy," I muse, and he spits out tea he just sipped.

"Daddy?" He blinks. "As if I'm a father? No, I do not have children."

I roll my lips in to bite back my smile. "Good to know." I giggle. "So you're super old and don't have children. What kind of god are you?"

"Of moon and magic," he answers with a soft smile. "Though mostly magic. It's a broad category, I know. Basically, I sense any magic in the world, but mainly witches." He winks at me as I grin.

"So you can sense my magic?" I ask, sitting up taller. For a moment, I stare at him, wanting to ask.

"I can," he says carefully, eyeing me.

Swallowing hard, I try to force the words out so I can learn the truth about what I am and the darkness that seems to plague only me, but in the end, I chicken out. "That's cool," I say lamely. "So you know a lot of covens?"

"I used to. We have withdrawn from this world in the last century. It's just easier to maintain balance that way. In all honesty, I haven't checked in with my people in a very long time. Covens run themselves, and witches are very good at keeping order . . . sprinkled with a little chaos. It leaves me with lots of free time. I feel more like an idea now rather than something important."

Sadness tinges his words, making me scoot closer. "So why don't you find something that makes you feel important again?" He blinks at me, so I continue. "I use my ability to help others with spells and potions. I like feeling successful and needed. The demon has, well . . . the demon. Agatha has the coven and her shop. Everyone needs something to give them purpose and inspire them, but moreover, it should make you happy. Without joy, are you really living?"

His head tilts as he eyes me for a moment. "Not for a long time." He glances away. "It is something all immortal beings feel after a while—the stagnant nature of our never-ending lives. We are doomed to watch those we love or care for grow and die. We are made to watch cities rise and fall, everything around us changing, but we never truly do."

"It sounds lonely," I murmur. "I don't think I'd like to be immortal. Yes, death comes for us, and the idea of dying scares me a little, but I think that fear is what keeps us moving, keeps us mortal, you know? We try new things, experiencing everything we can so that when death does come for us, we can say we truly lived. Our life spans are short in comparison, but I think it's possible to live many lifetimes within one if you try hard enough."

"Is that what you want? To live many lifetimes?"

"I want to be happy. It's a small dream, I know, compared to most, but it's true, I just want to be happy, loved, and cherished so that when the day comes and I return to the Earth, I know I can go without regrets. That's my biggest fear—that at the end, all I'll have will be bitter thoughts and what-ifs. I don't want that. I know how easily life can be taken away." I shrug. "Maybe that's silly."

"Never reduce your ideas and wants in fear of what others will say," he responds automatically. "That lessens your own worth and reduces your soul. Your dreams are not small, Freya, they are beautiful, and so are you." There's a knowing gleam in his eyes I can't look away from.

"It doesn't feel that way. All I have now are what-ifs and a million different roads taking me places, and I'm standing in the middle of them all, too scared to make a choice in case it's the wrong one. Someday, I want to take a step, but I want to know I'll be going down the right path," I say, my gaze on my twiddling fingers. When he's quiet, I lift my eyes. He's pressed to the edge of the barrier, watching me with a fond, soft expression.

"You will. I have never met someone as brave as you in my entire immortal life." My heart skips at that. I want to protest, but he doesn't let me. "Nor as singularly kind. I think, Freya, that when you make up your mind and accept all of you, you will have everything you want if you are strong enough to fight for it, and I know you are. I know you're strong enough to withstand whatever comes when you walk the path you choose."

"But what if I choose the wrong one?" I whisper.

"Then turn around and create another. Life is not so straightforward. If there's anything I've learned from my long years here, it is the ability to adapt and keep moving. Just because you make a choice doesn't mean you're stuck with it forever. You can always change, you can always go back or choose a different way. You are never trapped, Freya, not even with what fate gives you."

There's something lacing his words, something deeper, as if he's talking about something else. Shaking it off, I force a smile.

"I guess you're right. Anyway, what hobbies do gods have?" I ask, and he chuckles as he leans back, letting me change the subject, but something about what he said sticks with me.

Accept myself . . . Haven't I?

Is that why I'm stuck, never quite moving forward?

What happens if I do?

It feels as if something has always been holding me here in this spot, and part of me thinks that if I break free and move forward, something terrible will happen.

Why?

CHAPTER 15

"I'm hunting a mask for my little witch, hunting a mask so we can kill a bitch," I sing as I skip through the forest surrounding the coven. I found a faint trail at the edge of the barrier, and it led right into their land. Hagatha was right. It passed through without setting off alarm bells.

Nothing should be able to do that . . . .

Nothing but death magic.

I don't tell my little witch that yet, not until I'm sure. It would only worry her, and her voice goes all high and weird when she's worried. Plus, she won't let me play. She'll be all, "We need to save the world, demon, no time for thinking about our kiss."

Our kiss.

It's all I can think about—the way she tastes, the soft moans she made in my mouth, and the way her curves fit perfectly into my hands. Heat is all I know, yet I was scorched under her desire.

Demons take what we want, and we do what we want, yet I have held back my desire for my little witch for so long, I couldn't anymore, especially when I saw the darkness riding her. I can still taste it now, the death pouring into me, bringing me to life and killing me at the same time. What would it be like if I fucked her?

Would she shatter into mist?

Would she wrap it around me and drain me dry?

I shudder in desire. Fires, I could only hope so, and one day, I will find out. We are destined to explode, the little witch and me. I didn't know it all those years ago when fate brought me here. I was only here to uphold the deal, but somewhere along the way, that shifted to needing to protect her. The deal was forgotten, and all I care about now is her, but for a demon, loving someone isn't good. It never ends well, yet I can't seem to stop myself.

My little witch stole every dark, fiery edge of me without even realising it. I am her weapon, her saviour, and her damnation, and one day, I will be her lover. No one else could withstand her needs, not as strong as they are becoming.

It's selfish, but a part of me likes that I could be the only one who's able to withstand her power. Maybe Phrixius, the ass, could, but he's a god and is all high and mighty. There's no way he would let himself break his rules and take my witch, so that leaves me.

The quicker I get this hunt over with, the quicker I can get back to her and we can finish what we started.

It's what speeds up my hunt, my powers flexing across the land. It's been a long time since I've used so much, since I've been stuck at the coven. It makes me sigh in bliss to feel them flexing and being used again.

Whistling happily, I slip through the trees before deciding I should look the part. With a click of my fingers, my outfit changes, and I'm wearing a dramatic suit and a bowler hat with a moustache and a cane. It's much better suited for a detective on the hunt.

The cold edge of death magic is faint, so I focus on it fully, letting it lead me on a merry chase. It's a few hours of walking since I don't want to lose the trail and have to double back, and I get bored and hungry, so I create a corndog, milkshake, and burgers along the way, eating as I go. I ignore the wild wolves and ancient beasts I feel watching me the entire time. They won't touch me, not with the mark upon me, the one that no one else sees but me.

I am protected, at least for now.

It doesn't stop them from being interested though. I must present a tasty snack. I wag my finger at one persistent, feral wolf, and when it bares its teeth, I click my fingers. "Bad wolf." It shrinks down in size, changing colour until it becomes a furry little rabbit. "See how you like being hunted," I say as I continue my journey.

My mind is split between my witch and the death magic I'm following.

It can't be a coincidence, can it? Did someone feel her?

Do they know?

No, they can't. She's growing stronger, but she's contained. I made sure of it. So why now? The only thing that has changed is that fucking god. The sooner we get rid of him, the better. He brings nothing but bad omens, and he's annoying. He also keeps winning in my games and beating my scores.

I hate the way he looks at my little witch as well. It's the same way I look at her. He's supposed to be above all that, be all godly and shit, but I can see through him. He craves the magic inside her, wants to taste it and control it. All gods are the same. They crave power, and nothing is more powerful than my little witch—even if she doesn't know it. Maybe that's why he's sticking around. Regardless, once this hunt is through, I need to find a way to get rid of him for good—oh look, shiny rock.

I pocket the glowing stone to give to my witch. I know she likes things like this. I pluck a few herbs and wildflowers as well that she's running low on. Usually, she goes and gets them, but I know it drains her, so this way she can spend more time focusing on her spells and playing with me. That's the only reason why. No other reason.

"Seriously, I'm tired of hunting now. Those detective shows make it look way more fun!" I yell to no one. "I could be balls deep in my witch right now. Okay, probably not, since she'd kill me first, but I could be making my moves or taking a nap, but no." Using magic, I make my pitch higher. "Track down the mask, demon. Do this, demon. I'm so pretty that it's distracting, demon, so I make you agree to everything." Snorting, I sigh as I stomp through the hillside.

"We get it, with your ominous death magic and stealing a very naughty mask while probably harbouring malevolent plans to end the world, but could you make this easier? Like, come out and monologue me to death. I've been practising my, 'You won't get away with this.' Honestly, my witch would find it super impressive. She'd finally realise she loves me, and we'd spend the next ten years in bed, or on the floor . . . or against the wall."

There's no reply, so I stomp harder, following the never-ending trail like I'm a fucked-up version of Hansel and Gretel. At least those fuckers got sweets and almost got an epic nap in a fire. I'd kill to be shoved in an oven right now and let a witch eat me—specifically one witch.

Oh well, hopefully if I bring her the evildoer or some information, she might eat me either way. I could cover myself in sweets. Humming happily, I speed up my steps. The trail seems to get stronger the closer I get to the city. The flow of the death magic increases, and I run now, knowing I'm close.

The rolling hills give way to ancient trees, and once through their midst, I find myself in an overgrown, long since abandoned graveyard.

"Creepy, I love it." I nod, looking around. "Love what you did with the place. It's giving hobo chic vibes. Very in."

The church leans to the side, the windows broken and the doors smashed open with what looks like dried blood creating a trail inside. There are at least five overturned graves, with soil and bits of casket scattered around as if something inside wanted out.

"You know, if I wasn't a demon, I might be scared right now," I mutter as I follow the trail through the graves, avoiding the open holes as I head towards the church.

At the doorway, I glance in. "If anyone is in there hiding, come out now. I hate surprises," I call, but nothing moves, and I grumble as I glance at the sky. "If one of you fuckers sets me on fire for stepping in here, I'm going to be really mad. My girl doesn't like BBQ that much."

Placing a hesitant foot on the first step, I wait, and when I don't burst into flames, I skip inside, following the blood trail. I guess the holy ground isn't so holy anymore, or the gods simply don't care that a demon is desecrating it. That thought comes to a screeching halt, though, because I suddenly realise it's already been desecrated.

"I'm all for a bit of grave robbing, since the dead fuckers don't need it, and I get fucking with the church because fuck gods, but damn, you really brought down the property value," I remark. There is blood splashed on every wall, like someone took a bucket of paint and just went to town.

"It's very evil Bob Ross," I mutter as I head past overturned wooden pews, spying crosses flipped upside down nearly everywhere. When I reach the pulpit, I frown.

The trail ends here, and when I glance around, I almost groan.

I was right, and that doesn't bode well for this world or my little witch.

There is a pentagram made of blood and bowls of something I don't want to look too closely at spread around its edges, which still glows with death magic—strong death magic. In the middle of it all is a rotting hand, the skin falling off and decaying. It's a strange yellow colour, the fingers curled as if grabbing something. It's just sitting there, like a fucked-up arm-wrestling machine.

"Do not move. Do not fucking move. Do not move," I mutter as I carefully step over the blood just in case it's a reaping circle. Picking up a broken chair leg, I prod the hand. I'm not proud of the scream that rips from my body when it jerks, clenching the wood and stealing it.

"I told you not to fucking move!" I yell at it, shuddering like spiders are running all over me. "That's just creepy and rude. Who the fuck leaves a still moving and very dead arm in a church? Is it a warning or an interior design choice?" I wait, but there's no answer. "You can't speak, you're an arm. Some good you are!" I huff before an idea hits me, and I perk up. "But we might be able to use you to track whoever did this. My witch will be so happy. Okay, nice arm, come with me." I magic a bag because there is no way I am carrying that thing. It seems angry.

"Nice arm, that's it, come with Uncle Demon. You'll like where we're going. It's less satanic murder house, more cosy witch core.

That's it . . ." I grab the wood and jerk, plopping the moving hand into the bag and quickly shutting it. "Nice undead arm."

As I leave the church, the hand claws at the bag, hitting my side and ass in its attempt to get free.

"Hey." I smack the bag at my side. "No grabbing the goods. Only my witch can do that."

If my day wasn't bad enough, I'm now being felt up by a rotting hand. Oh well, beggars can't be choosers.

CHAPTER 16

freya

I almost forgot it is the full moon tonight. The spell is done, so I can free Phrixius from my binding spell. Why am I sad? We were bonding and getting along, but he's a god, not a pet. My demon is still out hunting, and I hope he's okay. The silence is way too loud without him, but I don't focus too much on that.

Instead, I hoist my bag with everything I need higher and smile at Phrixius. "I'll be back." I don't tell him where I'm going in case it doesn't work and he's still trapped. I don't want to get his hopes up. I don't think I could handle him being disappointed in me.

He nods with a soft smile and returns to lounging and reading his book. I take one last look at the beautiful god before leaving my cave. I remind myself he's not mine. I'm not collecting supernatural beings. Phrixius is an immortal being more powerful than nearly every other creature in this world. He cannot stay with a lowly witch just because I like him.

He's funny, cute, smart, and a good listener. Did I mention he's cute?

Oh well, at least I still have my demon, wherever he is.

It's probably good he's not here tonight. He would mess with the spell and we'd end up doing something worse, so I resign myself to doing this alone and head through coven grounds and out the blood circle. I don't want any other magic messing with what I'm about to cast, so to be sure, I head a good distance from coven lands and sit atop a nice hill overlooking nature. The moon is full, its light spilling across the grass and me.

For a moment, I just soak in the beauty of nature, looking up at the moon I'll never be able to look at again without thinking of Phrixius. That saddens me a little, even as it reassures me that I'll still have it when he's gone. I'll be nothing but a note in the history of his life, but for me, he'll be a whole chapter in mine.

Sighing, I open my bag and begin to set out the casting circle I need. I add the candles and tree branch, careful with their placement, then I add the herbs and oils. Once that's done, I cleanse myself before stepping inside and kneeling before the bowl of bubbling liquid.

Despite its appearance, I know it's cold to the touch, and I submerge my hands inside, closing my eyes as I push my intention into the spell.

Freedom. I want freedom.

I want the chains unleashed and the bindings to break.

I repeat it like a mantra, over and over, as I sit under the full moon.

Opening my eyes, I tug my hands free and produce a small ceremonial dagger then slice my thumb, letting the blood flow in the moonlight.

I add my blood since the binding is linked to me, so it should free him for sure. I watch it drip into the bowl as I repeat my incantation.

Freedom. I want freedom.

I want the chains unleashed. I want the bindings to break.

I feel the magic working through me and into the spell before flowing out into the world, searching for its target. My eyes shut as I focus on the increasing power. It pours out of me and into the earth, searching. A frown tugs at my lips when it seems to stop, surrounding something, and I urge it to move on, but it ignores me, growing stronger and darker. The once glowing spell turns pitch black, like the darkest shadows or the deepest ink.

My eyes open, and I pull my hands from the spell, panicking. The magic only continues to grow, and I watch with shock as the bowl flips, the contents pouring into the grass and seemingly absorbing into the ground.

Oh gods no, what's happening?

It only grows in strength, seeming to swirl around me in darkness until I can no longer see the moon. All I see are shadows. They circle around me, blocking everything, and my heart stills in recognition.

Something in that darkness calls to me, recognising me.

The darkness only thickens, something within letting out a primal roar that seems to shake and quiet the earth around us.

Suddenly, from that blackness, two bright red orbs appear high in the air and close together, almost like . . . eyes.

They are eyes.

The shadows seem to part, admitting a creature straight out of your worst nightmares. There are hands and limbs everywhere, and so many red, blinking eyes. It's tall and white, made of shadows, but somehow, lingering within it, I feel death.

It watches me and suddenly seems to shrink, changing shape as effortlessly as water, forming a more familiar figure akin to a human. Its skin lightens to a deep purple with shades of black. Shadows writhe across its huge chest, abs, waist, and legs, covering it. Its arms are long, unnaturally so, and it has black claws. Its face is shaped similarly to a human's, but it's too sharp, and thin eyebrows arch above its red eyes. Its ears are pointed and much too large to be human with bones threaded through the cartilage and lobes. Hair flows down its back, longer than mine and as dark as midnight, but I am sure I see flames licking along the locks. Its arms are as wide as my body, but when they lift, I see spikes running down the backsides, almost like shark fins, but sharp and deadly looking. Fangs jut from its bottom lip as they part.

It is a creature of midnight, evil, and death.

It's horrifying and beautiful.

One of its hands lifts, reaching for me as I stare, silent and shocked. "Mine." The voice is a growl.

"Little witch?" my demon calls from somewhere beyond.

The creature jerks at the sound, the shadows sucking back into it until it stands before me on the grass. With one last look, it turns and races away from me.

"Little witch?" My demon sounds worried, but I can't answer.

As I watch the creature race into the shadows of the trees, I groan and cover my face. "What have I done now?"

"Freya!" my demon shouts as he falls to his knees before me, his hands scrambling over my body. "I couldn't reach you. Are you okay?" The panic in his voice makes me glance down at him then to where the creature went.

He follows my gaze, his hands still on my cheeks as we kneel under the full moon. "What was that thing, Freya?"

"Evil," I croak, "and I freed it."

CHAPTER 17

I want to say goodbye, but I have no choice. I feel the gods calling, and I know something must be wrong. I want to resist, to stay, but I can't. As much as I am enjoying my time here, I cannot forsake all of my duties.

Maybe I can return before she gets home and she will not question how I got out of her trap. I have a feeling Freya would be very angry if she realised I could leave at will after she put all that effort into the spell.

I linger for a moment, looking around at the cave that has somehow become my refuge, my happy place in this ever-changing world. I found my purpose here. I found my excitement for this world and magic again. I found that the littlest things can bring happiness, like watching a film with someone you care about, joking with a friend, or just being together.

I will miss the companionship because deep down, I know everything will change tonight, although I am not sure how. I need to leave even a piece of me behind so she knows I have not just abandoned her, so I tread over to her workbench, wave of my fingers, and a carved statue appears. It's a figurine of her grinning at me. She looks so beautiful and kind that my heart aches.

Wherever I go, I know I have been changed now, all by one little witch.

She will never know how close I was to giving up until her call. Despite what she is and what she is capable of, she is still so pure, kind, and carefree that she makes me want to be better.

That starts with now and answering the call. After all, it could affect her.

With one last look around, I leave the cave and the witch behind.

Just as I appear on our meeting island, I feel something ripping through the magic on Earth—something dark and evil.

Something that never should have been born.

My eyes widen, but I do not say anything as the other gods turn to face me.

"Finally," Vanessa snaps. "Now let's talk about what we will do about Mors."

I nod, but my gaze is on Earth, worry filling me. Is my little witch okay?

DEMON

Swallowing hard, I glance back at my pale witch. "Well, that isn't good," I joke. "Are you okay?" I ask again.

She nods. "It didn't hurt me."

I help her to her feet, and both of us turn to look at the trees it disappeared into. "I say we get the hell out of here before it comes back or, worse, someone finds out and blames us."

"We can't leave it wandering about." She turns to me.

"Do you know how to find it?" I ask, eyebrow arched. "No, so let's regroup at home. Besides, we are ages away from anywhere, so it's not like it's going to go all Godzilla."

"I never should have got you the TV," she grumbles but nods, though her eyes go back to the trees. "What was it though?"

"Honestly? I don't have a fucking clue," I admit, and that's the truth. I have never seen anything like that before, and I don't think anyone has, which worries me more because that creature was not attacking her, it was reaching for her. It's clear that whatever spell she cast tonight called it, and I need to get her away before it comes back.

"I leave you for a little while and here you are, giving birth to creatures." I shake my head as I grab her and stand. "This is why we should stick together." Just as I stand, my bag opens and the hand launches out, lunging for her.

I grab it midair as she screams, and I smack the back of the hand. "Bad evil hand."

"What the fuck is that?" she screeches, scrambling back across the grass.

"Really? That creature didn't scare you, but this does?" I huff as I use it to wave at her. "It's our way of finding the mask, duh. Now come on."

She blinks at the hand, and I shove it back into my bag and grab her hand. Usually, I wouldn't show off or use my powers, but I want her away from this place, and with a snap, I transport us back to her cave. She stumbles away, glaring at me since she hates when I do that. I plop her bags down and shove mine into a drawer, then I draw a protection rune across it. I watch it glow bright red before it sinks into the wood so the hand can't escape or, you know, strangle us in our sleep. When I turn back, however, Freya is staring at the empty area where Phrixius was.

Surprise fills me. He left? Why? He didn't seem like he was going anywhere, not that she knows that.

"Huh, at least the spell worked," I say, trying to cheer her up, but she's staring at the space with a strange sadness in her gaze.

She sighs. "I suppose."

"Little witch," I murmur.

She shakes it off and turns to me, smiling, but it's tight. "We have bigger issues to deal with, I guess, like the thing I unleashed or that hand and the mask."

I nod, but instead of getting into any of that, I head her way and wrap my arms around her. "I'm sorry you're sad." No matter how annoying he was, she was growing attached to him, and yes, I'm selfish and happy he's gone, but not at the cost of her happiness.

I would do anything to keep her from ever feeling a drop of pain ever again.

She softens in my arms, and I kiss her head. "He'll be back."

"You think?" she asks, sounding so lost and unsure.

"Nobody can resist you, little witch, trust me on that. In the meantime, how about we save the world from evil? Hmm? Does that sound fun?" I lean back as she chuckles, her eyes lighting up once more, and I can finally take a full breath as her sadness retreats.

She nods. "Let's do it."

"First," I say seriously, "we need superhero names."

Her laugh fills my heart, and I know if Phrixius comes back, I'm going to kick his ass for making her sad.

CHAPTER 18

freya

"Really? This isn't some practical joke or some weird demon shit, is it?" I ask, my hands propped on my hips as I stare at the very old, abandoned, creepy church. The place looks like serial killer heaven or a demon's lair.

"Hey, I have more style than this," he mutters at my side.

"Hmm. You prefer soft blankets and large TVs. Who knew demons were so lazy?"

"Exactly—hey, I am just a demon with particular tastes, okay? I like to be comfortable and warm," he protests at my side, "but this is where I found the hand."

"The one currently in my underwear drawer," I remind him. It had been a whole argument, but we might need it, so the hand stays.

I was sad Phrixius left, or more accurately, that I freed him. I mean, he didn't even stick around to say goodbye. We have more pressing matters, however, as my demon reminded me, like hunting down the mask and then stopping the creature I might have accidentally summoned and released, which is why we are here, at the church. I can be annoyed at the god later. We're not dumb though. We waited until morning. I don't know why, but it feels safer. After all, dark magic works best at night, or I'm presuming. I don't actually know, but that feels correct. It's totally not because we were both scared of what could hide in the dark.

Not at all.

"Then let's do this." Rolling my shoulders back, I head towards the church, demon in tow. I don't hesitate at the door, knowing if I do I will run away like a chicken.

I remind myself I'm a badass witch with a demon sidekick.

I stop on the next step, turning my head to find him so close our cheeks touch. His hands are on my shoulders as he dogs my steps behind me. "Are you using me as a human shield?"

"Well, better you than me, little witch," he mutters.

"You are a demon."

"That doesn't mean this place doesn't give me the heebie-jeebies," he mutters.

"Heebie-jeebies? That's not very demonian."

The huff he lets out makes me smile, but he straightens and moves to my side. "How would you know? You only know one demon, which is me. Maybe we all say stuff like that."

"Sure, sure. Are they all such scaredy cats?" I ask.

"Woman, look at this place and tell me you're not creeped out. Like I said, even demons have standards. I mean, have they ever heard of a housekeeper? And the blood sacrifice? All wrong. Where's the screaming virgin and the—"

"Okay, okay, enough." I slash my hand through the air, plunging us back into silence as we head to the altar at the end. "I mean, would it kill them to have some curtains and soft lighting?" I say nervously.

"I know, right? Maybe a rug? Even some artwork would be fine." I know we are chattering out of nerves, but we can't seem to stop. When we reach the bloody altar, we both turn silent.

"See? Creepy," he whispers.

"Creepy," I agree. "What did it do?"

"I don't know. It felt . . . wrong and dark. It was different from me, but powerful. I tracked it all the way here. Whatever they are, they are using some seriously strong dark magic. The only thing that could get through the barrier is—"

"Death magic," I murmur. "You don't think . . ." I glance at him just as there's a loud bang, startling us.

We both let out a scream at the sudden noise, and before I realise what has happened, the demon jumps into my arms and I'm holding him up as we face the threat.

Which happens to be a pigeon, cooing in the open doorway where it flew in and knocked over a metal post.

"Really?" I look at the demon as I grunt under his weight and drop him. He poofs away in midair, reappearing next to the pigeon and looking down at it with an unreadable expression before glancing at me.

"No," I say straight away.

"Why not? It could be a cute pet, and you already said no to the crocodile," he snaps. "Look how cute—no! It flew away. Come back and let me love you!" he shouts after the bird that is flapping away.

"Smart bird," I mutter.

"I just wanted to love it. I could have got it a little hat with matching horns. It could have flown into battle with me or shit on people I don't like. What we could have been." He sighs wistfully.

"If you're good and help me stop the end of the world as we know it from happening, then I will consider letting you get a cat."

I jerk back when he appears before me, grinning widely. "Really? They are the height of indifference. I love them so much, and they are so cute."

"Uh-huh, I know. I had to watch the presentation you made on them. Remember last year when you tried to convince me? Now, can we get back to why we are here before whoever left this suddenly appears and strips skin from our bones and wears it like a cape?"

"Okay, okay, fine, save the world first, pets after. Either way, whatever did this is long gone, but it proves one thing," he offers.

"What's that?"

"They knew what they were doing," he says, looking around, "and they knew where and how to get that mask. If this is real and this is death magic, then there is only one type of person who could pull it off." Our eyes meet as I swallow.

"Necromancer," we both say reluctantly, as if giving life to the word will make them appear.

Necromancers are the darkest of magic users, using blood and sacrifice to reanimate the dead, often creating armies. It's said they can even control people using their magic, though I'm not sure how true that is. There is a reason they were hunted into extinction. If one is here now, then we are all fucked.

I swear I hear something that sounds suspiciously like a . . . groan?

"Did you hear that?" I hiss.

"Stop trying to scare me. It won't work," he snaps before his eyes widen and he darts behind me as the noise comes again. "I heard it this time. Quick, little witch, save us."

"After this is over, we are talking about the fact that you use me as a shield," I warn as we slink to the front door and look out. The groan comes again, louder this time, and we head around the back of the church, only to stop. Our mouths drop open.

There are more overturned graves here, but stumbling between the headstones is a . . . zombie.

My demon groans. "A fucking zombie."

The zombie in question is about six feet, probably well-built when it was alive, and missing one of its ears. Its skin is a decaying yellowy colour and seems to be sliding off its frame. "It looks like melted Jell-O," I comment.

"Like when you accidentally put someone's favourite flowery plastic plate in the microwave," my demon adds.

"I knew that was you!" I snap, turning on him before glancing back at the zombie as it groans again, smacking into a gravestone and falling over. As it does, one of its leg bones snaps, making us both wince, but it stumbles back to its feet, dragging the bone behind it like it's nothing.

"I mean, you have to give it credit, it's determined. Once, when you hit your toe, you were down all day," I remark. "But if this is the thing that stole the mask, then I expected . . . I don't know . . . more? How did this get in and out unnoticed?"

"It seems disoriented, like when you get lost without a map," my demon observes helpfully, disappearing and reappearing on top of a gravestone, kicking his legs. "Come here, little zombie. That's it, good zombie."

I watch in open-mouthed fascination as the zombie stumbles towards my grinning demon. "You'd be better with a dog than a cat."

"That's it, good zombie. No, no biting. I taste delicious, but it's not that type of party." He snaps his fingers and rope appears around it, thrusting into the ground and dragging the zombie down to its knees. It groans, looking around as if it's confused. Are all zombies like that?

From the stories I've heard of necromancers, I thought the undead armies were intelligent, sure, and strong. This one is smelly and slow. As if following my thoughts, my demon hops down and circles it, cocking his head as his forked tongue darts out to taste the air.

"Black magic for sure, but long gone. I think its master cut its strings. The only reason it's still alive and moving is because of the spark of power they used to bring it back," he muses, cocking his head. "I wonder if its master can still affect it or see us through it."

"We better not find out. Let's . . . Wait." I still. "Why would they see us through it?"

"Well, it might be useful," he starts with a sly grin.

"We are not keeping this one! It will shed its skin everywhere. It's enough that I have a demon who files his horns in my bathroom," I warn, pointing at him. "I draw the line at zombies. We have an arm, that's enough."

"Good point, this one isn't missing an arm."

"Which means . . ." We both look at the zombie in horror. "There are more of them out there." My eyes land on the overturned graves. "A lot more, and this is only one cemetery. There must be hundreds in a fifty-mile radius."

We share a look, and at the same time, we say, "Fuck."

"So this is a necromancer, and he used a zombie to steal a mask that is possessed by evil spirits, and they probably plan to take over the world, right? Just to get us both on the same page."

"Sounds about right." My demon scratches his head as he peers at the zombie. "We should go back before whoever is behind this returns. We can't just leave it here like this though, can we? That's cruel."

"Alright, let me see if I can cut the magic." I move closer, wrinkling my nose at the stench. My demon is right. It's cruel. This was a person.

"Wait, no, just leave it. I was wrong." He appears before me, his spread arms blocking my path.

"No, you're right. This was someone's loved one. We should lay them to rest." I slide under his arm, but he appears again, stopping me from getting too close.

"No, leave it. It doesn't care."

"Demon, what is going on?" I ask, crossing my arms and narrowing my gaze on him.

He's unnaturally serious for once. "It's fine. Let's leave it. We don't know what you are playing with or what that magic inside will do. We don't want to risk it."

I tilt my head, watching him. "That's not the reason. You are lying to me."

"I'm a demon. I lie all the time," he counters, but his eyes shift away.

"Not to me, and not about important stuff." Stepping closer, I force his eyes back to me. "Why don't you want me to free that thing?"

"Because I'm scared," he admits softly, peering into my eyes like I am pulling the truth from him. His voice is pained. "I don't know what your darkness will do when it touches that thing, and I don't want you to find out."

"My darkness?" I whisper.

"The one you hide, the one I feed on when it becomes too much. The darkness we don't discuss, the one you are afraid of. I don't know what it will do to it, and I don't want to, nor do I want whoever is behind its strings to see you, so leave it," he begs. "Please, Freya, let this one go. Let's go home and forget this ever happened."

I can't. I stumble back, my heart hammering. My entire body turns cold and clammy. "The darkness, you know what it is."

He swallows, dropping his arms as he stares at me. "Freya—"

There's a groan, and the zombie falls to the side, pathetic and abandoned—just like me. Maybe that's why I do it, or maybe I want to know once and for all what I am.

And that is how we end up adopting a zombie.

Every time I get close to the zombie, it focuses on me, seeming to grow stronger. I hide on my bed, watching it. We locked it in a cage, which my demon created out of thin air. Once I'm not close, it seems to go back to being dormant, but it's more than that. It's the feeling I get when I draw nearer. The darkness inside surges up as if called to it.

It terrifies me, but I'm tired of running.

I freed something evil, and a zombie recognises me.

My demon knows, and I need to as well.

My ears seem to buzz, and my soul tells me to stop and turn away, like watching a car crash, but I can't. I need to know. I have to know. All this time, I thought I was just battling something everyone had inside or an effect of my magic, but the way the demon was talking . . . It's like he thinks it's more.

His fear should have me crawling back to bed and ignoring it as best as I can, but I'm so tired of pretending and hiding from the truth. Maybe if I know, then I can stop whatever is inside me.

"Demon," I call, but he ignores me, pretending to read a book. He doesn't realise it's upside down. "Demon, do not ignore me." With a twist of my fingers, I burn the book to a crisp and drag the chair closer so he's before me. He warily meets my gaze.

"How about I cook us some—" He tries to hop up.

"Sit down," I demand, and he slowly sinks into the chair. "Tell me what you know. Now, and I mean it."

"I know, that's what scares me," he mutters slowly, watching me carefully. "Knowing will not help, Freya. It will only make it worse, as if acknowledging it will give it power."

"I live with this thing inside me, it has enough power already, so tell me. I want to know what you know. Please," I beg, taking his hand.

"I feel like I'm going crazy all the time, running from something inside me that I can never outpace. I need to know what will happen."

"You have hidden from it for so long, without realising you released it via pleasure to stop it from building up. You have spent your entire life like a clenched fist, but if I release that fist, I don't know what will happen," he admits. "I sensed it when I first met you."

"You know what it is?" I press.

"I suspect, but I will not tell you in case I am wrong. You do not want to live with that." He holds his hand up to stop my anger. "What I do know is that it is strong and dark. It has an edge to it, like my magic. It's born from darkness and evil, but that doesn't mean it's necessarily evil."

My body goes cold all over, while my skin seems to erupt with a thousand goosebumps at the same time. My heart begins to ache like it's shattering inside my chest and those broken pieces are cutting me open from the inside.

"Evil . . . I have something evil inside me," I whisper.

"Darkness is not all evil, and evil doesn't mean you will become so. Look at me. It's what we choose to do with it that matters, Freya," he tells me, cupping my cheeks so I'll look at him. "I am worried, though, because darkness senses darkness, and I think whoever is behind this could feel your magic interact with theirs if you used it on the zombie. We just need to be careful while we are hunting, that's all."

"I'm scared," I admit, and he presses his forehead to mine, peering into my eyes.

"I know, but I will never let you get hurt, little witch, not ever." He vows it so vehemently, I believe him, but that's not my biggest worry.

I whisper my deepest fears between us. "But what if this darkness gets out and I hurt someone else? What if I become evil?"

"Then we will be evil together."

I can't help but laugh, and he grins, his lips quirking as he watches me, and then he leans in, kissing me softly. "You will always have me, little witch, and we will stop this together. When it's all over, we will figure out what you are safely."

"Together." I nod.

CHAPTER 19

Freya is quiet, clearly a little shocked as we lie in bed. Her hand is playing with mine, but she's not paying attention. When she speaks, I startle at how sudden it is.

"Why are you truly here with me?" she queries. This is not the first time she's asked, but it is the first time she isn't angry or sad, just curious. Her eyes lift to mine and beg me to give her something to understand.

I could lie to her or distract her like I have in the past, but I do not want to. I don't want to lie to her, not after today, so for once, I give her some of the truth.

Taking a deep breath, I stare into her eyes, which I know better than my own. I never expected it to become like this, but I wouldn't change it. I would never go back and undo what I did, because it gave me her.

"A very long time ago, someone made a deal to save your life. I'm keeping that deal and repaying it," I admit.

She blinks. It's clearly not what she expected, but it's the truth. I still remember that day as if it were yesterday, the blood we used to seal it and the way we bound my soul to hers for eternity—not that she knows that. If she dies, it will destroy me. If I die, then she will die. We are forever linked, but she's scared enough, so that's all I tell her.

"Who made the deal?" she asks, searching my gaze for answers she doesn't truly want.

"When you're ready, I'll tell you," I promise.

Her face closes down, and with a huff, she flips over, trying to ignore me.

Chuckling, I move closer, spooning her as I wrap her in my arms. "One day, not never, little witch. I promise you that."

"Whatever, demon." She tries to scoot away, but I drag her into my arms.

"You need to sleep. Tomorrow, we will hunt your creature and the masked necromancer, but tonight, just rest. I have you."

It takes her a while, but she relaxes into my arms and finally falls asleep, snoring ever so softly—a noise I have memorised.

As she does, I lean in like I do every night. "Adder, my real name is Adder." My name gives power, but this little witch already has power over my soul, body, and heart. If we are honest, she always has. Giving her that last shred of me does nothing, and I have the strangest need for her to speak it one day and call me hers.

CREATURE

The darkness welcomes me, even as the creatures dwelling within the forest, ones that feel stronger and older than me, keep their distance.

What am I?

Where am I?

I do not know. I feel more like somebody's thought, but I am real. I glance down at my hands. Hands, how do I know the word?

I do not know. All I know is that my eyes opened to find that woman before me and the darkness surrounded me, calling to me. Who is she? Is she the one who called me?

Was it her?

What am I?

These questions plague me as I wander a world I do not know, yet simultaneously seem to know everything about. Even now, I feel her calling to me. The darkness within her seems to match the one I feel flowing through my veins, yet she looked . . . scared.

I feel another call, something different and earthy, and it blasts through the forest, awakening all the creatures. It's a cry for help, something instinctive. It screams of pain, terror, and anger.

Wolf. Something tells me it's a wolf.

Turning, I lumber towards that call with nothing else to do.

CHAPTER 20

I should be focused on the issue of Mors and his mate being somewhere on Earth, trying to escape the other gods' wrath, but I cannot seem to care. Let the others handle it. They do not need me, nor do I want any part of this.

I do not see who he is hurting by being in love. Mors clearly loves her, and she loves him. Only true love would bear such sacrifice. She was willing to kill us, and he was willing to forgo everything for her. That kind of love cannot be broken. Even a fool like me knows that.

Gods are not made to love, but it seems Mors has found a way. I'm jealous, but despite all that, I hope they win. I hope they conquer the obstacles the others are throwing their way. If anyone can, it is Mors and the woman who stood against us. Besides, I have a feeling they will not be the only ones who will stand against the others.

No one even notices when I disappear and reappear on my own island. They are locked in their own hatred and self-righteous justice. I know whatever happens next will not be good, but I will let them fight this battle. It is not one I wish to focus on.

The only thing I care about right now is Freya.

Is she okay?

What is she doing right now? Is the demon protecting her? Staring out into the clouds surrounding my island, I can't help but reach for her, wanting to see her. I know I shouldn't. I disappeared and I didn't even say goodbye. She's probably very angry about that, and that I lied to her about being trapped.

If she figured that out, then she might ask why and demand to know why I was so interested in her. I can't very well admit it's because I know what she is or the fact that I am supposed to report her and then kill her for being born, yet I haven't. I've protected her. I hope that if she can control what she is, like she has been doing all this time, then she will stand a chance, and I want to give her that. She deserves a chance at life. It's not her fault she was born the way she was, and if anyone can conquer this, it's her.

I have to believe in her, in the goodness of this world, or it's all for nothing. I have to believe in love, just like Mors did. If the god of death can face it for love, then so can I because Freya is something important. She's the only being who has ever brought me back to life and reminded me of the beauty of this world I had long since forgotten.

Even now, everything looks different.

It's as if I'm seeing it all for the first time, even though I have seen it a thousand times. How is it possible that things I took for granted now seem important after meeting her? The call of the trees, the butterflies floating around me . . . She made me see the world again, and someone who understands the beauty of life doesn't deserve to be destroyed simply for what could happen in the future.

Maybe it's foolish, but I don't care. Like Mors, I am taking a leap of faith and trusting my emotions.

Turning away from the beauty, I summon a portal with my mind and step through it as I walk through my island. I'm going to keep an eye on her just in case.

That's the only reason why.

When I reappear outside her house, it's early morning. Stepping silently inside, I take in the changes in the room. It remains the same, the same earthy scent mixed with the herbs of her spells, but there is a new smell that's quite distinct.

My nose crinkles as my eyes land on a cage in the corner.

Am I too late?

Has she already sunken into the power and been consumed? The creature in the cage is one I have seen many times back during the dark wars. They were used as soldiers and cannon fodder by the necromancers trying to stop our cull. We ripped them apart as easily as paper, though they were strong fighters, but more simply replaced them.

This one, however, looks old and forgotten, lacking power like those soldiers. Is she simply figuring it out, or was this done by someone else? I have to know.

I find her sitting up in bed, rubbing her eyes.

"Phrixius?" It's one of the only times she has said my name, and I cherish it, the sleepy rumble going straight to my heart.

How can evil look so beautiful?

"Holy shit!" She leaps to her feet, stumbling as she stares wide-eyed at me. Her hair is braided, creating two horns on her head. "It is you, but how? Why? I freed you. The spell worked—oh gods, are you here to take revenge?"

"Well, look what the gods dragged in," the demon remarks as he sits up. "Couldn't come at a more sociable hour? I was having great dreams about my little witch's mouth—" He's flung through the wall, even as he laughs.

Freya watches me. Her eyes are still bright, and her skin is the same. She doesn't look like she has given in. So what's with the creature?

"I apologise for the time. It shifts differently here than in my realm." My eyes land on the zombie again. "I see you have been busy." I word it carefully, and as the demon climbs out of the hole his body made, I meet his gaze. He shakes his head, and I let out a sigh of relief.

It wasn't her.

If not her, then who?

"You don't know the half of it," the demon calls, "but it's too early for this shit. If we are going to discuss the world ending, I need coffee."

I gape. "Wait, the world ending?"

"Yeah, just another Tuesday—wait, Wednesday, right?" He chuckles.

"You're back," is all Freya blurts.

"Caffeine would be good, I think," I respond, rubbing the back of my head, more confused than ever.

Sipping the coffee, my only human vice—well, that and my desire for the little witch sitting opposite me—I can't help but sigh deeply. "So a necromancer stole the mask, you tracked it to the zombie, and now you are keeping it to see?"

"Don't forget the hand," the demon reminds me.

Freya nods rapidly, still staring at me, and she leans in. "Why are you back?" She shares a look with the demon, who snorts knowingly. "Not that I'm not happy to see you, but—"

"Are you happy to see me?" I ask, sitting up taller.

"Well, yes." She blushes. "Anyway, you're back. Why?"

"To check on you." I shrug. "So, anything else new other than a necromancer clearly out to start the dark wars again and capture the power in this world?" They both share a guilty look, and I sigh. "Spit it out."

"Well, when I was freeing you, I might have accidentally . . . freed something else," Freya offers with a tight smile.

"What else?" I ask.

"I'm unsure. It was a creature, and it had claws, was wrapped in shadows, and had red eyes," she says quickly.

"Nothing I've ever seen," the demon offers helpfully.

Pinching the bridge of my nose, I eye them. "Anything else?"

"Nothing," they say in unison.

"Okay, this creature, where is it?" I glance around like it might appear.

"Well, erm, it got away," Freya answers.

"So there is an unknown dark creature on the loose as well as a necromancer?" I summarise.

"Pretty much." The demon nods, toasting me. "Told you that you would need caffeine."

Sitting back, I eye Freya in concern. If she raised this creature, then does this mean her control is slipping and her dark powers are taking over? Not only that, but if she is determined to track this necromancer, can she maintain control? I worry she cannot fight what she is forever, and then I would have to do my duty and end her. I have never been as sad about the thought of death for a mortal being as I am at the thought of Freya dying.

"I will help you stop the necromancer and capture this creature. As the god of magic, it's the least I can do." Plus, if I am there, then maybe I can stop her from falling into the darkness inside her and keep her alive. It's like walking a tightrope, but I have to try.

"Really? You'll help us?" She brightens. "That would be great. We weren't doing so well."

"Hey!" the demon protests, but she spares him a look. "Yeah, okay, he can be zombie bait. So this is the team, huh? A demon, a witch, and a god. What could go wrong?"

What indeed?

CHAPTER 21

"So how do we track a necromancer?" I ask, looking between the demon and Phrixius.

"In the past, we simply followed their trail of destruction. However, they usually found us, wanting to claim our power," Phrixius admits. "After the great dark wars, any that were born went into hiding, and then we tracked them down. We can sense their powers if we are close enough, and they leave telltale marks throughout the world. When death touches down, things wilt."

The demon snorts. "So basically, he doesn't have a clue."

"I didn't say that." Phrixius huffs.

"No, but you were thinking it, magic man," the demon says. "You said tracing their magic, so what about Bobby the hand?"

"Bobby?" we both ask incredulously.

"Yeah, I named it. It felt weird just calling it 'the hand.' What about Teddy over there?" The demon points at the groaning zombie.

"Teddy and Bobby? You named the zombies." I groan, rubbing my head. "Sometimes I wonder what goes on in your head."

"It's usually a montage of pictures of your boobs or moans." The demon shrugs, eyeing Teddy—no, shit, I mean the zombie. I just gape at him, and he winks. "So we use the zombie, track down the bad guy, kill him, destroy the monster, and then have lots of sex. Sounds like a plan."

"Demon—"

There's a noise, and I turn to see Phrixius raising his hand.

"Yes?" I ask, confused.

"The lots of sex part, am I to be involved?"

I gape further as he trades looks with the demon.

"You know what? There is too much testosterone in here. One of you needs to leave for a moment," I order, crossing my arms. "Before I turn you both into neutered cats."

That does the trick. They both grab their junk. "Rock, paper, scissors?" the demon suggests.

"What is that?" Phrixius asks. "A trap?"

"A game, you moron. Fine, just say one. Three, two, one . . . Paper!"

"Scissors." Phrixius frowns, confused. "Do I need to conjure some?"

"Bloody gods." The demon points from me to him. "I will be back though." Suddenly, he's gone, which surprises me. I expected more of a fight, but maybe he can see how close I actually am to turning them. I'm not used to being alone, not with the demon here, but add in Phrixius and it's a lot. It makes my head ache.

"Okay, so let me think. How can you trace the magic in a zombie?" I murmur, moving closer to check on it. It hasn't moved in a while. Is it dead—erm, deader? It's leaning against the bars, almost like it collapsed. Maybe the magic inside it finally gave out?

"Freya, no!" Phrixius yells as I press my hand to the bar above its head, intending to check on it, but as soon as my hand hits the bar, I scream.

Darkness explodes within me, the thing caged deep inside blowing through me like a storm. It flows from me to the bar, trying to get down to the zombie, but I am ripped away.

I feel myself falling then someone wraps around me, but I cannot see anything.

"I can't see!" I shout. "Phrixius, I can't see!"

I can't . . . Everything is black, like I'm drowning in darkness.

It's consuming me, eating me from the inside out.

"I'm here, Freya. I'm here." His voice is hard, and warm hands press to my cheeks, making me realise how cold I am.

"I can't see!" I sob, the tears leaking down my cheeks. I can feel my limbs, but I feel like I'm falling inside myself, and part of me knows if I hit the darkness, I will never come back again. "Phrixius, make it stop. Please, please help me."

"Hold on, baby, I've got you." Suddenly, warmth infuses my lips, breathing life back into me.

Phrixius.

I can taste him as he forces my lips open, his hands gripping my cheeks so hard I feel them bruising, but I want more. His tongue tangles with mine as he kisses me.

As he does, the darkness starts to recede. My vision clears, and heat returns to my body. It felt like I was being plunged into ice. It was what I imagine death would feel like. I couldn't see or feel. I was ice-cold, but as he kisses me, he forces heat back into my body, chasing away the darkness until my chest loosens. I shakily lift my hands and hold him closer.

I can see again, although my vision is still blurry. I'm in his arms on the floor, his face above mine, and as I keep blinking, he comes into view. His eyes are closed, and he's so close, his lips moving against mine. His eyes open and hold mine, but he doesn't stop, and I realise he's not just kissing me . . .

He's draining me of that darkness.

I can see it moving between us, a dark fog passing between our lips. My eyes widen, meeting his once more as he continues to kiss me until he pulls back. I can see that shadow of darkness darting across his eyes, blinding him until he blinks it away.

"Are you okay?" he asks, searching my face. "Freya, speak to me."

"I'm okay." My voice is hoarse, like I was screaming.

Was I?

I don't know. The last few moments feel like a fog was wrapped around my head, obscuring everything but that cloying darkness. I shudder at the reminder of the feeling, swallowing hard as I nod. "I'm okay," I repeat more to myself than him.

He relaxes then, stroking my cheeks as he watches me recover.

There's no darkness anymore. I'm left panting and weak, but there's no darkness, yet his eyes drop to my lips, and with a groan, he leans in and kisses me again. I kiss him back.

My hand slide up into his golden hair and tug him closer. All my fear and worry morph into desire—desire he stoked. I was ice-cold, and now I'm burning hot, unable to get close enough. I climb him, knocking him back to the floor.

He goes willingly, moaning into my mouth as my hands slide across his body hungrily. I perch on top of him, rolling my hips. Desire storms through me, and I can't stop. My entire body ignites with sensation, craving the taste of vitality on his lips and his warmth.

"I've got you." He groans as my lips slide across his cheek and down his neck, making him gasp. "It's okay, Freya. It's normal. It's your magic trying to bring life back to your body—" His words end in a moan as I bite down. He's trying to be good and help me, but I don't need nice.

I need hot and heavy.

I need life, just like he said. I don't know how I know that, but I do.

I bite harder, the desire inside me only growing until I burn with it, unable to lift my lips from his skin. My hands wander, ripping at his shirt until he's bare chested and all his glistening, gold skin is below me.

My lips slide lower and across his chest. I bite his nipple, and he bellows, his hands landing on my hips.

My demon is suddenly there, his hand in my hair. He forces my head back until I can see him. "Naughty little witch, are you playing without me?"

"Please." I wind my hips into Phrixius, digging my nails into his exposed chest.

My demon's eyes flutter to Phrixius, and something passes between them. "Shh, little witch, we've got you. Let go, we are right here."

"I need . . . I need . . ." I whine, unable to think straight.

"I know," he whispers seductively, licking my lips as I groan.

"You've got us," Phrixius promises, sliding his hands higher, caressing my sides as my demon licks my lips, teasing me. Phrixius's hands grow bolder, gliding along my front and tugging down the top of the dress so it falls to my waist, leaving my chest exposed. I shiver in want, and as the cold air touches my overheated skin, his hands massage my breasts. I groan and kiss my demon back. The caresses turn rough and needy. He tugs down my bra then plays with my nipples, sending electricity straight to my throbbing clit.

"Please, please," I mumble, and my demon deepens the kiss, swallowing my pleas. His forked tongue licks at mine as a hot mouth lands on my chest. I feel Phrixius's muscles tighten under me as he sits up, running his lips along my collarbones and then down, right where I need him.

His hot lips wrap around one of my nipples, drawing it deep into his mouth. He grips my other breast, twisting my nipple meanly. I moan into my demon's mouth as he tilts me farther back, so I'm practically lying against him, giving Phrixius better access.

If I had been thinking clearly, I might have stopped this, but I need them too much. My own hands pull at my dress, trying to get it up, but my demon slaps them away with his tail before wrapping it around my wrists, binding them together and jerking them above my head.

Phrixius groans, sucking my other nipple into his mouth, and the sudden pleasure makes me cry out as my back arches. Chuckling behind me, my demon reaches down and grips either side of my dress.

"Do you want this off, little witch?" he whispers in my ear, making me shiver as I nod. My gaze clashes with Phrixius's as he licks my nipples, driving me wild.

"Words. Tell us what you want. Tell us how badly you want us. The demon and the god. Beg for it. Beg for the sinner and the saint."

"Please, please touch me. Fuck me. I need you both inside me," I admit without a hint of shame. I need them to remind me I'm alive. I need them to make it better in a way only they can.

"Good girl," Phrixius praises, licking down my stomach to play with the edge of my dress. "I think we should do as our little witch asks, don't you, demon?"

"Hmm, she did beg so sweetly, and I do like seeing her impaled on a cock." He chuckles, and suddenly, my dress is gone. I'm bare before them. The demon presses against my back, the god to my front. I'm caught between good and evil, sinner and saint, and it's never felt so good.

My demon's tail keeps my hands up, trapping me as my god slides his hands farther down, touching my hips. I feel my demon's horns as he bites the back of my neck. "You begged, Freya. There's no going back now. You get what we give you . . . what I've been wanting to give you for years. Tonight, I'm not stopping until I'm buried deep inside you, claiming what's mine."

I couldn't protest even if I wanted to. I'm so tired of fighting this want.

I give into it, and I let it burn me up as my god lifts me. "Keep her in the air. You can manage that, can't you, demon?"

"Please, god." My demon snorts as he lifts me with his tail so I dangle in the air from my wrists. I kick my legs, but Phrixius catches them and throws them over his shoulders, pressing a gentle kiss to my skin as his eyes meet mine once more.

"I want to taste the magic of this pussy, so be good and let me worship you like thousands have worshipped at my altar."

Who am I to protest?

I couldn't even if I wanted to as his mouth seals over my cunt, and he sucks me like he's sucking the life out of me. I cry out, and my demon's hands slide around my front, cupping my heavy breasts and squeezing hard.

"Look at him, my nightmare tamer. You have the god of magic on his knees, desperate for a taste of your cunt. Look at what you do to us."

Whimpering, I roll my hips, dragging my cunt across Phrixius's face as his eyes meet mine. His hungry gaze steals my breath, and then he licks a long line down my cunt.

"I have tasted everything this world has to offer, but you? Your taste is more magnificent than even the nectar of the gods," he purrs, then he drags his tongue across me again before pushing it inside my greedy cunt.

My demon bites my neck, and the juxtaposition of the sweet, soft touch and the hard claiming one makes me cry out.

"No wonder your demon is hiding you." He groans against my cunt. "One taste and the world would be yours. One moment between your thighs and they would lay everything at your feet."

Panting, I tug on my hands to try and touch him, but I'm hoisted higher. Wrapping my legs more solidly around Phrixius's head, I press him deeper, needing the life inside him.

He sees it, and he gives it to me like a merciful god, fucking me slowly with his tongue before he speeds up. He uses it in a way I've never felt, and it seems to grow inside me, vibrating with magic. I feed from it, soaking it in as they bring me back to life.

His fingers slide across my messy cunt and rub my clit until it becomes too much, and I scream my release to the night. Both of them encourage me, their wandering hands squeezing my curves. Phrixius's tongue pulls from me and slides lower to circle my ass as his fingers push inside me, fucking me through my orgasm.

My eyes close, and when his tongue pushes inside my ass, I lose it, grinding into his fingers and mouth while arching my chest into my demon's hands. They don't give me a moment of reprieve, my desire spiralling once more. The darkness is replaced by a fire so strong, I burn in it.

It grows, and when Phrixius pushes a third finger into me and shoves his tongue deep, I fall into that heat with a scream. I squirt all over my god's face. He groans, finger fucking me through it.

Pulling his tongue from me, he slides his fingers from my cunt and licks them clean. "Enough to slay a god."

I fall, the demon releasing me, and luckily, Phrixius catches me. My wrists sting as blood returns to my hands, but I don't have a minute to recover. I'm suddenly ripped away, turned, and yanked down onto my demon. My eyes widen when I meet his glowing eyes, seeing the fire in them.

His tail flicks down my back and slaps my ass. "I want to see you ride me. It's all I think about, little witch." That is the only warning I get before I feel his cock move by itself, seeking my heat. My eyes widen in horror and fascination when it finds my channel, and with a wicked grin, he drops me onto it, impaling me on his cock.

I scream. He's too big, too different, and as I wiggle, trying to escape, his cock only seems to grow, burying deeper, like it's intent on getting as far as it can. It's strange, feeling it move inside me, but I'd be a liar if I said it didn't feel good.

I gasp as I writhe on top of him. His hands urge me on as he watches me with those evil eyes. "Perfection," he praises. "Look at how you take me, little witch. You were made for me, made for the darkness, made for the different." I lift up, but he drags me back down, fucking me.

The spikes on his cock seem to drag over my nerves as he thrusts into me, the pain and pleasure making me scream for him.

He might be evil, but he feels so damn good inside me.

He told me once I crave the touch of monsters, and I know he's right. I want the freaks. I want the weird. I want it all.

I want him.

His tail slides lower, parting my cheeks and rubbing my asshole until I scream for him.

His abnormal cock slides deeper like a tendril, all the way to my cervix, stuffing me full as he lifts and drops me onto it. His tail slides around my hip and up, and despite Phrixius's softness, my demon slaps it across my breasts, whipping me with it.

I gasp, and he does it again as I clench down on him, dripping.

"You love the pain, don't you? You want to wear my marks. You want me to rip you apart as I stuff you full of my cum." His tail whips across my breasts again, hitting my nipples. I cry out as red welts form from the force. "Admit it, it's what you think about when you're sleeping in my arms. Every time you went and fucked another, watching me as you did, you were imagining it was me inside you. It got you off, didn't it?"

"Yes," I admit as I lean down and suck the tip of his tail into my mouth. His eyes narrow, and he pulls it free and whips it across my chest in quick succession. Huge red welts form, the pain making me scream even as I ride him faster.

"More," I demand breathlessly.

"Anything for you, my little witch." He smirks as he slaps my chest, and I look down at the red marks, moaning as I run my fingers across them. The sting makes me tighten to the point of pain on his cock.

His tail slides down and around, flicking over my asshole again. "I've imagined having you every single day of my life, but nothing could compare to seeing you on top of me, dripping for me. I've waited too long, little witch. I need all of you."

My eyes flare as he pushes his tail inside my ass, spearing me with it as he works it as deeply as he can. The stretch added to his abnormal cock has me screaming, and I barely remember moving, but I ride him, desperate as a sudden orgasm rips through me. He forces me higher, fucking me harder, and that fire inside me doesn't abate.

It only grows.

I grip his horns, and he groans as I tighten my hold and use them to fuck both his tail and his cock.

"That's it, little witch. Ride me, make this demon yours. Claim the night and flames." He groans, urging me on while he licks over my welts.

He slides his forked tongue across my chest, making it hurt as I clench down on him. Leaning across him, I lap at his horns, knowing they are sensitive. He growls, hammering deeper into me, forcing me to take it as his tail presses farther inside me.

"Mine, you are mine." He pants against my chest before he bites down. "Mine," he roars into my skin as he slams into me so hard it hurts.

Leaning back, I whimper as I watch him in the throes of pleasure.

Fire burns inside me as he pumps me full of his cum, his skin seeming to flash red under me. The sight has me tumbling over the edge again, following him into my release.

Collapsing, I slide from his body and onto my back next to him, covered in sweat, but I'm so fucking high, I giggle until hands land on me. My eyes open as Phrixius smirks at me.

"Didn't think you were done, did you? You had the sinner, and now you get the saint."

Phrixius kisses up my body, licking the welts from my demon. The difference makes me cry out. The pain, pleasure, and softness after the hardness leaves me confused, yet still so needy. I need everything they have. It's like I need to drain their essences to breathe.

"You taste like raw magic, Freya," he murmurs as he slides up my body, lifting my hips until I wrap my legs around his waist.

My eyes widen, and he pushes inside me, his huge, hard cock filling me. He rolls his hips as his mouth meets mine in a flurry of kisses. I groan, tasting the pure magic on his tongue. Lifting my hands, I grip his shoulders, meeting his thrusts with my own despite having my brains fucked out by my demon. The fire burns hotter, and I swallow his power, feeding on it as his hips speed up.

I have to break away to pant, and he leans back with a cocky smirk that does something to me.

I don't know what I expected from the god of magic, but I should have known better than to assume it would be normal.

I scream as something clamps down on my clit. Teeth dig into the sensitive flesh. The sudden pain turns into a burning pleasure, and when I look between our bodies, I see a glowing clamp there. "God," he reminds me. "I can play with your body all night, witch. I can create anything I want to heighten and prolong your pleasure, and I intend to."

"Show off," my demon mutters.

"No, this is showing off." Without even a word, two more clamps appear on my nipples, and my screams bounce around the walls, and then a glowing chain slithers down my body, attaching to them before hooking to the one on my clit and pulling taut. With each roll of Phrixius's hips, it tightens. The pain is so extreme, I feel tears slip from my eyes, yet my mouth begs for more, speaking praises that my god drinks down as he watches me with that cocky grin.

The chain grows tighter and tighter, until the pain pushes me over the edge once more. I don't know if I'm going to black out or come, but my body decides for me, clenching on his cock so hard, he groans as I squirt around him. My release is so strong, I writhe below him. He slows his hips, fucking me through it, but it's too much.

I hit him with some magic, and he slides from my body as I flip and try to crawl away—prey trying to escape the predator intent on destroying me and making me his.

I scream when hands drag me back. "Where do you think you're going, witch?" Phrixius asks as he impales me on his cock again and lifts me onto my hands and knees, hammering into me as those glowing chains tug my clit and nipples.

I scream as I explode again.

He bellows behind me, following me into ecstasy, and fills me with his magic cum that I feed on until I finally pass out.

CHAPTER 22

freya

I actually blacked out.

When I came to, they were both holding me, my pussy sticky with cum, but it was so fucking good, I know they ruined me for any other monster. They helped me clean up and gave me water. Phrixius tries to heal my welts, but I decide to keep them, much to my demon's joy.

I really didn't mean to have sex with both the demon and Phrixius—okay, maybe I did. It wasn't planned though. I expect things to be awkward after, but if anything, it seems to have brought my demon and the god closer together. They haven't fought yet, so that's something. They do keep me away from the zombie, however, and I appreciate that. I shudder at the memory. I don't want to feel that again. I'm also feeling too raw to even discuss what happened, and they seem to take that hint.

I refuse to be ashamed of my response or the fact that I took them both. Sex is natural, and we all enjoyed it. I won't regret it. Hell, I'd do it again if given half the chance. I have no qualms that the demon and god have ruined me for my usual hookups. No matter how strange the monster, none will compare to how I was fucked tonight.

Clenching my thighs together, I try to focus on the present and not the feeling of my aching cunt, but as usual, my demon knows, and he winks. Luckily, he focuses on Phrixius and leaves me to my musings.

The god is sitting before the zombie, touching it through the bars. His eyes are closed as he tries to trace the magic. He mentioned it could take a while, since the remnants are old and lingering, not fresh and clear. It's strange that he didn't have a reaction like I did, but maybe it's because he's the god of magic.

That's what I tell myself, anyway, as I watch him.

His eyes open, and he turns to us, his eyes still glowing. "I have the trail. Take my hand."

"I don't do guys, sorry," the demon replies.

Sighing, I grab my demon and haul him over, grabbing Phrixius's outstretched hand.

"What will happen—" I scream as I am ripped away.

This is not like when the demon transports me. It's like magic wraps around us and rips us from time and space, and then suddenly, we are set back down, still holding one another but in a completely different place.

Is it night?

How?

The sky is dark—no, not night, I realise with horror. The darkness is smoke from fires. The flames lick at buildings' walls.

We are standing on top of a small grassy hill with a village spread before us. I don't know where we are, but the village looks ancient. The structures are made of thatched roofs and clay walls, and the fires are burning it all. There are no screams, though, no signs of running or panic, and despite it only being a small village, I know there should be someone.

"Where is everyone?" I whisper, a bad feeling building within me.

"I don't sense anyone," my demon murmurs, taking my hand as I step forward. "Be careful, Freya. Remember what we are hunting. They could still be here."

"They aren't. They are gone, and the trail is growing colder." Phrixius sighs and wanders away. We follow him, stepping into the silent, burning village. It feels like it's frozen. There's a teddy on the ground, and wooden toys lie forgotten where they were dropped.

Clothes still blow on lines strung between houses, and buckets near the well are overturned and leaking water, but there are no bodies . . . no people.

I just hope they managed to escape before the necromancer arrived.

The demon clicks, and the flames disappear, leaving smoking cinders and charred remains of houses. The smoke still fills the air, and I bat it away to see, my eyes stinging from it.

"Stop." Phrixius stops us, his arm spread in front of me, and he turns, blocking my view. "Don't look, Freya."

I blink, trying to clear the smoke. "What?" The smoke clears behind him, and he tries to cover my eyes, but I move past him, seeing what he did.

My heart stops, horror coursing through me at the sight in the middle of the village.

They didn't get away. They didn't escape.

They are all dead.

I gasp in horror, stumbling back as I try to make sense of it, piecing the scene together like a macabre puzzle.

The tree that remains in the centre of the village is a horrible sight, with bodies spread on its twisted branches. They range in age from old to young, and I even see a baby cradled in one of the branches, looking like it's sleeping, but blood covers its chest and its mouth is slack.

They are all dead. They were killed and hung like this to be found.

I heave as I turn, throwing up on the grass. A hand rubs my back as tears squeeze from my eyes. "Who could do this? Why?"

"Evil," Phrixius says. "Pure evil. They did not need to die, but the person wanted their deaths. Instead of letting them go after destroying their village, they chose to kill them as a warning."

"To whom?" I ask, wiping my mouth.

"To us," Phrixius murmurs, his eyes locked on the tree. "This village is where the last battle of the dark wars took place. It was built by their ancestors, and this tree was planted with magic after the last necromancer was killed. It was a sign of life, of rebirth. This is a warning." He turns and picks his way through the village.

I stumble after him, needing to get away from the tree and the smell of death that fills my lungs. He seems to know his way, and we find ourselves behind the village where an old graveyard sits.

Now, all the graves are overturned.

"They committed one more crime," he whispers. "After burning, killing, and desecrating the tree, they stole their lost loved ones for their army—the last disrespect they could offer. Whoever did this is powerful and old enough to know the stories of the dark wars and be angry about it." He glances at us, looking worried. "They are trying to bring back the dark nights when death spread across the land. They are trying to reclaim their power and territory, and with the mask they stole, they can. It holds the souls of the necromancers from the past. They are channelling them and joining their powers. This isn't one person anymore. This is an army. This is the dark wars all over again, and they will not stop until we are all dead or enslaved."

We cannot leave the villagers like this.

I cannot change what happened, and I know it's not my fault, but I can't help feeling an immense sense of guilt. What if we could have stopped them? I cannot change the past, but I can change the present.

Ignoring my demon's pleas, I climb into the tree and carefully lift the baby from the branch before I gently lay him on the straw my demon magicked for me. Then I climb back into the tree, making sure to memorise each face. I know they will haunt me, but I want them to. This one is a little girl, her hair in braids. A branch is thrust through her chest. As carefully as I can, I pull her free, catching her as she falls into my arms. Grunting, I lift her and climb down, laying her beside the baby.

Silently, Phrixius and my demon help me, climbing higher than I can and taking the bigger bodies. They don't use magic, and neither do I. Enough magic has been used on these people. They deserve the respect and love of being cared for after what they endured in life. I will not defile them in death.

Once they are all out, I turn to Phrixius. "We should bury them."

"We can't," he says, looking at them sadly. "I want to, but I can sense the remnants of the dark magic used to kill them inside them. If we bury them, he will be able to call their bodies back from the grave even years from now. To honour them and allow them peace in death, we have to burn them so he cannot do that."

"I hate that. They deserve to be buried," I snap, looking them over, "not to burn in the flames that stole their homes."

"Let me," my demon calls, taking my hand. "I will make it quick. They won't feel a thing, my little witch, and it will protect their spirits and their peace. Let me help you."

I turn to him with a nod. I take his hand, and we step forward. He's solemn for once, and even he looks angry and disgusted at what happened. Demons are creatures of evil, but not this evil.

With a click, flames appear in his hand, and he blows them across the bodies. We stand there, the heat licking at us as it absorbs into the corpses and the magic flames swallow them swiftly, making it as respectful as possible.

When the flames recede and extinguish, all that is left is the burnt earth, and I know it will stay like that for an eternity, scar for what happened here. Good.

"They are at peace," Phrixius murmurs.

I nod, and they wander around the village, searching for any others, while I turn to the tree, standing before the bloodstained branches.

How could someone do this?

How could someone kill innocents all because of an old grudge? These people did nothing. They were killed because of their ancestors' actions. How is that fair?

I might not agree that necromancers should be killed at birth, but I'm starting to understand why some feel that way. If one is capable of such death and destruction, then what would an army of them be capable of?

Phrixius appears at my side, but I can't look away from the tree, something akin to fury igniting within me. The gods let this happen.

Gods . . .

"Shouldn't you tell the other gods?" I murmur, still staring at the tree.

"Not yet, not until I'm sure," he replies, and I glance at him in confusion as he cups my cheek. "Doing so would put you in danger. I will not allow that. Trust me, Freya, to handle this."

"What does that mean?" I whisper, staring into his shining eyes.

"Trust me," is all he says, and I nod as my demon returns.

"There is nothing else left."

"Then let's leave this place."

I nod again, and Phrixius takes us away from the horror, but I swear it follows me back home.

I swear I can still taste the smoke and blood, and I know I'll never be free of it.

I have been changed and scarred like that earth.

CHAPTER 23

She's right, I should tell the other gods, but if I do, they will come to Earth and hunt for the necromancer, leaving nothing unturned, and they will find her. They won't care about my reasons or my hopes.

They will slaughter her.

I cannot let that happen. It is selfish, but I have to protect her. I know I can hunt this necromancer alone, and I will do it quickly before it draws the gods' attention. No doubt Mors already senses something amiss. I will do everything I can to protect Freya.

My eyes fall on her. She's standing, silent and seemingly lost. She is sad and horrified by what she saw. It shouldn't make me happy, but it does. It shows me exactly why I'm doing this. She's not evil. She's not darkness, not like that. She cares, and she showed that much tonight. Even when the darkness took her earlier, she caught it and called to me. I still remember the panic in her voice. I'm just glad I was here to bring her back from it, but it had been close.

We need to be more careful because the closer we get to this person, the more her powers will react. We cannot lose her along the way.

She turns and walks to her bed, falling into it before wrapping herself in the bedding. I hear her soft sobs moments later, and my heart breaks for her, but I let her feel it as I meet the demon's eyes.

"We have to keep her safe."

"Then let them go, let them kill. I will not risk her," he snaps.

I wish I could give up on the rest of the world for her like he can. That is the difference between us. This demon would forsake this world for her, uncaring as it burns, but I can't. The best I can do is try to protect her.

As my eyes find her again, I cannot help but move closer, something nudging against my mind.

"Phrixius?" the demon snaps.

My magic screams, and as I lay my hand on her, I gasp, thrown into the dream—no, a nightmare is claiming her. It rings with truth and a touch of fate, as if we have already lived it.

"Now, little witch," the dark voice calls, the husky timbre making me shake.

For a god, he truly is a patient man, being held in my trap for so long. When I set it and cast a summoning spell, I didn't expect this, but I had nowhere else to turn. The magic in me called something dark, and I need help or it will be the downfall of my coven, my court, and the world as we know it.

"From the beginning once more," he urges, sitting cross-legged.

He disappeared a few days ago, and I panicked, but he returned, which begs the question—if he can leave, then why hasn't he?

"I told you," I say as I pace. "I don't know how I called it, and neither does the demon that feeds on our magic. When you left, I was trying to rid my coven of it. I thought if I could show them, I could banish the demon, and we would be okay, but I called something much worse." I peer at him. "I called something wrong, something dark and dead. Please, Phrixius, please help me."

I feel the demon I speak of pushing from the shadows as if the world pauses when such evil emerges. A cold chill goes over me as the demon's heat meets my back. The god stands then, anger furrowing his brow as he meets the demon's eyes—the eyes of the demon I've been haunted by my entire life.

"He cannot, but I can. I told you, little witch, just make one pesky little deal and I'm yours," he purrs in my ear. His voice is smooth and relaxing, making me sway into him. I want to give into the bargain he has been peddling since I turned eighteen, one I can never agree to, but for a moment, I falter.

"No," Phrixius snaps, his fury breaking me from the spell the demon weaves around me, and with a furious look at the chuckling demon, Phrixius steps from the spell circle, righting his suit, and doesn't stop until he stands before me.

Their powers surge through me, leaving me breathless.

"I will help you. You called and trapped me, after all," he counters.

"What could a god know of such dark, evil things?" the demon retorts.

"More than a lowly ground crawler," the god replies, my head aching from their power.

Something dark, evil, cold, and dead grasps my ankle and yanks me down, and with a scream, I reach for the demon and the god, but it's too late.

The thing I called forth rips me from my cave and into its grasp.

I yank us both from the dream. She gasps, jerking up, her eyes wide. "What was that?" she asks.

"That was magic. That was the past mixing with the future—a foretelling, a warning . . . like your déjà vu," I mutter, staring into her eyes. If that dream claimed her within seconds, then it means it was waiting for her.

"We should place some defences around this place." Standing, I turn to the demon. "The creature she called is coming for her. Help me."

We move to the cave entrance, both of us debating how best to protect her. "I can use my magic to create a barrier. It should even keep other gods out." It's something I should have done before. "I don't know how it will react to you though."

"If we add my blood, it should allow me to enter. Either way, I'm tied to Freya, so it might recognise me," he replies as I nod. With my hands raised, I begin to lay the protective ward. It's born from ancient magic older than even me, but as I do, something tickles my senses, making me freeze.

Something stirs the air, something dark, ancient, and powerful. We both turn in horror.

Freya is standing with her arms wrapped around her in front of her bed. She tilts her head as we both turn. “What?” she asks worriedly.

Suddenly, a long, midnight-black hand reaches from under the bed, wrapping around her ankle and yanking her down. She screams, clawing at the floor before she is dragged under.

I leap over, slamming my magic down to stop the creature, but it’s too late. I don’t feel it anymore. I flip the bed with the demon, and we both freeze, our eyes wide.

There, like a still glowing, healing scar, is a closed portal.

It’s what the creature came through and used to steal Freya.

CHAPTER 24

I hit something hard with a scream, the impact jarring me and cutting off the noise as the air is forced from my lungs. Magic fills me, and I fling it at the creature as it lands in front of me. The portal it conjured on the ceiling is closing. I get up as it's flung away and leap at the portal, trying to get back through. If I didn't call it, then I can't reopen it, so I need this one.

I'm hit by something huge and hard—the creature.

It tackles me, making me cry out as I hit the rocky ground again. I feel the stones cut through my dress and into my skin as it pins me, and I'm left to watch the portal seal, my escape taken away.

I'm trapped with the creature that stole me far too easily.

Its eyes glow red, and the beast is so big it takes up the entire space above me as I lie here, pretending to be weak all while I conjure a spell.

"Please don't eat me," I cry, shielding my face with my hands.

"Eat you?" the dark voice replies, wrapping around me and tightening like a net as clawed hands grip my thighs. "I think I will."

I scream as I'm forced under the creature, and I fling the spell. He roars as the spell hits him, and with wide eyes, I watch as the magic absorbs into his skin without even a scratch.

It absorbed my magic.

It shouldn't be able to do that. Only I can absorb my own spells. That one should have knocked it out for hours. "How?" I whisper.

"I am part of you." It sniffs me. "You smell like mine."

"No, bad creature." I smack his head as he sniffs my crotch. I squeak when he snarls but then smack him when he tries to bury his head in my crotch again. "No," I say, pointing in his face. It's probably a dumb choice, but I'm not left with many options. "What do you mean you are part of me?"

Honestly, he hasn't eaten me yet, and I can only be terrified for so long. Don't get me wrong, I'm still scared, but I'm growing braver. Also, I don't know when I stopped thinking of this creature as an it and turned it into a he, but the appendage pressing against my leg definitely indicates it's a he and very happy to be where he is.

Great, a pervy creature. I really do have problems. My sexual kinks even made a creature of evil hot for me to fuck. My demon was right.

He watches me, and if I overlook his menacing, terrifying appearance, he's almost . . . good-looking in a monstrous way, not to mention huge.

"Why are you important to me?" he asks, his head cocked. "Why do I feel you at all times? Why can I sense you? Why do I ache without you?"

My eyes widen as he speaks. "Erm, yeah, I made a bad spell. I can fix it and put you back—"

"Why would I want to go back?" he murmurs, lying on me and sliding down my body as my eyes blow wide. "No, I don't want to go back. I want you. I need you. You're mine."

"I think my demon and god would have something to say—hey!" I yell, kicking at him as he rips my dress off me. My stomach churns in panic, but he captures my leg and pins it to the ground. His glowing red eyes land on my pussy, which is barely covered by a scrap of lace.

"Don't you even dare!" I squeak.

He tears off my underwear just as easily, and he sniffs them before stuffing them into his mouth. I watch in silent horror as he eats them.

"Did you just eat my underwear?" I snap. "They were expensive—"

"They tasted like you," he murmurs, sniffing the air. "Something smells delicious."

"No, bad. Don't." I try really hard to stop my moan, but he lowers his head and licks along my cunt. His tongue is rough and has some sort of spikes along it that almost hurt, even as they feel good.

No. Shit. What the fuck is happening?

"Please." I try to kick him again, to close my legs, anything, but he's too big and strong. He flattens himself against me, inhaling between my thighs as my cheeks heat in mortification and, to my shame, desire.

I really am fucked up.

"It's here. This smells delicious. Is this why you offered to let me eat you?" he murmurs, and without waiting for my response, he slides his tongue across my cunt and stops at my hole. "What is this?" His clumsy innocence shouldn't be hot. I should be horrified.

I freeze, words stuttering out. "My vagina," I whisper.

"Vagina." He tests the word. "What is it for?"

"Erm, so . . . Okay," I stammer as he watches me, waiting. "You know what? Nope, not having this conversation. Get off me." I try to shove him again, but he slaps my hand away. I throw my magic at him, but it just absorbs into his skin. I'm as weak and useless as a human, and I'm at his mercy. He seems to like that, exposing his teeth in a smile as his tongue slides inside me, exploring.

My back bows as he shoves it so deep inside me, I feel it hit my womb. My scream rips through the air, and I'm ashamed that it's one of pleasure, not pain. His tongue is so thick, it's like a cock, the spikes pressing against my walls like a massager.

How the fuck did I go from being kidnapped to being tongue fucked by a creature born just a week ago?

"Stop," I demand. "Stop it." I try making my voice harder, but he ignores me completely as he pulls his tongue out and swallows.

"Tastes delicious." He drops between my thighs, the sudden weight making me grunt, and then thrusts his tongue back inside me.

Whimpering, I try to fight the desire working through me from his touch, tinged with horror, but I can't as he tastes every inch of my channel and then slides his tongue out and lower. I don't even scream as he thrusts it into my ass. The sharp pain makes me black out for a moment.

When I come around, his tongue is back in my cunt, uncaring that I was unresponsive. I really do try to fight, but when his tongue glides over my clit, desire spasms through me. My walls clench as I come embarrassingly hard.

He stills, moving lower a second later as he licks at my cream sliding from my passage. "What is this?"

"Release," I say, shame filling my voice. "You made me come."

"Do it again," he orders. "I want more." He licks at every drop of my cum.

"I can't, please." I writhe, hitting the stone below me.

"Again!" he roars, lashing my clit with his tongue like he did when I came. It hurts, but he doesn't care. His tongue scrapes over my clit until I come, screaming once more. I yell from the force, and he groans, licking at my cunt with a happy sound as I collapse. I'm exhausted and so ashamed, tears leak from my eyes.

Humming, the creature lifts his head, watching me with glowing eyes, and then he moves up. "Do they taste as delicious? So many of your holes leak." His tongue darts out, tracing my cheek and tears. "Different." He frowns.

I nod, watching him. My eyes narrow when I feel his cock press against me. God knows what the thing would be like, but luckily, he's happy licking my cheeks, forcing the tears back as I smile. When he moves again, he rubs against me.

"Need more," he murmurs. "Hungry. I need something."

It's so innocent, such a naive way to explain desire, but that's what it is. He needs to come.

"If you let me up, I can help," I cajole.

He frowns, pinning me harder as he rubs against my pussy with something foreign, something I don't think I would survive. "Let me help?" I ask softly.

"Hungry," he whines.

I nod. "I can help with that."

Slowly, he sits up and back, letting me scramble to my knees, and my eyes land on the cock protruding from his body. That motherfucker would kill me, so then why does my channel clench in want?

He's easily the size of my arm and completely a monster. His length is the same colour as his skin, but a brighter purple at the tip that seems to open wide like a flower, moving and seeking. The base of his cock is surrounded by tendrils, like that of an octopus, with suckers waving in the air.

Swallowing hard, I slide closer on my knees and glance up at him, but his head simply tilts as he watches me. I stop when I'm close enough to reach out, my hand hovering over his cock. It seems to seek my heat, writhing and growing as it reaches for me. The tendrils wrap around my wrist, dragging me closer as its suckers taste my skin, and he groans, the flower head of his cock pressing to my palm. Black oil, like precum, smears across my hand, and it seems to absorb into my skin. It tastes like magic and pleasure, darkness and evil.

"Hungry," he growls, and his hips move innocently.

"I know, I'll help," I coo, trying to keep him calm so he doesn't just ram it into me and kill me. Keeping my eyes on his foreign length, I wrap my hand around it and squeeze.

He roars, his back bowing, so I tighten my grip and slide my hand up and down with hard squeezes. Those suckers pluck at my skin, and more of that black oil spills from his head. I rub at the flowerlike tip, and he roars, spilling more from the head. Lifting my hand, I taste the darkness, and my cunt clenches in ecstasy as the flavour fills my mouth.

"It's okay, this will help," I promise, panting now as I jerk his cock harder, watching that darkness spill over my hand and arm like a continual release. The suckers grip my skin, and I can't help but wonder what they would feel like on my cunt. My hips rock despite my horror, my desire winning as I stroke him.

Touching him makes me wet, and I am needy despite the fact I just came twice. I shouldn't want him or be wondering what he would feel like inside me, but I am.

His arms wrap around me, dragging me closer, his hips thrusting his length into my hand as he lifts me into the air like I weigh nothing to get me closer. He licks my face as he snarls and groans.

Shadows dance across my skin, conjured by him, his magic tasting my flesh until I'm whimpering and my cream slides across my thighs as I work him, but if anything, he only grows harder, like steel in my hand.

It's not working.

"Hungry," he hisses. "Hungry."

"I know." I meet his gaze, my cunt clenching at the look in his eyes. "I can help, but you have to go slowly, okay? Let me lead."

He nods, either unbothered or not understanding.

His naive innocence has a weird effect on me. I let him lift me higher, and I grip his cock harder. I line him up with my entrance as he watches me with confusion. I told myself I wouldn't, but I need to come. I need to feel him. All my shame is gone, replaced by desire.

I can tell myself it's for him, but I'd be a liar.

I want to feel that inside me.

Maybe if I fuck this creature, he won't kill me. It's my excuse, even as my cream slides down my thighs. Pressing my entrance against his tip, I dig my nails into his arms and hold on as he watches me.

"This is called sex. It's what my cunt is for. This will make it better, and it will make you feel good," I mumble.

"You too?" he asks.

"Me too, if you let me set the pace," I warn as I slip him inside me. My eyes roll back at that first inch. Something wet suddenly squirts into me, and I pull back to see black, inky cum slipping from his cock and my channel. Despite it, he remains hard, but it helps slick the way, and I moan, sliding farther onto his waiting cock.

He's so big it hurts, and with a roar, he grips me and slams me down onto his length, forcing me to take all of him. I gurgle and choke, agony tearing through me as I scream and try to pull away. The flower head seems to grow inside me, expanding to the point of pure pain, and I scream and batter at him.

"No, no, no!" I shout.

He holds me there, forcing himself deeper, and those tentacles writhe across my cunt, stroking me. One finds my clit, and the suckers attach to it like a greedy mouth, applying constant pressure, as another slides down and sucks my asshole.

I go from begging to be released to begging for more within seconds.

The tendrils make my eyes roll back into my head, and before I realise it, I'm lifting myself up and ramming back down. It hurts, but it feels so fucking good I can't stop. I need it badly. The suckers drive me higher towards pleasure, and that inky cum I feel spilling in me constantly feels like magic, making me even more wild until I'm riding the monster desperately.

"Yes," he hisses. "Need this, feels good. Wet, so wet, delicious." His words are raw and hungry, and his fangs sink into my shoulder, pinning me as he hammers into me.

It sends me over the edge, and I scream my release loudly as I come so hard I black out.

When I come to, I'm limp in his arms. His fangs are gone from my shoulder, but his cock still rams into me, making me whimper.

He lays me on the rocky ground, slamming his claws into it on either side of me to keep us still as he hammers into me as I remain limp, unable to move. Agony and pleasure race through me until I cry out again.

The tendril sucking at my ass worms its way inside me, slithering deep, and my back arches. The stretch of the tendril and his cock are too much.

"Please, stop, stop!" I scream, but despite my words, I push down to take him deeper as the sucker at my clit massages my bundle of nerves, making constant waves of pleasure course through me until my words no longer make sense.

Snarling, he pins me to the rock and slams into me. Agony mixes with such pleasure, I scream raggedly, yet I want more.

He roars, and I feel that flower spurt deep inside me, coating my walls and leaving me writhing as I come again. Pulling from my aching cunt, he flips me and yanks my ass into the air. My scream rips through time and space as he rams his cock deep into my ass along with his tentacle.

I feel myself rip, and the pain makes tears flow down my face as I scream and fight, but just as quickly, his cum fills my ass and seems to heal me, magic sealing me back together around him as he hisses and snarls.

He fucks my ass so hard, I feel sick, and yet I push back, and when one of those tentacles slides deep inside my pussy, I cry out, "More! More!"

A second and then a third pushes inside my cunt, stroking my walls as he fucks my ass.

"Hungry, hungry, need you," he roars. "Mine, mine, you're mine."

"Oh gods, please!" I beg, unable to take any more, but he forces himself so deep inside me, I know I'm rearranged around him, and when he roars, that flower squirting deep in my ass, I come. I bear down on his cock and tentacles, squirting around them before collapsing.

I kick at him, and he pulls from my ass. I slump into the rock, coated in sweat, blood, and cum. My heart is hammering so hard, I'm surprised it hasn't exploded.

"Hungry," he growls, his tongue darting out to taste the sweat on my spine.

"No more or you'll kill me," I rasp.

He sighs and tugs me back into his arms, stroking my body. The magic in his skin seems to soak in my pain and heal me.

"I will wait for you to be hungry again." His hand slides down, covering my messy cunt.

Holy fuck, he's going to kill me with sex.

This is definitely not how I thought this would go.

CHAPTER 25

Phrixius and I explode into the cave where we tracked the creature. Luckily for my little witch, I am tied to her soul, and after fighting to conjure another portal, we followed that tie to this mountain. Phrixius was a very bad sport about climbing, but I couldn't risk us evaporating up the side and plunging to our deaths. I would not look good flattened, so instead, we climbed while he complained, but we are here now. We storm into the dark oval entrance, only to come to a stop, our war cries dying on our lips as we share a confused look.

"Well, it looks like we didn't need to rush to save you. We could have stopped for that iced coffee like I wanted, but no, somebody said it wasn't important." I glance at Phrixius, wagging my finger. "Now, don't you feel silly for worrying? Plus, it looks like she needs some caffeine after that . . . workout."

Freya's face flushes as she struggles to sit up, but the creature holding her tugs her back down, narrowing his red eyes on us, but he doesn't appear angry. A good fuck can do that to a guy.

"I am so confused." Phrixius's face is red as he meets Freya's eyes and tries to be a gentleman.

Leaning in, I whisper, "Need me to give you a book on sex, buddy?

See, the penis goes—" He throws me a glare as I cackle. "I told you she likes to fuck monsters. Pay up."

"You bet I would fuck the monster that abducted me?" Freya snaps.

I blink at her anger. "Yes?" I reply slowly. "I wasn't wrong, was I? Now we both get to benefit since Phrixius owes us a whole island."

"An island?" she scoffs haughtily. "Wait, nice bet, I could use a holiday after all this. Can it be somewhere warm?" she asks Phrixius.

"Can we focus please?" he snaps. "This creature abducted you. We thought you were in danger."

"So did I. I thought he would eat me," she begins.

"Oh, he did that for sure." I chuckle.

They both pin me with exasperated looks while the creature in question just snuggles closer to her. "What, a guy can't have fun? I was riding in here to rescue you, so at least let me enjoy this since I didn't get to kill anyone. I guess we don't have to worry about the creature eating and killing people—wait, I'm not sharing the bed with that thing. It's huge and looks like a cover hog."

"Mine," the creature snaps, tugging Freya closer.

"Ours," I retort. "We share here, buddy."

"Share?" he asks slowly.

"Share." I nod. "I guess it works out. She has three holes—"

"Oh my fucking gods, please stop!" she yells, and we all fall silent. She struggles from the creature's embrace, pointing at him when he tries to drag her back. "No, bad, stop. Give me a minute." Despite being totally naked and dripping in monster cum, she stands, propping her hands on her hips and looking every inch the defiant witch as she watches us. "Right, enough. I can fuck whomever I want, and I don't want any judgment or arguments. Understood?" She glances at me.

"Understood, little witch." I nod with a grin. "As long as I'm one of them."

Huffing, she looks at Phrixius. "Understood?"

"Understood." He nods quickly, glancing at me. "I didn't even do anything—"

"Enough," she snaps, and the god actually closes his mouth. She looks at the monster then. "Understood? I don't belong to anyone."

"Mine," he snarls.

She snarls back, and despite the shadows now leaking from him in anger or the fact that he's huge and clearly evil, she points in his face. "No." Her eyes narrow. "I am my own, and if you cannot accept that, I will never touch you again."

He shrinks back, his shadows receding into him. "Fine." He pouts.

"Good, now that's sorted, I need clothes."

"Why? I like the cavewoman look you are—" I fly back into the wall, hit by her magic. Groaning, I get to my feet and snap my fingers, swiftly dressing her. "So rude to your rescuers."

"So we are . . . accepting this creature?" Phrixius asks cordially.

Freya shrugs. "He's harmless."

"It is an entity of darkness and unnatural. It shouldn't even exist. It feels ancient and wrong," Phrixius admits, and we all stare at the creature who is busy rubbing against Freya's leg like a house cat.

"Terrifying," I comment drily.

"I want nothing but this woman, Freya." It drags her name out to a hiss, and I don't miss the way her cheeks heat, making me grin. My girl really does love to fuck monsters. God, she's amazing, but I pretend to be put out.

"So now we are sharing three ways. There are only so many days in a week—"

"Three ways?" Freya interrupts, looking at Phrixius, but he says nothing, and she rubs her head.

"You are all idiots." She stalks past us, bursting from the cave. There's nowhere for her to go, so I don't worry, but I do step closer to the monster, letting my expression go cold and dead as I channel my power.

"If you hurt her, I don't care how long it takes, I will find a way to rip you apart and scatter your soul across the world so you will suffer for eternity." I blink then smile. "Welcome to the family, killer."

"I have only killed some." It frowns. "Are we not supposed to?"

"Oh yeah, you'll fit right in." I glance at Phrixius to see him watching the entrance anxiously. "What is it?"

"Did you feel that?" he whispers, his eyes widening as he looks at me. "That call?"

My heart stops and stutters. I was so focused on the creature, I didn't feel it at first, but I do now.

Darkness and death.

It's a scream, a call in the air.

We both rush from the cave to find Freya's eyes completely black as she floats in the air before collapsing to the ground in a slump.

"Freya!" I scream in horror, dropping to my knees at her side and pulling her into my arms. "Little witch, wake up!" I demand, shaking her, but her eyelids don't even flutter. "Freya, please!"

CHAPTER 26

freya

My eyes snap open suddenly, and I blink at the complete darkness.

The last thing I remember is leaving the cave, needing space from all that testosterone, and then . . . something happened. Something was whispered into my ear, burrowing in my brain, and then . . . nothing.

What happened?

Did I pass out?

Frowning, I try to move, but it's like I have no body or it's frozen. I cannot even feel or see anything but darkness. Panic fills me, and I scream internally for someone, anybody.

Suddenly, flames burst to life, blinding me for a moment before they die down, and I can see. When I do, horror and fear explode through me. I'm not in my body nor anywhere I recognise. I'm in the dark someplace. It has to be underground, if the rock above and around us is anything to go by, but stretched below and before us is an entire underground city.

It's dark and empty.

I say us because before and to the side of me are hundreds of unmoving zombies. They are lined up and waiting like soldiers ready for battle. I want to scream, but I can't. I'm trapped inside one, seeming to use their eyes to look out. Flames jump along the wall in a long line, illuminating more, but the darkness is so thick, most of it cannot be penetrated, and it leaves everything in an unnatural, shivering shadow.

From one of those shadows, a figure emerges, and I pray to the gods they cannot see me inside this zombie. They are tall, clearly male, and dressed in what looks to be ornate armour, which is black with spiked vines. Pale skin shines underneath, and I see black, bulging veins. I cannot see his face, however, which is covered by a mask.

It's the mask from Agatha's shop.

Even now, I hear the souls trapped inside calling to me.

I watch in terror as the necromancer turns away from the zombies. He stands above the city at a black stone altar. There are bowls and skulls across it, and blood seems to drip endlessly from the slab to the floor.

There is so much blood, you could drown in it.

As I watch, he reaches behind the slab and drags a wailing woman onto the altar. My heart freezes as I scream.

"Please!" she cries, trying to fight him, but he pins her down and produces a curved, wicked blade from the table. Her scream bounces around us until my ears feel like they are bleeding, and his laughter follows it.

He lifts the blade, holding her with his other hand. "Your sacrifice is for the greater good. You will serve a bigger purpose. Do not fear death, for it is my friend." The knife slices down so fast, I swear I barely see it. It cuts through her chest, even as she screams and chokes on blood. He drops the blade for a moment, plunging his hand into her chest as her arms fall limply to the side, her head turning until her empty eyes meet mine.

If I could cry, I would, but all I can do is watch as he roots around in her chest, the sound of snapping bones filling the air. He grabs the blade once more and stabs, pulling it out of her wound.

I fight to get free, calling my magic, but it's like there's a block between it and me. The figure turns, the blood-covered blade held in the air with a heart speared on the tip.

Blood magic. Death magic.

He seems to be searching for something before turning back to the altar, and as I watch, he holds up the heart and whispers something before carving into the organ and carefully placing it back in the open chest of the woman. Picking up a needle and thread, he sews her up and presses his hands to her skin.

I watch in fascinated horror as the woman sits up, still bleeding but dead. Her eyes are cold and empty, and her mouth is still open in horror, so he reaches up and shuts it.

"Welcome to my army," he murmurs. "Now stand with the rest." Obediently, the woman slides from the table, stumbles over, and gets into line with the rest of us.

Oh gods, please. I want to go home. Please, let me go.

I reach for my magic again to get out of here when he turns abruptly. "I feel you." I freeze. "I can taste your magic in the air. I know you are watching me. Where are you?"

He wanders over, blood dripping down his arms to the floor, making my stomach roll. His eyes run over his zombies, searching, and I panic. I try to hide as deeply as I can, but I don't even know how I got here or how to get back.

He stops before me, and I want to run, but I'm trapped.

That masked head tilts, and I know he's smiling as his hand grips my zombie's face. That mask fills my vision until I see black eyes that delve into my soul, seeming to tear me apart as agony rips through me. "I see you, witch."

I jerk awake with a scream, my hands scrambling across my face and body as I blink and look around.

"Freya, Freya!" Panicked voices fill my ears as I scramble back, trying to wipe the blood away from my face, but there's none. Breathing heavily, I meet three worried gazes. Phrixius, my demon, and the creature kneel before me in my home.

"Little witch," my demon says softly, "it's okay. You're okay now.

I don't know what happened. I couldn't reach you. It was like I couldn't follow you—"

"He saw me," I croak.

"Who did?" Phrixius asks softly.

"The necromancer. I was there, wherever he was. I saw him, he—" I swallow, tears falling down my cheeks. "He killed someone and brought them back as a zombie. There was a whole army, and he saw me. He saw me."

"Freya, are you sure?" my demon asks, and I nod as I wrap my arms around myself.

"I'm sure. He saw me. He fucking saw me."

CHAPTER 27

They share a knowing look, apart from my creature who comes closer and sniffs me, wrinkling his nose. "You smell like death and blood."

"What is it?" I ask of Phrixius and my demon when they remain silent.

They turn back to me. "He knows who you are," Phrixius murmurs as they watch me.

"What?" I snap, panic lacing my tone. I don't like the way they are eyeing me like they pity me. "What is it?" I press, my heart still racing so fast, my body is shaking.

"Freya, I need you to calm down," Phrixius says, placating me.

"Stop talking down to me and tell me!" I shout, and my power bursts from me in a wave of black magic. It slams into them, sending them flying back as I gape. Lifting my hands, I see smoky, black shadows dancing around my fingers. "What is happening?" I cry, looking at them as they get to their feet.

"Little witch." My demon comes closer, taking my hand and allowing the shadows to crawl up his arm, and Phrixius takes the other, absorbing the shadows into his skin. It lessens my load, letting me think clearly, as if they are taking it into themselves. "Breathe, that's it, in and out."

I nod, sucking in desperate breaths.

"I am not talking down to you, Freya, I promise. I just want to keep you calm. I do not want you to get hurt."

"Or more likely, have me hurt you," I whisper, realising I could have without meaning to.

"Hurt me. Kill me. I'll come back because I am a god." He shrugs. "I could not bear you hurting yourself. That's it, breathe for us. We are right here, and you are safe. Everything will be okay."

"Please, tell me what the hell is happening to me. What is this power inside me? Why can I see him? Why can he see me? What's happening?" I whisper, glancing between them. It's clear they know.

"Freya," Phrixius begins.

"Please," I beg, meeting his eyes. "I need to know what's happening to me. I feel like I'm going crazy."

"You're not crazy," my demon replies. "You are just coming into your powers—the ones you have held back for so many years. They are getting stronger, and it means you're losing control more often, but you are doing an amazing job of holding them back. It's why you've been needier and reaching for us, letting us help you subconsciously without realising it."

"What powers? My witch powers?" I ask.

"Freya, you are not a normal witch. You are a necromancer," Phrixius tells me as he watches me with a sad look.

I laugh. "I'm not a necromancer. I'm a witch, a dark one for sure, but I'm just a witch." I trail off as they stare at me with stern expressions. "I can't be. They would have killed me. Right?"

"No, because I protected you," my demon mutters as my eyes swing to him.

"You can't be serious. This isn't funny," I snap.

"It's not a joke, Freya. I wish it were. Don't you feel the call to the grave? This darkness inside you is waiting to be used. When you were in the graveyard with your demon, did you not sense the bodies there? When you touched the metal bars, you felt the zombie calling to you, reacting to your magic. You can see the necromancer because his magic calls to yours. It's the same as yours."

"I'm not like him—"

"No, you're not," he murmurs when I start to panic again, "but you are a necromancer, Freya. I sensed it the first moment I met you. That's why I stayed, worried about your powers overwhelming you."

"Or more likely what I would do," I whisper, my eyes going to my demon. I beg him wordlessly to tell me this is a joke.

I can't be, right? He's so serious for a change, and he's right. I feel everything he said. I always thought I was just a really dark witch, and I tried to ignore it, but what if they are right?

What if I'm a necromancer?

"How long have you known?" I ask, my voice cold.

"Since I met you," my demon admits, and my bitter laugh makes him wince.

My gaze goes past them, unfocused, as I try to put the pieces together. "Why am I alive?" All necromancers were killed, so the fact that I am alive, even with the demon protecting me . . . There has to be a reason why I was kept in this coven when I should be dead.

Agatha . . . She came here after the mask.

Does she know?

Do they all?

"We can get into that, little witch, but it's going to be okay. We are right here. You need to know, you're right, because if he knows who you are, then he'll come for you. He'll want you, and we need to keep you safe, which means not keeping you in the dark . . ." His voice carries on, but my ears refuse to work.

They are serious.

Necromancer.

The word rings in my head, and my soul revolts. No, I can't be. I'm not like him. I don't kill people and bring them back. I'm not evil.

No, it can't be true.

I'll prove it.

I leap to my feet and rush to the zombie, pressing my hand to its head to prove to them and myself I'm not evil.

That I'm not a necromancer.

"No!"

I ignore their bellows.

As soon as my hand makes contact with the zombie's decaying skin, I regret it. All that power flows through me, and something within me reaches for the spark within the zombie. I can see it, like a flower or a vine dying and decaying, but that darkness within me feeds it. It grows, blooms, and spreads, and when I jerk back, the zombie turns its bright eyes to me, it's skin fuller.

It's more alert as it waits for me to order it.

I can feel its life force like a shadow, a whisper in the back of my mind.

Oh gods.

I turn and throw up, understanding what I did and what I am.

I look to them to see their horror, and I can't handle it.

I run, but this time nothing is chasing me except the truth—the truth I wish I never knew.

CHAPTER 28

I watch her go, my heart squeezing at the panic in her eyes. With a thought, I hold back the demon and the creature. "Let her go. If we try to trap her, she will panic more. Let her breathe."

"She shouldn't be alone," the creature begins, understanding despite being recently created.

"She won't. Demon, go after her in a moment." He frowns at me. "I might be a god, but she is one of my people and she needs help. You two have a deeper bond—you understand her more. She needs you right now."

"One of your people? Is that what you told yourself when you fucked her?" He smirks, but then his expression sobers as he looks at the entrance. "I'll go, but what about the necromancer? He's going to be a problem."

"He needs time to find her, so we have a little bit of a head start. I will work on securing her home from him to give her a safe space. The creature can help me . . . . You need a name." I frown at him.

He shrugs. "Whatever Freya wishes to call me. I am hers."

Rubbing my head, I flick my fingers at the demon. "Go, you both give me a headache." I smile at them. "Demon, make sure our girl is okay." It's the only way I will admit to feeling more for her than I should because he's right.

This is about more than being a god. This is Freya and a bond we have created without meaning to.

The little witch has become important to me, very important.

I watch him go, and then I look back at the zombie. He's watching me, looking bright and fresh once more. "She's powerful."

"I could taste that," the creature murmurs.

"She might even be one of the most powerful necromancers I have encountered." My eyes go back to the exit. "I just hope we can save her. Come, you can help me place some wards to keep her safe."

"The necromancer?" it asks.

"He will get in if he really wants to. We need to find him first," I reply. "To do that, she will need to embrace who she is to stop him—something I don't think she is ready for, but we might not have a choice."

DEMON

She is easy to find. Phrixius is right, not that I would ever tell him that, but I know her well. I know everything about my little witch, since I have been with her from birth. There are no secrets between us, and as I appear at her tree just inside the barrier, I spy her curled up against its trunk, looking out at the forest beyond.

Not many of the witches come here, so it became her safe haven when she was younger. It's where she always comes to think, and now is no different. For a moment, I just watch her, wondering how I am going to get through to her. I feared how she would react when she found out.

If you are told your entire life that necromancers are evil and should be killed, then you find out you are one? It's a lot to handle. My little witch's morals cannot handle this. She does everything she can to be good and helpful, but now she's learned she is expected to be evil. I'm lucky because I was born a demon, and being evil is what I do best. It's who and what I am. It's in my nature, but not hers. She's fighting against two halves of herself—who she wants to be and who she was born to be. I really don't know which side will win.

I walk rather than appear next to her and sit at her side. I press my leg and arm to hers, knowing she appreciates physical comfort more than most. She is turned away, but I see the tears falling down her cheeks.

"I always knew I was different," she whispers. "I thought if I tried hard enough and fought long enough, then I could be just a witch. I tried too hard to ignore that . . . that darkness inside me. I thought if I didn't look, it would go away." She laughs bitterly, her gaze landing on me when she turns her head. "I'm a foolish, naive witch, aren't I? Like a child hiding under a blanket, hoping the monster won't notice them if they don't look."

"It's not foolish, little witch. It was wishful thinking. We cannot fight what we are born to be. I was born as a demon, and you were born as a necromancer. Both are supposed to be evil, but I like to think we can choose who we are." She snorts, and I take her hand. "I mean it. Yes, I do bad things. I like the darkness, and I make choices most would consider evil, but I don't go around skinning children or anything. There are shades of grey within the dark, Freya. It's not all black and white like this world would have you believe. We can still choose the type of person we want to be, even if we cannot change how that happens. You were born into great power—dark but great power. You choose how you use it."

"And if I can't?"

"You can. I know you can. You are the strongest witch I have ever met, and you have been fighting this your entire life." I lift our joined hands. "You're not alone. I am right here. If it ever becomes too much, reach for me. I will take your burdens, and I will swallow that darkness for you."

She's quiet for a moment, watching our hands. "Phrixius probably wants to kill me. That's why he's around." She glances at me. "And you are here because of a deal, right?" She laughs, and the cold sound sends my heart into overdrive. "I'm evil, aren't I?"

Gripping the back of her neck, I turn her face to me, my eyes dropping to her lips as I move closer.

"Then let's be evil together," I whisper against her lips.

Her eyes slide shut, and she relaxes into my kiss. The moan I swallow makes me grip the back of her neck harder.

She whimpers and climbs on top of me, straddling me, and I wrap my tail around her to keep her secure. Our tongues tangle wildly, and the kiss is filled with passion and love.

Our hands race across each other before she lifts her dress, and before I can tug my mouth away, she impales herself on my length. My grown fills the air as her cunt grips me. She groans, taking me deeper, and I look down to watch her work herself farther on my length.

Her bruised lips are parted, and I can't resist. I yank her closer, kissing her once more. She slips deeper onto me, and I wrap my tail more securely around her, helping her ride my cock until we find a rhythm.

It's hard and fast as my claws dig into her skin, keeping her against me. My forked tongue laps at her mouth. She grips my shoulders, drawing blood as she pulls her mouth away, moaning my name. I suck and kiss down her throat, feeling her cunt clench around me. Her head falls back on a moan as I bite down at the junction of her neck and shoulder so hard I taste her blood.

"Demon," she begs, and I slam her down as she cries out.

Our thrusts speed up, both of us racing towards the precipice of pleasure. Her shadows wrap around me and sink into me, making me shudder. The pain is ecstasy as she flays me alive, yet I fuck her faster, needing more.

Her hips swivel with each thrust, and I know she's close. When I slide my lips up her throat to her mouth, I can't help but grin. "Come for me, little witch. Let go. Let me have all of you."

Her eyes open, meeting mine, and I nip her lip. "Come."

She cries out, splintering at my order, and comes all over my cock, taking me with her. I bellow my release to the night sky as I fill her with it.

Panting, I press my head to her chest and listen to her racing heart. I stay like this for a moment before I meet her eyes as I kiss her chest.

She smiles and slides into my lap, curling into me, and we both take in the night air, our bodies still shaking with pleasure.

She needs to know, when everything else is changing, that I'm her constant.

Holding her in my arms, I kiss the top of her head as she sighs. "You are right. I am here because of a deal. My soul is linked to yours. I know you have always wondered and asked . . . . It started as a deal, but it's so much more now. I don't know when I started to fall in love with you, but I did. Demons are not supposed to love, but I love you, Freya, with every dark shard of my wretched soul. That's why I'm here. Deal or no deal, I would be right here, at your side. The deal doesn't make me love you. It doesn't make me need to see you smile or make me crave your happiness and pleasure. It's just a deal to be near you. I could keep it and never see you, but I want to see you. You are the brightest part of my day, of my life, and without you, I would cease to exist."

She looks up at me, her eyes wide. "You love me?"

"I do, with every fibre of darkness inside me. Where you go, I go, evil or not, Freya. I'm here, and I'm not going anywhere. If you want to burn this world, then we'll do it together. If you want to fight every day to be good, then I'll be right there with you, trying."

She smiles and leans up to kiss me.

"I love you too," she says, caressing my cheek. "I don't know when I fell for you, but I did, and I can't deny it. I love you, every part of you."

"If you can love me, Freya, then you can love yourself. Give it time," I tell her as I kiss her head. I want to dance on the spot for her admission, knowing how much that cost her, but I don't. I hold her tighter as she leans away.

"If you love me, then tell me who made the deal."

Groaning, I close my eyes. "You tell a witch you love her, and she thinks that means you'll tell her all your secrets."

Huffing, she settles back in my arms. "Fine, but one day?"

"One day," I promise as I kiss her head. "For now, let's just soak in the peace. I have a feeling everything is about to get a whole lot more complicated."

"You mean because there's a necromancer tracking me down to join his evil legion and take over the world?"

"Yup, you would look good with a crown though," I remark, and her laughter fills my soul, letting me know it's all going to be okay.

CHAPTER 29

freya

"That's it, keep reaching for it. It's like you would use your witch powers. It's the intention that matters and how you wield it. It comes from the same place, but you locked that necromancer side away a long time ago. We need to free it slowly so it cannot be used against you or take you by surprise and leave you weak. I was hoping we could keep it locked away forever, but clearly we can't, so you need to learn to control it. First, we'll release it, just like that. Nice and slowly, like opening a door an inch at a time. You are doing great," Phrixius instructs.

We sit opposite each other, our knees touching.

My demon took the zombie and creature for a walk to give us some peace since they keep sending my powers into disarray. I calmed down after my demon held me, and he urged me to come back. Neither Phrixius nor the creature commented on it. They simply smiled and welcomed me back. None of them looked at me differently, and Phrixius wasn't hesitant to touch me or be around me.

I keep my eyes closed, focusing on his words. Now that I'm looking inside myself, I see the darkness I was hiding from. At first, I jerked away with fear, but his soothing voice urges me to reach for it.

As if it were waiting for this, it surges towards me, making me gasp as my body jerks.

"Relax and do not fear it. It is a part of you, nothing more. It is controlled by you, not the other way around. That's it, just breathe and let it flow through you. Do not block it or retreat. Fear is your biggest enemy. It will sense heightened emotions and react."

Nodding, I try to relax, but as that darkness surges through my veins, it feels like my whole body fills to the point of bursting, like a balloon. The power is so strong, I'm surprised I'm not floating away.

This is so much more than I could have ever imagined, and the dark edge feels like vines slithering through my skin. Its sharp edges dig in, taking root. It's ready to be wielded. I don't know how long I sit here, fighting through it, before it finally stops.

It sits just under my skin, which feels too tight, but it's still and I can take a deep breath. My eyes open and clash with Phrixius's.

He nods. "You're doing amazing, Freya," he praises. "Okay, you have released it. Now you must learn to control it. Just like your normal powers, it reacts to what you want and feel, so you need an iron fist. If you get mad, it could mean someone's death. You need to be aware of that at all times. Imagine a wall, any is fine, and build it inside yourself."

"Around my power?" I ask with a frown.

"No, around your soul. You must be strong. Think of the strongest wall you can and imagine it surrounding you so nothing can penetrate it, and then step inside it."

I do as I'm told. It takes a while, and the wall crumbles a few times, so I change from wood to steel. Once I'm inside it, I open my eyes and meet his.

"Good, now every time you feel panic, scared, or angry, imagine it bouncing off that wall and back in until you can control it," he murmurs.

My back aches, so it's clear we have been here for hours.

"We'll take a little break, and then we will try to block the other necromancer and practice control. Unfortunately, we do not have time to go slow or take it easy. You need to learn as quickly as you can. I don't specialise in necromancy, but I have met enough and know their history, so I can help a little."

Nodding, I watch him as he stretches his arms up.

"Why haven't you killed me?" I murmur. "You're a god, one of magic. It's your job to stop necromancers . . . so why didn't you kill me?"

His arms drop as he eyes me, thinking how to respond.

"I should have. It's my duty," he admits. "But I couldn't do it. You were not what I was expecting when I felt the call. You are good. Deep down, you are good. You are not evil, and you haven't given into the darkness. I was just hoping I could save you and that you were strong enough to fight it. Maybe we can change history for the better this time. I never liked having to end a whole kind just because there is magic in them. As the god of magic, I understand it all has its place, but the others feared it. I was hoping if I were here, then I could help somehow and that I could save you. I have seen so much death, Freya. For once, I wanted life. I wanted to believe in hope. I wanted to believe in you."

"Why me?"

"I don't know," he replies. "There's something in you, something different. Despite what you are, you still fight to be good. You're so strong and filled with life, even with death at your fingertips. You are a perfect blend of naivety and anger, sinner and saint, witch and human, good and bad. If anyone stands a chance, Freya, it's you, and I want you to win. I believe you can. Without hope, what's the point of living?"

"For a god, you believe a lot in this world. I thought they were all ancient and had given up?" I joke.

He laughs, laying his hand on my knee. "I nearly did. When you live this long, nothing is exciting anymore, but then you came along. For better or worse, you brought life back into my world. You reminded me why I protect our people and what it means to be a god. You know more about living and happiness than even a god, Freya. Never forget that."

I lean in and place my hand on his. His eyes widen, and I drink in his reaction, but I need to know. "And you fucked me because you want me or because you were worried about my powers?"

I need to know where I stand with him before I get too attached. I like him, and I like spending time with him. Where my demon encourages me to be mischievous and enjoy life, Phrixius slows me down and reminds me to smile and look around.

I'm starting to adore him and the way he looks at me despite what I am, and I need to know before I get hurt. There is a lot going on, but I still want the answer, and I'm not afraid to ask.

I've lived in the dark my entire life, and I refuse to anymore.

"Both," he answers. "I saw you struggling, and at first, I wanted to help absorb some of it for you so you didn't fall into the darkness, but then at the first taste of you, I was lost. There is a reason the demon sticks around, Freya—you are addicting. Yes, I want you more than I have ever wanted any being in a thousand lifetimes. It's a terrifying thought for a god, but it's true. I want you even now . . . maybe more now. I want to taste your darkness. I want to see you shatter and come apart for me. It's dangerous, but I want it."

"Then do it," I say. "Test me, test how I can control myself now with these powers while we play. If anyone can stop it and keep everyone safe from me, it's you."

"And what if I want to keep you safe from the world?"

"Then do that too. Show me how much you want me," I purr as I lean in, sliding my hand up his thigh as I hold his blazing eyes. "Remind me I'm alive and that I'm good."

He needs no more prodding, and we tumble to the floor. Our lips meet in a flurry as we drag our hands over each other.

I feel his magic hit me, ripping off my clothes so I'm bare, and I return the favour. I strip him with a thought, and our bare bodies press together.

Our kiss never breaks, not even as his hand slides down my side and across my thigh, hooking around my leg and lifting it as he breaks our kiss and kneels between my parted legs. I meet his eyes as he turns his head and kisses my calf before sliding his tongue up my thigh. I arch up, and he kneels, his tongue inching higher and higher.

Reaching down, I grip his hair, wanting him there. He grins at my impatience but gives me what I want. His tongue drags over my cunt until I cry out. He lashes my clit before slipping it inside me and fucking me with it, thrusting it deeper before pulling out and moving to my ass, where he circles my hole as I shudder.

I feel his magic push inside my pussy, fucking me like a cock as he licks my ass until I can't handle it. I explode with a cry as I clench around his magic. He slides up my body, still fucking me with magic, but my release only seems to have unlocked more power inside me.

Snarling, I hit him with it, and he falls back as I pounce, straddling him. I grab his cock and sink onto his length, taking what I want.

My hands hit his chest, and I roll my hips, taking him deeper.

Phrixius's eyes narrow, and I fly back from his magic, a net across my back as he tugs my hips up and slams inside me. He impales me on his cock, my scream filling the air. I push back and take him deeper.

So much pleasure arcs through me, I cannot even breathe. He uses the magic that fills him like a weapon, clamping onto my nipples. Pain and pleasure collide, and I weep beneath him.

Gathering all my power, I hit him with it and free myself from his hold. I manage to flip to my back before he's on me again.

"I'm a god, remember? I can handle anything you throw at me. You can scare everyone else in the world, but not me," he warns as he lifts my legs and thrusts his length back into me. Wrapping my legs around his waist, I grip my breasts, tweaking and twisting my nipples as he watches me.

"Fuck, Freya, just like that. Goddamn, I could never deny you anything."

"No?" I reply, an evil grin curling up my lips. "But you said you can handle me. Let's see."

The darkness rises, wrapping around us and tightening like a vice, claiming his power and death, and he narrows his eyes. His power pushes mine back, but I pour more into it, testing him even as I arch and cry out when he bottoms out inside me.

He hisses as the darkness slams into him like a weapon, then he reaches down, grips my throat, and slams my head back to the floor, cutting off my air so the darkness retreats, wrapping around me protectively.

His hand tightens on my throat as he snarls above me, keeping me on the verge of death as he hammers into me.

It's so fucking hot.

His power tames me, and it also allows me to let go.

I shatter, screaming his name, and as my cunt grips his cock, he roars my name as he pumps his release into me.

When the pleasure frees us, we slump together, and he kisses my throat even as I chuckle. He meets my gaze and starts to laugh as well.

A noise makes us turn our heads to see my demon, creature, and the zombie at the entrance. There is a metal dog leash attached to the zombie with his name bedazzled across the collar.

"Really, I have to walk your pets while you two fuck?" We both look at my demon, who shakes his head. "I'm disappointed. You could have at least let me join."

"Or me," my creature adds.

I laugh, feeling happier than I have in a very long time.

"Good, again," Phrixius demands, and I close my eyes and focus on his magic trying to seep inside me. I block it once more, my eyes popping open with a grin. "Very good. We'll keep practising that every day, but for now, we need to test your abilities."

"I don't want to," I admit.

"Hiding from them won't make them go away. Being a necromancer doesn't mean you're inherently evil. Unfortunately, those who came before you chose that path, but the powers themselves are over death and reanimation. There is beauty to that and even joy," Phrixius explains. "Let's start here." He makes a flower, the purple rose wilted and long since forgotten. "Bring it back to life. Make it beautiful again."

Taking a deep breath, I focus on the rose. He's right. I can't hide from what I am, which means I need to train to know how to control it.

The worst choice would be to leave it alone and not understand its strengths and weaknesses. That won't help me at all.

Closing my eyes, I reach for the flower, letting the dark vine inside me unfurl and reach through towards it. It hurts, and I screw my eyelids tighter together. I can taste my blood in my mouth, but I keep going. Silently, those vines seek death, not life. It is not how I thought it would be. It seems to crave the decay in its petals and wants to consume it, turning it into power.

I thought necromancy was about reanimating life, but this seems like it wants to use death. It scares me so much my eyes fling open. Phrixius is grinning at me, completely unaware. "Good, Freya!" I follow his gaze down to the flower, which is now fully blooming, bright with life and a future.

As I stare at that alive flower, I start to wonder if necromancy is truly evil, but as the vine slithers back into place, fed and happy, I shiver in horror, knowing it can be. That feeling, even a little, let me know how easily it could be corrupted.

It wanted death. It didn't care how it got it, whether from something already passed or still living.

"Again." Phrixius conjures a whole plant this time.

I'm hesitant, but I follow his instructions. The more control I learn, the better. I don't want something like that living inside me unchecked. If it truly is evil, and if I am destined to kill and slaughter, then I'll do my fucking best to stop it. I will not let it win, which means learning control.

I'll practise so much it never consumes me. I'll show them all. I have no other choice.

Hours later, I'm covered in a cold sweat and exhausted. I practised until I couldn't lift my hand anymore. Magic takes a toll, and new magic is wild and harder to maintain. My bones ache and my skin feels uncomfortably tight as I crawl into my bed. Phrixius and my demon are watching me, both worried, but I wave them off.

"I just need to rest a little, then I'll carry on."

"Rest," Phrixius says. "You cannot afford to be weak."

I am glad he's taking this seriously, even if we both know why. He doesn't want to kill me. He wants me to beat this, and so do I.

My creature, who was happily eating, polishes off the bowl and heads my way, climbing into my bed. My eyes widen as he wraps himself around me, purring happily. "Erm . . ." I try to scoot away, but he clings on tighter, and honestly, I'm too tired to fight him. I just slump into his warm embrace, letting it comfort me after a long day.

"We can't keep calling you creature," I murmur.

"You call me demon," my demon mutters.

"Only because you won't tell me your name!" I snap before glancing over my shoulder and softening my tone. "Do you have a preference on a name?"

"Whatever you wish to call me, I will cherish." He presses even closer. I feel his length hardening, but I choose to ignore it and the flash of desire that slides through me.

"How about third wheel? Annoying? Inappropriate?" my demon starts, so I flick my fingers and sew his mouth shut. He mumbles something behind it as he begins to unwind the magic, giving me at least a few moments of peace.

Turning in the creature's arms, I look up at his monstrously handsome face and try to think, but the first word that pops out of my mouth is equally as strange but almost fitting. "Sha?"

"Sha? Isn't that just a sound?" Phrixius asks.

"No," I reply. "I heard it once, a long time ago, in a fairy tale." I snuggle deeper into the bed, a wide yawn splitting my face. "The elders were telling it to us to scare us, describing a big bad monster coming to eat little witches." A soft smile curves my lips.

"He ate you, that's for sure," my demon interrupts, but I ignore him.

"So I am . . . the villain of this fairy tale?" Sha asks.

"No, not to me. When they told us how this creature was made, I always felt sorry for it. I always felt it was not the monster, but the victim of the witches' own greed. He was an outcast who was alone and confused. He just wanted the same thing they did—peace—but they wouldn't let him have it. He was different, and I guess I always liked that. It's still my favourite story."

"Sha." He watches me. "Then that is what you will call me, after the monster that first stole your heart."

"I knew you had an obsession with monsters, but you had that fetish as a child too? I would say it's sick, but I'm quite proud—" My demon's words cut off again as I sew his mouth shut without looking.

"I'll get the scissors," Phrixius says, making me laugh as I bury my head in Sha's chest, letting him hold me protectively.

Sadly, he cannot protect me from what lives inside me.

None of them can. It's up to me, and that fear follows me into my dreams.

CHAPTER 30

freya

I don't know how long I sleep. One second, I'm unconscious, and the next, I'm jerked awake by a scream filled with horror and fear. Blinking in confusion, I turn my head. My demon is already on his feet, as is Phrixius, both of them standing near the entrance to my house.

Sha growls behind me, holding me tighter.

Struggling from his arms, I sit up in my bed as their eyes find me. "What is it?" I whisper. There's a tightness in my chest I don't like as awareness spreads through me. My skin feels wrong, as if I'm standing too close to a fire and about to get burned.

It's power, I realise.

It's pure power and stronger than anything I have ever felt, and it's so dark, it's choking me. Fear pounds in my head. It can't be. It can't—

My zombie groans and lumbers to the bars, seeming to answer an invisible call. As I watch, its eyes change, turning completely black. I leap from the bed and head over.

"Sit down," I order with panic.

"Freya," my demon warns, tugging me closer to him so my back hits his front. "Don't."

"Sit!" I order, lashing out at the zombie with my magic, but it ignores me, its head turning to the entrance, and despite the bars, it tries to leave.

"Necromancer," I whisper in understanding. The necromancer is here, and he's taken back control of what I stole.

Another scream fills the air, ripping into my shocked stupor, and then another.

Tearing from my demon's arms, I grab my cape and pull it on as I stumble to the entrance, needing to see. If the necromancer is here, then that means my coven is in danger. Is he attacking? Are they dying while I waste precious seconds?

Both my demon and Phrixius catch my hands as I rush past, yanking me back. "It's him. It's the necromancer!" I snap.

"I know," Phrixius says calmly, "which means he's here for you. Stay here, where our protections will keep you safe."

Pulling my hands away, I glare at them. "There is no guarantee they will work, and my coven does not have those same protections. I will not hide here while they suffer at his hands. I have seen what he is capable of, and I will not let them stand alone." Ignoring their outraged expressions, I rush from my house, their shouts following me.

It doesn't surprise me when all three appear at my side moments later. Without a second thought, I fling a blocking spell over them so no one else sees them. The coven might be under attack, but me being seen in the presence of a god and a creature won't help things.

They stay by my side as I run through the empty streets. A bad feeling builds within me until I burst out of the last road to find the coven there. They are all gathered, ready to use their magic.

"What's happening?" I ask as I push through the crowd to Agatha's side. She's pale but standing tall. She simply points, and I follow her gaze to the invisible barrier, my own eyes widening as my heart stops.

Standing at the edge of the barrier is a legion of zombies—the same legion I saw within that underground city. They stand like soldiers waiting for orders. Their undead bodies don't even move an inch. There are so many of them, they continue into the darkness of the trees beyond.

"They haven't attacked?" I whisper.

"Not yet, but it's only a matter of time. Where there are zombies, a necromancer follows." Agatha grits her teeth and glances at me. "I should have known when the mask was taken. I was a fool. I wanted to hope I was wrong, but I wasn't." She glances back at the coven and lowers her voice. "We do not stand a chance against a necromancer. Even with all our magic combined, we cannot defeat such evil. We will be dead by dawn." She says it calmly, confidently, but there is terror in her eyes that I have never seen before.

Our steely elder fears nothing, she always knows the answer and the path, but as she looks back at the zombies, she is silent and afraid.

"What do we do?" I ask. "We can't just stand here and wait."

"There is nothing we can do. We'll fight until our last breath and pray to the gods they take our souls far away from our bodies so when he steals them for his army, we do not have to watch or be trapped within."

"Agatha, what do we do? Do we run?" someone calls.

"There is no point. They have surrounded us. We would not get far."

"What if we create a portal—"

A flash of magic fills the air, and Agatha sighs. "He will block it. We'll fight. There is no other way. Barricade the younglings and elders in their homes behind barriers as strong as we can make them. Everyone else, stay with me." She looks at me, seeming to debate something. "Go, Freya."

"What?" I shake my head adamantly. "No, I'm staying here—"

"Go." Her eyebrows lower in meaning, and my heart freezes. Does she know he's here for me? "Before it's too late."

I stare into her eyes. "Whether or not I'm here, he will kill you. I cannot and will not live with that. If I die, then it will be at your side. My coven. My family."

"Child." She squeezes my hand. "We will always be your home, even if it might not have always seemed like it. Now let us protect you this time. Go now." She glances behind me. "And wherever you are, demon, go with her and keep her safe."

It's the second time tonight I am speechless, my eyes going to my demon who gives me a dark, serious look. "She knows about you."

He says nothing, and neither does Agatha. There's a groan from the zombies, and I jump, realising now is not the time. Turning back to her, I drop her hand. "I'm staying, and that's final."

I dismiss her penetrating gaze and the truth prodding at me. Later, I'll confront them, but for now, we need to face this threat. The necromancer is here somewhere. He has to be. What does he want with me?

More importantly, why aren't his soldiers attacking?

I saw what he did to that village, and I have no doubt he will do something like that here.

They crossed the barrier before, so why aren't they now?

It's then I realise they are waiting for me.

All of their eyes turn to me, and when the voices come, it's his in their bodies.

"Hello, witch, I have been waiting for you."

I try to ignore the goosebumps that erupt on my skin or, even worse, the vines within me that are starting to move, recognising his magic. It doesn't care if he is evil. It doesn't care that we are enemies. All it cares about is it feels like death and magic and it wants it.

"Leave," I demand, stepping forward.

Agatha tries to pull me backward, but I ignore her and step away again, feeling my men at my back. They won't stop me, even if they want to—they know better. I might be acting tough, but inside, I'm terrified.

"Witch, that is not a nice way to say hello, especially after we came all this way." The voice is a whip, cutting into us, and the zombies shuffle forward a few steps—a threat.

"A necromancer throwing a tantrum!" I yell, scanning their ranks, looking for him. Why am I antagonising him? I know reasoning with him won't help, but pissing someone off like this isn't a good idea. Honestly, what will he do to me that he hasn't already planned? "Take your soldiers and leave."

After we came all this way? This time, his voice is in my head, dark and sticky like oil. *For you, travelling so far to find you? That's quite rude. We are not enemies, witch.*

"Yes, we are," I answer aloud. "When you threaten my home and my coven, we are enemies."

I fall to my knees in agony as something stabs into my brain, and then his roaring voice cuts through my nerves. *They are not your coven! They are holding you back! They are nothing but naysayers. Where were they when our kind was slaughtered? They hid and helped. They are not your friends or family, witch. They are your enemy. I will show you that.*

Hands help me to my feet, and worried voices reach me, but my eyes lock on the zombies now steadily marching towards us with intent and death in their eyes.

He's going to kill everyone here because of me.

"Stop! Leave!" I demand, but it's clear he's done talking.

Swallowing my fear, I glance at Phrixius, then my demon and Sha. "We have to do something."

Phrixius nods. "We will stop him. I have stopped necromancers before, and we will again."

There will be so much death, and we still might not win. For all the gods' strength, Phrixius cannot lower himself for what needs to be done to end this. He doesn't have the darkness and death in him.

I do though.

I can stop this.

My gaze turns the zombies'. If I take them away from him, he will flee, right? I took one once—yes, it was older and only one, but how much harder could it be? Regardless, I need to try. I cannot risk any of my men or my coven.

If I don't, everyone here will die.

He will kill them to get to me. I cannot let them be slaughtered.

I meet Phrixius's eyes again. "I have to try," I say without explanation, and his brows furrow in confusion before his eyes widen.

"Freya, no!" He reaches for me, but I dance out of reach and turn to the approaching zombies. This might not work, but I have to give it my all. I cannot stand by and let this happen.

All the death I feel in the air belongs to me. It calls to me . . . . It is me.

I denied it all my life, but I cannot deny the truth anymore. I am a master of death, reincarnation, and reanimation. I am a necromancer, and these soldiers will be mine.

Taking a deep breath, I step farther away from my coven and my men, so their magic doesn't interfere with what I am going to do.

I centre myself, remembering what Phrixius said, and reach within me to those vines, filling them with my intentions.

Control. Take them over.

Make them mine.

I repeat it as they flow out of me, growing in power and strength as if they have been waiting for this moment. It hurts, like a thousand tiny cuts lashing my body, and I shudder and sway, but I stand strong as they grow and consume, reaching for the zombies. I expected resistance, but the darkness just keeps spreading.

There is so much of it, I have no idea how I kept it inside.

It bursts from me, ripping me to pieces so I bleed from a thousand cuts.

My body is one big open wound, but something in me knows if I stop now, it will be much worse. All that darkness needs an outlet. There is no going back.

I've let it go, I've released it, and it is hungry.

Everything they worried about and told me makes so much sense because no matter how much intention I pulse into that magic, it feels wild, evil, and dark.

Hands land on my shoulders and my back, grounding me. Their magic infuses mine as they lend me their strength and power. I am able to regain control, aiming the darkness where I need it.

When it hits the first row of zombies, I gasp loudly, my eyes opening wide. I don't know why I expected it to be invisible, but I watch in horror as the inky black vines crawl up the marching bodies and slide into their eyes, mouths, noses, and ears. I rip into them, but they continue to march as it burrows deep until I feel the spark of his magic.

With my hands held out, I turn and close them into fists. The vines consume that spark, snuffing it out and ripping them apart piece by piece. I watch in horror and fascination as the zombies split into limbs and pieces, and they fall and stop, but the ones behind them keep coming.

Rolling my shoulders back, I stand taller and open my palms again. The vines seem bigger, growing with power as they hits row after row, doing the same. Sweat beads on my skin and rolls down my body, the exhaustion making me pant, but I still stand, killing with the vines. I don't take them over, not like before—no, I tear the life from them until limbs scatter the grass before us, yet they keep coming.

The veins only grow stronger, their ends attached in my soul, draining it of life, and I sway under the power.

"Enough," Phrixius barks. "It's killing you. Pull back."

The soldiers are still coming. "No, I need to finish this," I grit out, my voice sounding strange.

"Little witch, stop," my demon pleads.

I shake my head, even as my vision seems to darken, and I know I'm running out of time. Magic always has a price—the stronger, the steeper. This death magic could kill me. I need to end this now.

Do you have the means, witch? comes his taunting voice. *I don't think you do, and when you're out, I will take all of their souls and make them mine. I will use their bodies to haunt you and remind you of your loss every time—*

"No!" With a scream, I thrust my hands forward, shoving everything I have into that one last move.

The remaining zombies explode, torn apart by a tidal wave of thorns that physically raises the earth, tearing into the dirt as they go. It's so strong, and there are so many, it blackens the moon before they slam into me. I stagger into the men behind me, and they catch me as I gasp, unable to scream as the thorns once again fill my body. They hold too much power, and I feel like I will implode.

"We've got you. Give it to us," Phrixius demands. "Now, witch!"

My head is turned and lips meet mine. I pour the darkness into those lips until they rip away and another set replace them. I do the same, each moment that passes letting me breathe easier as they take the darkness and make it their own. When my head is turned again, my shoulders slump in relief as more power passes from me to them until I can see, hear, and breathe without feeling like I'm dying.

The thorns settle back inside me, satisfied and happy, leaving me cold and shaken.

What I was capable of terrifies me as I look around at the hundreds of scattered heads and limbs leading to me like a trail. All the zombies are torn apart, their sparks of reanimation stolen by me.

The necromancer chuckles in my head, making me whimper in pain. *Hmm, you are strong. Fine, I will leave for now. Consider this a victory, but I'll be seeing you again soon. You cannot fight the darkness that lives in us forever. Look at you. You're magnificent.*

I freeze, my eyes wide. This was what he wanted all along—for me to use my magic against him. He didn't want to kill my coven, though he would have if it got him what he needed. No, he simply wanted to rip open my magic and pour it into the world.

He wanted to make me like him.

"I will never be like you!" I scream, even as the bodies around me groan with life, reacting to my anger and horror.

We will see about that.

Suddenly, his power is gone, and I slump even more.

When I turn back to my coven with the help of my men, all I see are horrified eyes, and I know he took something precious from me tonight. I sway with exhaustion, and when I fall, something—no, somebody catches me.

"I've got you, little witch. I've got you."

I pass out right there in his arms.

The necromancer is gone, but I still remain, and I know nothing will ever go back to the way it was.

CHAPTER 31

Sha

The demon stands with Freya in his arms, and the moment her eyes shut, there are screams. The witches stumble back when they see Phrixius and me at the demon's side. Her spell is wearing off.

Moving closer, I lean down to check she is okay. She's exhausted. I don't know how it's possible for so much magic to be in a tiny body, but she was incredible. Watching her destroy a whole army just confirms that I was born to be hers and bear this burden with her.

"Let's get her out of here," Phrixius murmurs to us.

Nodding, we move towards the witches as a unit. They stumble back, bar the one my woman was talking to, who watches us sadly. When we breach their midst, they quickly part, creating a pathway between them. We walk silently, every eye on us.

I warn them with my glare. If anyone so much as dares to touch or attack her, then I will end them. I do not like the energy surrounding them nor the way they are looking at her as if she is their enemy, especially after she almost just died to protect them. Without her, those zombies would have ripped them to pieces, I would not have helped. I only listen to her, I only care for her, but she clearly cares for them.

I felt it in the magic she used to protect them, yet here they stand, as if she is worse than nothing to them.

Phrixius and the demon feel it as well. Both are tense, their eyes scanning the crowd, but they do not seem shocked.

"She's a necromancer," someone whispers. "We have to kill her—"

Magic lashes towards us. I step before Freya, and it absorbs into me, feeding the beast inside. I tilt my head as the change comes over me.

Gone is the humanoid form I took so as not to frighten my woman, my creator, and now I stand before them as the monster.

There are screams, and I lift one of my long arms to point a black-clawed nail at the pale female who flung the magic. "You attacked." My words are more of a growl, but she understands, scrambling to turn and flee, but the crowd is too thick. In two steps, I am before her, and the other witches scramble away as I lift her into the air with a hand on her tiny throat.

She's so weak and puny.

She kicks and screams, flinging magic at me, but all it does is make me stronger.

I know my witch would not want me to kill her, but she dared to attack my woman so she cannot live. I do spare her a more gruesome death though, since I do not want Freya to be angry at me. I simply snap her neck and drop her as I glare at the others in warning.

"I would heed his warning. He is a beast, and he answers only to Freya. If you so much as follow us or dare to attack us when our backs are turned, then I will not be able to stop him. He will eat you without a care."

Ah, permission. Reaching down, I swallow the witch's body whole, absorbing her magic into me before turning back to my woman.

Phrixius is wide-eyed. "I didn't mean literally," he whispers.

"You said so," I growl as I head over. "We go, yes?"

The demon chuckles, holding her closer. "Oh, you're going to be in trouble. I'm so glad it isn't me. Come on, let's get our witch home to rest."

I follow after them, confused. "Why will I be in trouble?" I force out the words as I shrink back into my other form, feeling too full after the snack.

"You ate someone," Phrixius hisses.

"Yes?" I ask, confused, and the demon chuckles.

"She won't like it. We don't go around eating people," he explains as we walk.

"But she attacked Freya," I rumble.

"Solid logic to me." The demon shrugs, and Phrixius just sighs, pinching his nose.

"How did I even get here?" he mutters, and I answer for him, wanting to be helpful.

"I heard it was a spell . . ." My words fall silent as they turn to me. The demon looks at the god with a knowing grin.

"Note to self, sarcasm is lost on the beast. Come on, Sha, before you have an all-you-can-eat witch buffet."

Ignoring his laughter, I follow them back to her home. No witches dare follow or attack us. Once inside, I watch Phrixius mutter something before the feeling of magic touches me. I follow the demon to her bed, where he lays her down softly and pulls the covers up.

Climbing in, I curl into her side while Phrixius lies beside her, watching her worriedly. His hand covers hers as if to check her life force. I expect the demon to join us, but he watches for a moment, his eyes hard.

Tucking her between us, I meet the others' eyes. I care nothing for them, but she does, so I will accept them. "What will happen now?"

I do not understand the hatred towards what she is, but I have spent the last few days learning as much of her history as I can. It is not good. They slaughter her kind.

If they so much as try to lay a hand on a strand of her hair, I will tear them to pieces. She is mine.

"I don't know," Phrixius admits. "They could tell the other gods or kick her out. No matter what happens, she's out now, and there is no going back."

"You are a god, make them forget," I demand.

"I cannot do that. I cannot interfere in their coven laws and magic, even if I want to," he argues, looking at her. "And I want to. I want to help her, but I cannot. My hands are tied."

"Mine are not," the demon murmurs as he leans down and places a kiss on her head before stepping away.

Phrixius catches him. "What are you doing?" he asks worriedly.

"Do not worry, god. I will not kill them. Look after our girl, and I will be back." He leaves.

DEMON

I know she is safe with them for now, which is the only reason I do what I do next. She will not be safe forever, not now that they know.

I appear in her home, and moments later, she enters like a hurricane, but she stills when she sees me there. I allow her to view me, just like my little witch did earlier without realising it.

"Demon," she hisses, but there's a tremor of fear in her tone. "Is Freya okay?"

I stalk towards her, and she backs into the door as I chuckle. "She is resting. Make it known that if any come after her, we will kill each and every one of them," I tell her. "You knew her truth all along. If you let them hurt her, physically or emotionally by trying to get her to leave, then I will expose you and kill you all. I will laugh in the flames as your whole coven and its lineage dies. I have lived amongst you for as long as she has, but I owe no loyalty to anyone but her." I slam my fist into the wall next to her before conjuring an image of her entire village burning. "Make no mistake, I have been well behaved so far, but if anyone even looks at her wrong, I might decide not to be."

"You truly are evil," she sneers.

"I am." I smirk. "Never forget that or that there is only one person in this entire universe I care about, and it is that little witch. I will do anything to keep her safe." I let her see the true depth of what I am capable of when it comes to Freya.

What I said is true. I have been behaving until now, but that can quickly change. This might have started with a deal, but Freya is my world. She is my reason for living. She is my everything. She is mine, and I will never let anyone hurt her.

She can hate me for eternity for slaughtering her people, but she cannot leave me, especially not in death.

"Is it just because of the deal?" she retorts, lifting her chin in defiance. "Do not tell me, demon, you have come to care for her." I do not speak, and she laughs bitterly. "What do you think she will do when she learns the truth?"

I slam her into the wall in warning, my magic binding her to it. Flames that do not burn crawl across her body. She pants in fear, her eyes wide as she tries to fight me, but she is no match. "Don't threaten me, witch."

"We want the same thing," she hisses. "To keep her safe."

"No, we do not. You would put the coven, your people, before her safety. Me? I will not. Nothing comes before her, and that is where we are different. Remember that." Releasing the flames, I step back into the darkness until I am just a voice as I wrap the shadows around me.

"This coven's lives now lie in your hands. Make sure to keep her safe or you will all die." I go back to my girl, crawling into bed and lying on her.

I need to feel her breathing.

The witch's words haunt me. When she learns the truth, what will Freya do?

Will she try to leave me? Banish me? Break the deal?

I clutch her closer.

No, I won't let that happen.

Freya is mine and has been since the day she was born, and she will continue to be until the day she dies.

CHAPTER 32

I know I am asleep, yet I cannot seem to fight the darkness wrapping around me. My emotions feel muted. I can't remember what happened, and I know I should be worried, but I am empty, wrapped within this fog that seems to squeeze me tighter and tighter.

Suddenly, it parts, and the necromancer is before me with the mask still covering his face. We stare each other down through the smoke. I should be fearful, but I can't feel anything. He slowly lifts his hand, holding it out to me.

"Join me, Freya," he purrs.

"Never," I snap, fighting to escape him and the seductiveness in his voice calling to that part of me.

"Aren't you tired of fighting who you are, Freya?" he murmurs. "Of what lives inside of you? Accept it and come home with me, where you belong, with your people." His hand is still held towards me, like a lifeline in the dark.

"You are evil," I hiss.

He laughs, the sound grating on my brain as he drops his hand. "Evil? You use that word so carelessly. Evil . . . You have no idea." The smoke around us parts, and the numbness I felt is stripped away.

We are inside a house. It's small but cosy, with a little wooden table with one leg shorter than the others. There are three place mats with cutlery before them. A multicoloured, handwoven rug is under our feet, and candles blaze around us. It's filled with warmth and happiness and so much love, I can feel it pulsing through the walls.

"I want you to understand," he says as he turns to me.

"I do not need to understand," I retort. "You have killed people—"

"As have most," he adds. "You call me evil, Freya, but do you understand the truth of that?"

A baby's cry splits the air, and we turn to see a woman smiling down at a baby bundled in her arms as she sits in a rocking chair. Her thumb rubs over the baby's ruddy cheeks, her smile so bright and beautiful it hurts. "There, there, Daddy will be here soon. I know you miss him, hmm? I do as well," she whispers before kissing the little head. "But he's protecting us. Do you know why? Because he loves us so much," she says as he starts to suck her finger.

"That is my son and my wife."

I turn to see him, and his mask disappears. I do not know what I was expecting, but it isn't the handsome, middle-aged man before me. His hair is dark, and there are lines around his thin lips and cheeks. He looks normal.

"They are both dead now, killed by those who hate us. They were slain right here in our home. I was not here to protect them. I simply came back and found their bodies."

I turn back to the baby and the woman to see her giggling at something he did, and something inside me aches at the pure happiness radiating from them.

"No evil being starts that way. We are all born innocent," he murmurs as he looks at his baby. He steps towards them and kneels, looking up with such longing it feels like I am intruding before he stands and steps back. "We are turned evil by people who hurt us. Mine is not the only story of pain. So many innocents died. Babies were slain in their mothers' arms and wombs. It's why we went underground, but even there we were not safe. Everyone was killed simply for being born as we were. Our children did nothing to deserve it. My child did nothing to deserve it." He looks at me. "He died, but you survived. Tell me, Freya, how is that fair? Should you have been killed at birth simply for being what you are? Or should you have been given a chance?"

I'm silent, lost and unsure.

"His name was Laurent, after my best friend—my best friend who died while trying to protect me. That name died with them. No one remembers them because even their memories weren't safe from the stigma. You call me evil, Freya, but I wasn't always. I only wanted to keep my family safe. We hid, we rejected our magic, and yet it was not enough for them. Most died in the massacre in our hidden city that day. Others were hunted across the world, and then I was the only one remaining, or so I thought. I never wanted to become what they called us. I hated the idea that we could be capable of such evil, but when I had no choice, when I lost everything, the darkness was all that was left. It welcomed me home. It stole the pain so I could survive. It kept me alive and gave me purpose."

"What they did was wrong," I say, pained as I look at the child. "But it does not make what you are doing right. We need to be better. We need to show them—"

"They will never listen nor care. Don't you understand?" he roars. "You can be as good as you wish, and it will not stop them. They will never let us live. They cannot because that means they must admit they were wrong and all those they slaughtered were innocent. They cannot live with that."

The room around us transforms, and I stumble back in horror. The candles are out, the front door is hanging off its hinges, and blood and scorch marks mar the surface. The once beautiful rug is destroyed, and the woman lies across it, turning it red with her blood. Her head is turned, her eyes empty and her arm outstretched, and I gag when I realise she's reaching for her baby.

"Do not look away," the necromancer demands. "If you choose their side, then you must watch."

His tiny body is at a strange angle, and his blankets are gone. For some reason, that worries me. Won't he be cold?

Then I realise he's dead too.

They both are.

"Evil is not born, Freya. It is created," he says as a younger version of him rushes into his home. The echoing howl of agony pierces my heart as he falls to his knees, clutching his wife and his baby to his chest as he sobs. The bag that was on his shoulder falls to the floor, the contents spilling free—baby formula.

The vision changes, and we are in the street. It takes me a moment to realise this is the underground city I saw before, but there are hanging lanterns, children's toys in the street, and open food vendors. It's filled with life, but then it changes once more.

All that life is gone.

Bodies litter the streets, and blood runs into the cobbles.

Houses burn, and screams fill the air.

It changes again, and I'm staring at the necromancer once more. He's panicked, sitting in the driver's seat of a car, the door open. A man stands before it, looking at him, his expression determined. "Go, my friend. You need to get back to your pregnant wife and keep them safe." He shuts the door and turns, racing with a gun raised to two figures who float in the air before them.

"Gods," he murmurs from my side.

He drives away, but we stay, watching as his friend fights and is slain with a flick of one of the god's fingers, a wound opening on his chest so deep, I see his beating heart. He glances up at the escaping car and smiles before falling forward, dead.

The visions keep changing. There are so many bodies piled up, fields of dead, and destroyed homes. I see so many corpses that I start to scream, sinking to my knees.

"Stop, make it stop!" I beg.

He walks towards me through the battlefield, the dead and dying surrounding us, their calls splitting my head and heart. There is so much death, I can feel it crawling into me. The horror and power wrap around my dark heart.

"Do you understand now, witch?" he calls as he stops before me, tipping my chin up. "How about now?" The scene transforms again, and I gag once more.

Children of all ages lie around us, broken and dead. We are in a church, the same church where we found the arm.

"They came here to hide and beg the gods to stop, but it didn't work," he whispers as he straightens, the edges of the vision starting to swirl with smoke once more.

His voice fills my ears as the vision fades. "Who is really evil, witch? Them or us? Those who were born with the capability to be, or those who forced them into it? We are not enemies, and you will understand that soon."

CHAPTER 33

I wake with a scream, fighting the smoke until I realise it's hands.

"Freya!"

I turn my head and meet Phrixius's worried eyes.

I didn't see him in the vision, but that doesn't mean . . . I turn my head and throw up on the floor. Hands rub my back as I gag, my body still feeling weak.

"Shh, it's okay. We are here." It's Phrixius's voice, and I gag harder. The idea of him touching me fills me with a sick feeling, as well as anger, and when the gagging stops, I sit up. I wipe my mouth, finding him so close I recoil. He tries to touch me, but I move away.

I hold up my hand to stop them as I pant. My stomach rolls as my gaze lands on Phrixius. "Tell me," I demand.

He frowns in confusion. "Tell you what?"

"Tell me you did not kill children. Tell me you did not slaughter babies in their mothers' arms," I order.

"Freya, what are you talking about?" he begs, sliding closer.

"Tell me!" I scream, and he falls backward as my power hits him. It rushes through me, so dark that I don't even realise I am floating above him with smoke crawling up my arms and legs until he gasps, but I cannot stop it. "Tell me you were not like them," I implore. "Tell me I did not let you into my body and my home when your hands are covered with innocents' blood. Tell me!"

A cut opens across his chest, but he ignores it as he climbs to his knees, his hands spread wide as he stares up at me with longing and pain.

"I do not know what you saw, Freya, but please breathe. You are going to hurt yourself."

I snarl, and another cut opens.

"I have killed people, Freya, I will not lie to you, but no, I have never killed innocents nor children. I participated in battles, and I have slain thousands in my lifetime, but not without provocation or reason and never innocents. Look into my soul if you wish. You can check it. I have blood on my hands, but I would never touch a child or someone who did not deserve it."

"They did. They killed children and innocents," I say as I float back to the bed, the smoke retreating at his conviction, and my anger turns to horror.

"They did," he confirms. "Many did."

Blinking through the pain, I face them.

"He is trying to confuse you and drive a wedge between us," Phrixius murmurs.

"It's working. Tell me it was all a lie. Tell me what he showed me was not how it happened." He's silent, and I laugh bitterly. "You can't because he showed me the truth, even if he did it to confuse me. He didn't lie."

"Freya, please listen. I am not saying what happened was right, it was not, but you must understand why they did it. The gods felt like there was no choice. One necromancer could bring down entire cities. You did not see that side, Freya, or the death and power they wielded with one hand. They could destroy the world, and some wanted to."

"Some, not all, yet you killed everyone! You killed innocents." The pain causes me to double over. "So much death. There was so much death."

"There was," he murmurs, moving closer, and this time I don't fight him as he pulls me into his arms. "I cannot change the past, Freya, but I'm trying to change the future. Please believe me."

"You want to know the worst bit?" I whisper as tears fall. "I understand why he's doing it now. If the world killed my child and love, I'd do the same."

"No, you wouldn't," Phrixius retorts, cupping my cheeks. "He has his reasons, and I'm not saying what happened is right because it's not —innocents paid for the crimes of some, and it's horrendous—but you would not do the same."

I meet his confident gaze. "Wouldn't I? Are you so sure? Wouldn't you? Wouldn't you want revenge against those who took the person you love away from you?"

"Revenge does not change what happened," he whispers.

"No?" I search his eyes. "Then what does? Have we really learned from that? My kind is still hunted and killed for existing. Nothing has changed. Maybe he's right. Maybe the world needs this to remind them that they can't just kill an entire classification."

"Freya," he snaps. "You are talking like him. You cannot kill innocents to make a point."

Is that what I was suggesting? I don't even know. I melt into his arms, crying for what I saw. "Then what do we do? How do we make it stop? When does it end?"

"I don't know," he admits. "I might be a god, Freya, but I'm lost in this too. I wish I knew. I wish I could tell you it will get better and that there is right and wrong, but the truth is, we are just existing in this world. Do you want to know what I'm hanging my hopes on?" He pulls away from me, cupping my cheeks. "You. You are my hope for a better future and change. I believe you can show them all that your kind is not evil. You are my hope, Freya. Revenge is not the answer, change is, and I believe in you. We all believe in you."

I swallow the pain, falling into his eyes as I nod, but deep down, I worry.

I worry I will let him down and that I cannot be the change he needs.

I fear I will be the same as those who came before me, and when it comes down to it, I will lose myself in the darkness with the rest.

I'm still feeling a bit . . . sensitive, emotionally and physically. Using my powers took its toll. The demon forces me to eat, and then they just curl around me in bed. I should face my coven and check on them, but I cannot bring myself to. Instead, I melt into their arms.

My brain ponders everything that has happened.

"I am so sick of finding out secrets. My whole life is a lie. Everything I knew was wrong. I need to establish a new faith, a new system." I turn to look at them. "If there are any more secrets or lies, tell me now. I mean it. I cannot handle this later. I do not want to be left in the dark anymore. That is a sure way to make me fall into that darkness." There's a pause, and my eyes flitter to my demon. "What is it?"

He looks guilty. "Freya . . ." The fact that he used my name makes me sit up.

My demon takes a deep breath as he sits as well. "The reason I made the deal . . . who I made the deal with . . . I did not lie. I did it to save you. Our lives are tied, but I never told you what happened, not really, for your own sake, but you are right. You deserve to know."

I stare, knowing whatever I'm going to learn won't be good. "Your mother made the deal." I startle at that. "Your father and mother had been on the run when they were attacked. He died, and your mother sustained wounds. To keep you safe, she used her magic to bring you both here, to her old coven, who had been kind to her even after she'd fallen in love with your father, a necromancer. She was dying and terrified because she knew they would come for you. She begged Agatha to help her. They called me together. She made a deal that I would protect you and keep you safe."

"What did you get out of it?" I whisper in horror.

"You, forever," he admits. "She gave the last of her life to save you, Freya. Agatha and I decided never to tell you. We knew it would hurt you and expose you to the truth. I guess we foolishly hoped by not telling you, you would never find out what you really are and we could keep you safe."

My laugh is bitter, and he flinches.

"I didn't tell you . . . because I was scared you would leave me."

"You were right to be," I state coldly as I stand and leave him behind.

Everything I know is a lie, even my life.

I was never meant to be alive.

CHAPTER 34

freya

I wander, lost and confused. The coven is asleep at this time, so the streets are empty, which suits me just fine. For some reason, I find myself back at the tree where my demon and I sat recently. I guess deep down, I always knew there was a reason he was here, but I didn't expect it to hurt so much.

I never even knew my parents. They were killed trying to keep me safe for simply being born this way, and the demon . . . he was supposed to protect me.

Hilarious.

I should know by now that everyone lies, everyone cheats, and everyone has a motive. I stare up at the tree, wondering why I get to live.

Was the necromancer right? Why am I alive when everyone else is dead? What right do I have to live when his son did not? I am not special. I might not be Phrixius's hope like he wants. I am just one of many. I got lucky.

I am just . . . *this*.

It shouldn't surprise me when he finds me. I knew he wouldn't let me go—he can't.

"Little witch," he begins.

I turn. "Do not call me that and pretend like you care."

"Care?" His brows furrow, fire crawling up his horns. "Of course I care."

"I am just a deal to you!" I scream as everything catches up to me. "Stop lying to me. Stop toying with me, please."

"I am not toying with you, little witch—"

"Stop! Just . . . Just go," I beg, my shoulders slumping. "Please, just leave me alone."

"No," he snaps, stepping closer despite my wrath. "Because you will convince yourself of things that are not true. You do not get to stand there and tell me I do not care. I have been by your side for your entire life, protecting you, sharing in your highs and lows, and holding you when you cried. I have been right there. I did not have to be. The deal brought me to you, yes, but I could have fulfilled it from a distance and never even been near you. I wanted to be in your life. I wanted your smiles for me alone. I wanted your darkness and your nights. I wanted to walk with you and share your life."

"And yet you lied to me. I do not even know your name," I snap, my heart pounding at his words.

Snarling, he gets in my face. "I have told you my real name every single night since I have been at your side, hoping you would hear it. You are the only person in this world who knows my true name." He drops to his knees. "Think back, think hard, you know it. I gave it to you just like I gave you power over me. Use it. Use me. I am yours, and I have always been."

"Because of the deal," I retort, feeling hurt.

"Because I love you," he corrects, his eyes wide with truth. "Because you made me love you—a creature that should not love or grow attached. My entire life is you, Freya. I was born as a demon, but you made me yours. You are my universe. Where you go, I go—not because of anything as easy as a deal, but because you are my fate. You are my everything. You are the heart I didn't even know I had. Do not dare tell me it's because of a deal. Look at everything I have done by your side, Freya, and if you can still look me in my eyes and tell me that I don't care, then I will leave like you ask."

My heart races. He will leave now if I ask him to. I will lose him, and something about that . . . hurts. No, it rips me to pieces. Despite how this began between us, this demon has become my home, my safety, and my happiness. He keeps me from falling into darkness with his mischievous attitude. He protects me, and he's there every night, just like he said.

Phrixius once said demons are capable of love. Did he know? Was I blind to it?

As I stare into his eyes, I realise yes, I was because I was terrified of the truth and what that means, but I'm done being scared. I am done worrying about what others will think and what that says about me as a person.

I am a necromancer.

I love a demon.

My whole life is crumbling, but as I stare into his hopeful eyes, I start to wonder if I could live like that.

Maybe that makes me a heathen.

"Adder," I croak, voicing the word in my head, the one that has chased me into dreams for as long as I can remember. "Your name is Adder."

He jerks, seeming to shiver as I speak it. "Yes," he hisses, his forked tongue darting out to wet his lips. "And I am yours."

Looking into his eyes, I give into the darkness. I pull him to his feet and crush him against me, my lips seeking his.

Deal or no deal, I am his, and he is mine.

Tomorrow might not come, I might be killed, but tonight I am alive and I am his.

His Freya.

His little witch.

CHAPTER 35

His little witch.

The thought floats into my mind as she licks my lips. I do not speak it out loud, but satisfaction fills me. I know what that means. The last barrier between my witch and me has fallen, and she has let me into her mind as well as her heart. All of her now belongs to me.

Gripping her tighter, I turn us and back her into the tree. She gasps into my mouth as my tail wraps around her wrists and pins them above her. I hoist her higher, and her legs wrap around my waist as I pull away, tracing her mouth with my forked tongue.

"Let me prove it to you, my little witch. Let me show you that I am yours and will always be. Let me show you that I love you."

"Adder," she murmurs.

My cock jerks as flames dance down my spine. "Say it again," I growl desperately. "Say my name again."

Her lips curl into a taunting smile. "Make me, demon."

Grinning, I tighten my tail on her wrists. "Never has there been a sweeter dare. You should know better than to taunt the devil, little witch, especially when you're his."

"Or he's mine." She grins, leaning back against the tree.

She's not wrong, I am hers, and I want her to howl my name for everyone to know. Keeping her pinned, I move closer and slide my forked tongue along her lips as she gasps and opens her mouth for me.

"Then let your demon make you, little witch," I taunt before I slam my lips onto hers. She moans, and I swallow it down as I suck on her tongue before tangling mine with hers, tasting her sweetness as my hands slide down her body possessively. This new connection between us drives us both to the edge of madness. She tilts her hips, begging for me, and when I slide my hand between her thick thighs, I feel her cream and I know I can't wait.

Forcing them wider, I conjure chains and wrap them around each of her thighs, forcing them wide open. She whimpers into my mouth before digging her teeth into my lip. I quickly chain her hands above her and slide my tail down across her wet cunt, then I slam it inside her. Her cunt adjusts swiftly as she screams, breaking our kiss.

Grinning, I lean back and take in the sight of her impaled on my tail, her pretty, pink cunt dripping and stretched around it. Her chest turns red, and her pink-tipped nipples jiggle with our movements.

There has never been a more magnificent sight.

"Adder," she moans, and the sound of my name on her lips drives me wild. I pull my tail free of her dripping cunt. It feels good, but nothing feels as good as when I slam into her, forcing my cock home until she screams my name for the heavens, her magic and darkness exploding around us.

Snarling, I fuck her hard and fast. The tree creaks with the force, but I don't stop. My witch's eyes roll back into her head as I slide as deep as I can, and when she comes, the earth shakes with the force, but I still don't relent. I slide my tail up and into her open mouth, letting her taste her release.

Her eyes meet mine as she closes her lips around the tip and sucks as I hammer into her cunt, feeling her pussy flutter around me. When I lean down and bite her breast, she screams around my tail again, coming all over my cock.

"Adder, please," she mumbles, then she slumps, but I don't relent. "Adder, Adder, Adder, I want to feel you. I want to feel you come."

It's a plea, and as always, I am helpless to resist.

Pressing my lips to hers, I taste her and her blood as I split her lip. "Say it again," I snarl.

"I'm yours, Adder," she cries, and I can't hold back.

I bottom out inside her and slam my tail all the way down her throat until she chokes on it, and my pleasure explodes. I pump her full of my cum as she gasps, clenching around me in another release. Our magic and minds mix until we are one.

When the pleasure finally abates, I slowly pull from her mouth and cunt. She hangs in my chains, panting, but she's smiling, even as blood drips down her chin and her eyes sparkle.

Sliding my hand down her body, I cup her cunt and rub my fingers through the mess there. "I want to spend the rest of our lives like this, playing, fucking, and reminding you." Pulling my hand away, I paint my name across her chest in our mixed cum. "So now you can never forget again."

CHAPTER 36

Holding hands, we head back to my house. The sun is almost up, and I'm betting the others are worried. I shouldn't have left like that.

I expect concerned looks and maybe some awkwardness, but Phrixius is busy cooking, and my creature is cleaning up. When we come in, they just smile at us and go back to work. "I might let you keep them around," my demon, Adder, whispers. That will take some getting used to. "That way we don't have to do housework."

I elbow him, but I laugh.

"Phrixius does look cute in an apron," I admit.

He winks at me over his shoulder, making me grin. Despite everything that is going on, I know I'm lucky to have found all three of them. This cannot last because Phrixius has his own life, but I plan to make the most of it while I can.

"I like your way of thinking." My demon chuckles, and I meet his gaze.

"Her thinking?" Sha asks, stopping before me with a wide grin. "Are you having naughty thoughts?"

"Was it the apron?" Phrixius laughs, and their teasing makes me blush as I glance around.

"I wasn't," I snap.

"She was." Adder smacks my ass. "She's a very sexual person, our witch. She has a high sex drive, so we can't leave her wanting, can we?"

"We should talk about the necromancer," I say, trying to divert their attention.

"Uh-uh, later." Phrixius takes off the apron and heads my way, and my eyes widen at him teasing me. He's usually so kind, but the wicked look in his eyes tells me he is planning something different.

I guess he's not so saintly after all.

I back up. "We really need to—" I gasp as magic wraps around me, and I'm yanked to Phrixius, his hands dropping to my ass.

"You just had your demon, so he can be last. Sha, are you okay with sharing your mistress?"

"As long as I have her," he growls, sliding his hands up my body. I shiver, remembering the way he touched me when he fucked me. I barely survived, so I don't know if I will survive all three, but I want to try.

Grabbing Phrixius, I yank him down for a kiss, and he laughs. The sound soon turns into a groan as he hoists me up and throws me onto the bed, appearing above me. With a flick of his magic, my clothes disappear and so do his.

Perks of being a god. "I love magic," I murmur as I look over his muscles.

"Good, because I plan on using it on and inside this incredible body. Let me remind you what your god is capable of."

My eyes widen, and a moment later, a glowing golden chain wraps around my throat. He coils the other end around his wrist and winds it up, using it to yank me up so I'm arched below him, my chest rising from the bed. His tongue traces over my lips hungrily. "You taste like cum and magic," he whispers. "My two favourite things." His other hand slides down and through the mess between my thighs. "At least you're slick enough for me because with the way you're watching me, Freya, I am not going to be able to hold back. We both know you can take it, but this pretty pussy has already been fed, so I'm going to feed something else."

My eyes widen, and a moment later, his cock slams into my cunt. He keeps me pinned with his glowing chain, watching me with that cocky smile as he rolls his hips a few times before pulling out. The chain loosens enough for me to drop back to the bed with a bounce.

He rolls me, and my head spins until we stop, and I blink up at the ceiling. He's now below me, and the chain is still wrapped around my throat, tightening and loosening with my pulse. It throbs in time with my pussy.

"Phrixius," I begin, but the chain tightens, cutting off my words, and then his big cock presses to my ass. He widens his legs, and before I can protest, he pushes inside my ass. I arch up to escape, but glowing chains criss-cross my chest, tying me against him, and then across my thighs, keeping me open as he pushes deeper. The pleasure makes me cry out, and I dig my nails into the bedding on either side of us.

He grunts below me when he can't feed me another inch of his cock, and I pant above him, shivering in pleasure. I love this, love him controlling me and taking my power away.

When everyone else would be afraid of me, he is not.

He pulls out and slams back inside my ass, forcing me to take him. The chains throb, and smaller ones bite into my nipples, twisting around them like vices. His magic strokes over me as another chain appears, slithering across my stomach and down my pussy. The warm throb presses to my clit, even as the links slide inside me, filling my pussy and pressing to my clit. He rolls his hips, feeding his cock into my ass.

I'm so full of him, I can't help but move, rolling my hips quickly.

His mouth slides across my throat before he nips at my sensitive skin there, sending pleasure spiralling through me. Fire licks at me, my nerves alight, until I can do nothing but gasp and ride him, needing more.

"You look good in my chains, necromancer," he teases, biting my pounding pulse as I cry out his name. My pussy clenches down on them, and they seem to throb harder. The insane vibration rolls through me until I can't hold back.

I come all over them and him.

He chuckles in my ear. "I'm just getting started, Freya. I would tell you to hold on, but you aren't going anywhere. You're mine until I'm satisfied." His voice is dark and dangerous, and it slides through me like flames.

His tongue licks at my throat, and he alternates between that and biting as he fucks me from below. When I clamp on him, he speeds up, pounding into me.

I cannot think, see, or hear.

All I can do is feel.

My body is alive, throbbing in time with the chains, until I'm slick with sweat and just a writhing mess. He fucks me through two more releases until I'm a sobbing.

His voice is tight with his pleasure. "You feel so good above me, taking me like this. Fuck, Freya, I pride myself on being a good man, a good god, yet you make me depraved as fuck. I want you chained to me at all times, pumped full of me." His voice is little more than a snarl now. "You make me a wicked god, Freya. I'd fall for this pussy and lose everything to be here forever. Don't you see what you do to me? You ruin me. You destroy me. You taint me, and I fucking love it."

"Phrixius!" I cry out before chains slither across my mouth, cutting off my words. I'm trapped, encased in him and his magic. Every inch of me vibrates until my body can't handle it and I shatter.

He roars below me, slamming into me twice before burying himself as deep in my ass as he can. My name is groaned in my ear as I feel his hot, magic-filled cum fill me up.

I must black out because when I come to, I'm still on my back but the chains are gone. Phrixius stands above me at the side of the bed, grinning at me.

"I meant what I said, Freya." He doesn't look away, but I feel the others drawing closer. "She's all yours. Let me watch as you fuck our witch."

My head jerks up, my eyes widening when I find Sha perched at the end of the bed, his cock swirling, searching for me. His eyes are so red they glow, and shadows roll across his skin.

Despite my body being limp, my cunt clenches in want at the sight.

Sha crawls up the bed, wrapping shadows around me, and I'm flipped. I scream as I'm forced face down on the bed then yanked towards him and straight onto his waiting cock. I feel it rip me and put me back together again. His suckers find my clit and ass straight away, knowing where to go. More slide up and seal around my nipples as he yanks me up and ruts into me.

That's what this is—rutting.

It's animalistic, and I can't help but cry out in pleasure, even as agony tears through me. I feel my blood and cum dripping down my trembling thighs, but I don't ask him to stop.

I don't want him to.

My head hangs low as I fist the bedding and push back, taking him so deep, he grows inside me.

"Mine!" he roars. "Mine, mine, mine!"

"Yours," I rasp just as a noise has me lifting my head.

My eyes widen as Adder appears on his knees before me. "I've had that sweet pussy tonight, and I think you'll be too sore to take me there. Aren't I kind, little witch? Open your pretty mouth. You'll choke on both of us until we are satisfied."

I open my mouth, and he smirks, tapping my chin with his thumb. "Wider."

I open it until it hurts, and he slides his cock deep, right down into my throat. He quickly finds a rhythm with Sha, and I'm pushed between them. I love it, crying out around Adder as he bruises my throat with his quick thrusts.

Sha jerks behind me. "Mistress."

"No. No, no!" I want to scream it. I was so close, but he can't hear me around Adder, and I feel the moment his cum fills me. He stays inside me, and the suckers have stopped. I whine around Adder's cock.

He groans and pumps his cum so far down my throat, I don't even have to swallow. I wipe my mouth before I look back at Sha, who seems dazed.

Eyes narrowing in irritation, I glance at Adder as he tilts his head, sensing something.

"Monster fucker, remember?" I tell him.

Slicing my nails into Sha's chest, I push him over and straddle him, and then I ride him hard, getting what I want.

"Mistress," he rasps. He's soft inside me, and I snarl. "I'm spent."

"No, you're not. I want more. It's your mistress's order. I'm not done yet."

"Yes, mistress," he hisses.

I rock atop him, and he finally hardens. "That's it," I purr as he bulges inside me. "Good boy, just like that. Stay hard for your mistress until I'm done, and only then can you come."

I ride him hard, knowing he can take it. I use him, winding my hips as I seek my pleasure. He whimpers and moans below me, his face tight, and I know he's holding back.

"You do not move, not until I come," I snap, my voice dark with magic that tightens on him and absorbs into his skin.

"Yes, mistress."

"Good boy." I grab one of his suckers, the bigger one, and I take it into my mouth, letting it suck at my tongue before I push it down and press it to my clit. I use it like a vibrator as I roll my hips. I use every inch of him, and when pleasure finally rolls through me, I can't hold back my victorious scream as I clench around him.

I slump back, my eyes closed. When I finally force them open, I see his chest heaving and arms shaking, but he doesn't move.

He did as I ordered.

"Now you can come."

"Yes, mistress, thank you."

I'm lifted off the bed as he slams up into me with a cry, his cum spilling inside me.

It goes on forever, and when he's finally spent, I can't hold myself up anymore.

I fall onto him as my eyes close, my body satisfied and heavy with sleep.

CHAPTER 37

"We still have to talk about the necromancer," my mistress mumbles around a spoonful of soup. She's in nothing but a silk slip that I can see through, her hair is unbound and messy, and her skin is still pink. She looks good enough to eat.

In fact . . . I start to slip under the table when her eyes narrow on me, and she points her spoon into my face. "I can see your thoughts, monster. No." She taps my cheek with her spoon. "Killing first, sex later."

"If I kill this necromancer, then I get to fuck you whenever I want?" I ask.

"Well, er . . . yes." Her cheeks turn a prettier shade of red.

"Then I shall do that now." I thrust to my feet, ready to track down this necromancer, when she starts to laugh. Grabbing my hand, she tugs me down and pushes my bowl closer.

"Eat. We will kill him together, and then we'll have a very long time to play, okay? Demon!" she warns, smacking his hand away from whatever he was doing. She looks to Phrixius for help, but he just shrugs and nods.

"If you were closer, I would have my mouth on your pretty tits, feeding from them instead of this bowl." Her pupils blow wide, and I watch as the god lifts his bowl and licks it clean.

Freya shoves back from the table, sending hot soup splattering everywhere. "Gentlemen—no, monsters, pay attention. Stop looking at my boobs, stop thinking about my vagina—"

The demon groans. "Now that you said it, I am—" She smacks his hand away again, darkness crawling along her skin as she points at every single one of us.

"Focus. We must track down this man, now," she warns. "Do not make me use my magic on you."

Leaning into the god, I lower my voice as her darkness crawls along the table. "I do not know much about other witches, but are they all this magnificent when wielding magic?"

"No, that's all our girl." He grins, and when the darkness touches his arm, he simply welcomes it, but he does sober up. "She is right though. We do need to focus on the necromancer. We might have held him back, but he wasn't defeated. We should push our advantage while he's weak and without an army."

"So how do we find this necromancer?" the demon asks, slinging his arm around Freya and pulling her into his lap, notching his chin on her shoulder. "How did you do it in the past?"

"The gods tracked down necromancers. You're the god of magic, so surely you must be able to. With all of us together against him, if we push him now, like you said, then we stand a chance." Freya nods as she leans back into her demon. Is she even aware she does it? Something dark and ugly rises inside me for a moment at seeing her in another's arms, but watching her relax like that, her shoulders unwinding, the emotion changes to something happy.

I would give her anything she asked for, and if she wants this demon and god, then I will chain them to her side forever as long as she will continue to be happy.

Phrixius sighs. "We did, and I can. My worry is that he knows that and it will be a trap."

"It doesn't matter. Trap or no, we have to end this now. We all know he'll want a new army, which means he will kill hundreds to get it. I might understand why he's doing this, but I cannot sit back and let it happen," she admits. "I cannot imagine the pain and suffering he endured, but I cannot condone his plan for revenge."

"If it comes to it, can you kill him?" Phrixius asks seriously. "After what you saw?"

"We have to, right? There's no saving him. I felt it in his soul. There's nothing left but anger and the need for blood. He's past redemption. I won't relish killing a man who only loved his wife and child, but if it means saving others, then I'll do it. My coven is in danger, but so is the world, and maybe if I can save them, I can save myself too."

"What do you mean?" I ask as gently as I can.

She turns to me. "I feel like if I lose to him, then I'll lose my soul and the grip I have over this darkness too. If we end this, then I stand a chance at having a future and being alive. I know it's not going to be easy, but we have to try."

"It will mean you will use your powers. We will protect you as much as we can and carry the burden of killing him so you do not have to go fully into the darkness, but we cannot save you from everything, and there is a possibility your control will slip again. Are you ready for that?" Phrixius asks. "Because if not, we can do this without you."

"No, he's one of us. It's my duty—"

"Not if it endangers your soul, it isn't. I will not put you in danger, not even for the world," Phrixius admits, his eyes on her. "I know I should not say that, since it is my duty to risk my life for this world and the magic within it. I was taught that one death for hundreds is no loss, but I'm finding, Freya, that if that one death is yours, then I would let hundreds die."

I glance between them as they stare at each other, and the smile that blooms over her face is magnificent. "But I will not. I cannot live with myself if I do nothing when it's me he wants. It's time we end this, don't you think? Then you can whisper sweet nothings in my ear like that all night."

Phrixius looks us all over and nods. "Then we will track him down. We'll go tonight before he has regrouped his army. First, I want you all to rest and eat. Tracking the necromancer is the easy bit, but killing one? That's much, much harder. He might be one, but one necromancer is worth an army of witches, and before the sun is up, all of us will be covered in blood." Phrixius rises and wanders away, and we watch him go, wondering how much blood this god has really spilled.

PHRIXIUS

Staring out at the coven from the entrance of Freya's cave, I cannot help but think of the past. Freya may think we are all monsters for what we did, but we had our reasons. He only showed her his past and the horrors that made him this way, but he did not show her the countless atrocities committed by his people.

I watched children be turned into monsters and then be used against their parents.

Mothers were replaced by nothing but empty shells with orders to kill before they were sent home, where they destroyed their families, knowing they could not fight back.

I had to watch friends turn into enemies. The necromancers' armies filled with their loved ones, and they could not even grieve because they were still there. There was no peace, rules, or laws for them. They did as they wished. Yes, the gods killed many, maybe even innocents, but the world would not be standing if we had not. I know that for sure.

I hesitated back then, hating the orders I had to follow, and although I didn't kill those innocents, I did not stop the gods either because I knew we either eradicated them or were eradicated.

They banded together, obeying those stronger than them out of fear. They were either with them or against them.

I am not saying it was right, but we did what we thought was appropriate. Knowing she thinks we are all monsters . . . it ruins me.

Perhaps that is why when she appears at my side, I offer her my hand. "Can I show you something?"

She lays her palm in mine. With a devastating smile, I tug her close and allow myself a moment of weakness as I press my mouth to her ear. "Take a deep breath. This might make you feel nauseous."

I take us away, appearing back on my island. I keep her in my arms as she sways, and when she pulls away, she gasps, looking around in wonder. I follow her gaze, seeing it as she does—the beauty, magic, and otherworldliness.

It truly is a place of wonder, even if I never wanted to admit that nor cared before.

"Where are we?" she asks softly, heading to the edge of my island and peering over.

"My home."

She glances at me over her shoulder before I join her at her side.

"This is the realm of gods. Here, we are free . . . and alone. Each of us was gifted an island upon our creation. It complements us. It is supposed to make us feel safe and protected."

"Does it?" she asks.

"No," I admit, unable to meet her gaze. "It just made me feel very alone."

She hums then is quiet for a moment. "So the gods hide here." Venom tinges her words, and I know the necromancer has already started to sow seeds of doubt into her darkness.

"Nobody is born evil," I tell her. "It is decisions that make us such." I feel her gaze on me as my eyes flit around the clouds. "That is our duty, and sometimes we make the wrong decisions. Sometimes we make good ones as well, but nobody ever remembers them." I turn to her, searching her gaze. "I know you hate them for what you saw, but you did not see everything. The horrors that the gods committed . . . those decisions were not made lightly. You did not see the future as we did."

"Phrixius—"

"We were not unaffected." I point to a far-off island. "His name was Albraross. He was the god of harvest. After the dark wars, he withdrew to his island and went mad. He relived those wars in his mind over and over, questioning if what we did was right. The lives he took, no matter how evil, haunted him."

"What happened to him?" she whispers softly.

"Gods, despite what you think, can be killed, and he ended his life rather than facing the truth. He could not live with it." I glance down at her. "Maybe there was another way out back then, maybe we could have done things differently, but I need you to know, it changed us all. We ended the war, but they started it. There was so much needless death, and as the god of magic, I felt every passing soul keenly. I felt the magic building in the world, ready to be wielded . . . It would have destroyed the universe, not just your world, Freya. When the ones who seek power have it all, do you think they will stop? No, they would have kept going. It does not mean we do not grieve or remember. We have the gift of immortality, and the price for that is a memory that will never stop. We have to live, every single day, with our pasts and what we have done. We can never escape it. We grow alongside the world, and we do what we think is best, yet we can never find peace. Cities come and go, and civilizations are destroyed, yet we stand. It is our duty and our purpose." I turn to her, letting her see the tears falling from my eyes.

"I have seen so much hate and destruction as well as beauty and happiness. I have lived with it for thousands of years, and I will live with it even when you are gone." I slide my hand over her face, absorbing her warmth. "You have the beauty of time, Freya, to live each day like it's your last because it might be. I do not have that. I know there will always be a tomorrow and that I will always be expected to keep going, even if I don't want to. Immortality is a gift and a curse, and it was only after meeting you that I started to realise that. I would give it up in a heartbeat for just a day at your side, truly living and free to make my own path, my own future. I am destined to watch as those I grow close to die. I am destined to be alone forever. I never understood that before I met you. I was grieving for the life I wished I could have. No matter what you think, I am jealous of everyone on Earth. All of you get to enjoy this world knowing in the end, it doesn't matter. I'm jealous of those who get to love and build a future and a life." Looking back at the world of gods, I can't help but wish I were not born this way.

"It is my duty, and I have done my duty for centuries. I have never once questioned our purpose or our cause." Looking down at her, I memorise her face. "Until you. Maybe that is why I brought you here, because I can't stand to have you think we are all monsters. We care so much, Freya, but our hearts have been broken time and time again, crushed under the weight of the laws we have no choice but to uphold. We are gods, but we do not have free will. It is just a fantasy. You humans dream of living forever, while we dream of living for a day. Ironic, isn't it?"

"I think . . . I think both sides made mistakes, and wars are won by those fighting for something." She sighs, taking my hand and pressing it to her cheek again. "I wish I could give you the life you want, Phrixius. I wish I could free you from your duties. I guess we are all bound one way or another by fate."

"I guess so," I murmur, looking into her eyes. "Which means meeting you. You stormed into my life, and I cannot be angry at that. In fact, I want to thank the Fates this once for giving me something precious, something worth fighting for."

"Softie," she teases, taking my hand once more as we stare out at the world, observing the peace. "We should get back. I suppose tonight will change everything."

"It will," I agree. I will never lie to her. For a moment, she looks worried. Turning her, I press my hands to her cheeks to tilt her face up to mine, and I give her my truth and my soul. I hand it over in the hopes it will be enough.

"I wish I could tell you that I would destroy this world for you and kill anyone who harmed you, damn the consequences, but I cannot. I am a god, Freya, but I would do something we cannot, something infinitely more dangerous. I would die for you, and I hope one day, that will be enough."

"Why?" she asks, searching my gaze. "Why would you die for me? We haven't known each other—"

"Time does not matter to an immortal. I knew from the first moment I met you that you would be important to me. In all my thousands of years, I have never met another like you. I care for you a lot, more than I have anyone before."

"Even knowing what I could become?" There it is, her true fear—herself.

"Even then," I admit. "I lied to myself. I told myself I stayed at your side in case you embraced the darkness, but the truth is, I stayed at your side because I did not want to be anywhere else, and if you'll let me, I'll stay there forever."

"Your duty—"

"Will still be here. I can do both," I tell her. "If you want me, that is?"

Her lashes flutter for a moment, and when her eyes lock on mine, they are warm with desire and happiness. "I want you," she states boldly. "I want any part of you I can have, even if that is selfish."

"It's not selfish when I want you to have it," I murmur, tugging her closer and lowering my face. "If you want me, little witch, then claim me." It's a plea rather than an order. I have reached for her every time, but in this moment, I need her to reach for me and give me a reason to fight for us.

When her lips press softly to mine, I taste the truth in her heart, even if she does not speak it.

It's a soft, exploratory kiss, and when it's over, I pull her into my arms, holding her tightly. I always felt like I was waiting for something, and this is it. I was waiting for her to fill my arms and my heart.

"When you gods want something, you really don't hold back," she teases from the shelter of my embrace, making me laugh.

"We better go back before your demon and creature storm the god realm looking for you." We share a look as we pull away. "We both know they would."

"And they would enjoy doing it." She smirks, pressing up on her toes to kiss me gently. The warmth of her lips stains my soul forever. "Take me home, Phrixius."

"Always," I promise.

CHAPTER 38

freya

Phrixius's eyes snap open and land on us. "I know where he is."

We all breathe a sigh of relief. Despite the demon's teasing, I think we were all worried Phrixius couldn't find the necromancer. He searched for hours. When we came back from his world, we all slept curled together—it was the best sleep I ever had. Our hands lingered on one another as if we knew we needed to hold on tight because tonight, we will face our biggest enemy yet. Anything could happen. It almost made us reluctant to release each other, but before the sun set, we sat down and protected Phrixius as he tracked the necromancer.

We are ready, or so I tell myself. Either way, it doesn't matter. We have to end this before any more lives are taken. I don't know what awaits us, but I know the necromancer will not go down without a fight, which means I need to be stronger, faster, and harder than ever before. I need to trust my magic and my men.

Combined, a demon, creature, god, and necromancer can do this, right?

My nerves do not disappear, however, even as Phrixius gracefully rises and holds out his hand. "Let us go." As I place my shaking palm in his, the others surround us. "Remember," Phrixius warns, "necromancers are masters of the dead. Do not trust anything or let your guard down. The grave will come for us tonight, and we must face it head-on."

Nodding silently, I hold his hand tighter, and then we are gone. My body twists and melts, and when we reappear, it is not where I thought it would be. We stand at the edge of a graveyard—a familiar graveyard.

A lone church with open doors faces us.

"This is the church we came to before," I whisper, sharing a look with Adder. "He'll be waiting inside. It's a trap."

"Yes." Phrixius nods as he steps over the invisible line we have drawn. "It most certainly is a trap." When he glances back at us, there's a slight grin on his face. "So let's spring it, shall we?"

I share a look with Sha and Adder, who grins, rubbing his hands together. "I like this version of your god. You should fuck him senseless more often." He winks at me and tugs me after them. "Into the creepy church we go."

"Don't hide behind me this time," I mutter jokingly, searching the graves in case he lies in wait. Something is different, but I can't put my finger on what. Maybe it's my own nerves, or maybe I'm just being a coward, but my steps slow. The darkness within me crawls and writhes as if sensing something I don't. My magic is ready to strike out at an attacker I do not see nor sense.

"What is it?" Sha asks, turning back and waiting for me.

"Nothing." Shaking my head, I start to follow them to the church once more. There is no point in hiding our approach, since he will have sensed me as soon as I arrived—I know because I can sense him. The touch of death waits for us inside. It calls to me like a taunting whisper on the wind.

Suddenly, I jerk to a stop, realization slamming into me as to why it looks different. "All the graves are empty."

They stop around me, seeking out what my brain has noticed. Every grave is a gaping hole. As far as the eye can see, there are no bodies, only empty caskets. I tread closer to one to check and swallow at the emptiness.

"Freya," Phrixius murmurs, "can you see if they are waiting inside? Be careful not to touch them. You could take control, but don't yet. We'll take him by surprise with that once we are inside, if you think you can."

Nodding, I close my eyes and reach out with those thorny vines. They touch upon the church, and I pull back. "At least forty inside," I tell him. "I can do it." Rolling my shoulders back, I nod at them. "Give me the signal, and I will snatch control of them so it's only him."

"He'll be weak from bringing so many back so suddenly, right?" Adder asks with a frown. "That takes a lot of power."

"Unless he did it before and left them behind. It wouldn't surprise me," Phrixius says. "Necromancers are tricky, intelligent beings. They know their greatest strength is also their weakness."

Inclining my head, I follow after them, carefully now, since we know what awaits us inside, if only slightly. The darkness of the night wraps around us as we move towards the church, the moon seemingly not reaching here as if afraid of what is inside.

We share a look at the door, and Adder leans over and kisses my cheek. "Be careful, little witch, and leave the killing to us. Give us a route to him."

Swallowing nervously, I watch as Phrixius heads inside, followed by Adder then Sha. Taking one last look behind us, I step over the threshold and into the church.

It is not how we left it. I don't know what I was expecting, but it is so much worse.

Blood still paints the walls, but there is more now. Words I do not understand cover every inch, even the floor and forgotten pews.

Standing against each wall are the decaying corpses of those from the graves outside, their dark eyes locked on us as they wait.

They speak as one. "Welcome home, heathens."

Standing between my men, I search for the necromancer, but I cannot see him. The candles covering nearly every inch of the ring spring to life, their wax starting to drip across the floor like blood. At the altar, a blood-red candle burns brightly, and I spy a beating heart atop it, pierced by a blade.

It's eerily quiet, and I hesitate for a moment before stepping from their midst. I feel the guys reach for me, but I tug away, treading farther down the path between the bodies and pews. "Where are you? I know you're here. I can taste you," I call.

"You brought friends," the bodies say together.

Wax drips down on me from candles hanging from the ceiling, but I don't let my hiss escape as it slides down my cheek and then pauses there, hardening like a tear. More droplets land on my shoulders, in my hair, and down my back, coating me like blood.

"You know why we are here," I tell him. Part of me hates what we are going to do, and I feel sorry for him, but he made his choice, and I am making mine. "I cannot be what you want me to be. I cannot turn my back on the world."

"It has turned its back on us!" they screech, and I stop myself from covering my ears. I feel blood sliding down my neck from them, but I stand tall, and when it stops, I step forward again, showing I am unafraid.

There is only one thing a man like him respects—power.

"Enough, talking will not get us anywhere. You have made your choice, and I am making mine. I choose this world and these people."

It's quiet, and I step forward, searching him out in the bodies. My gaze catches on something black. It's a robe, and my eyes narrow as I head closer. "Come out."

"Freya," Adder warns.

"I know," I hiss, and then I turn when there's a flash of black. He appears behind my men, and my eyes widen. "Behind you!"

He's gone just as quickly, but his army steps forward, their eyes turning to my men. "Now!" Phrixius tells me.

I slam my darkness through the bodies, taking control of them like I did my zombie, but his laughter rings out.

He appears before me, wearing a grin, and presses his finger to my forehead.

"Just what I wanted." Suddenly, the control I had yanks on me, and I tumble into the empty, cold grave.

It was a trap.

He wanted me to take control. He wanted to trap me inside them.

I feel my body, still and empty, as my name is screamed, yet I cannot see, feel, or move.

It was like when I was inside the zombie, only this time everything is dark. It closes around me like a cage, trapping me there with his power, which means . . . it can be broken.

I calm myself like Phrixius taught me, and then I flood my system with my own power, meeting his and ripping into it. I focus on pushing him back. It's like peeling tar, and I grow agitated but try to focus. If I let my anger get the better of me, he will consume me again.

It's a battle of wills, and I refuse to lose while my men are fighting him alone.

I don't know how much time passes, but it feels like forever, and when I finally manage to push back that last bit of darkness, I realise it wasn't me. It was him—he retreated.

He releases me, and I gasp as I slam back into my body, my eyes watering from the sudden shock. My limbs shake as I stumble forward. Everything is different—everything has moved. My head swings around in fear. I am standing in a ring of candles, with zombies kneeling before me, facing outwards, and my men are nowhere in sight.

Blinking, I look around the room, wondering how long I was out. Candles have burned down, but I don't see the necromancer or my men. "Guys?" I croak, so I clear my throat as I step from the circle, carefully avoiding the motionless bodies standing like statues. "Hello?"

There's a bang that makes me jump, and I whirl, my eyes narrowing in confusion.

There are three black caskets with chains wrapped around them. Zombies stand guard on either side, their eyes locked on me.

"Guys?" I murmur as I step closer, only to stop when there's another bang and one of the coffins jumps.

My ears strain as I move closer. "Freya!" The scream makes my heart stop.

Phrixius.

My eyes move to the other coffins.

Three.

Oh god. I rush over.

"Run! It's a trap!" he bellows.

I turn, ready to use my magic, but it's too late. He stands right behind me, grinning, and as I lift my hands to fling my spell at him, he blows a glittering black powder into my face. I cough as I fall back, my vision going dark, and then suddenly, darkness closes around me once more.

Only this time, it's sleep.

I wake with a gasp, my eyes suddenly clearing. Everything feels too hot, too tight, and my mouth has a horrible taste in it. How much time has passed? Where am I?

Where are my guys? Are they alive?

Fear fills me as my vision finally clears enough for me to see my hands, and my heart freezes in my chest when I recognise the buildings around me.

Necromancer City.

It stands tall around me, too tall, and I frown, realising I'm kneeling in the middle of a street. To my left is a shop, and to my right is a familiar door—his home. I'm kneeling outside of it.

How long was I out?

"Good, you're finally awake," he calls from inside the dark home, and then he fades into view at the door, stepping out into the lantern-lit way. He doesn't stop until he is before me.

"My men," I rasp.

"Oh, the three you came with? They are alive for now. They could be useful. They were easy to defeat." I frown, knowing they are unstoppable. "One threat to you was all it took, and they got into those coffins willingly, refusing to let me harm you. Foolish, they knew I would anyway, but they couldn't bear to be the reason you were hurt. I knew you were special. Look at you, you will be magnificent, and if you can turn them to our side, then you can turn anyone."

He crouches before me, his hand lingering above my skin. "Magnificent."

His hand lowers, hovering above my chest as I stare into his eyes. He threatened my men, and they did what he said so he wouldn't hurt me? No, Phrixius wouldn't risk letting him go like that, right?

"However . . ." He meets my gaze, and agony tears through me, his fist slamming through my chest, carried by his power. His hand wraps around my heart as I scream and writhe. "They cannot have this. It belongs to us. It's time to wake up, little witch. It's time to come home to us where you belong. This will make you weak. I will rip that weakness out of you."

The agony only triples, and I watch in horror as darkness crawls down his arm and seeps into my chest, wrapping around my heart.

"You cannot fight this." He chuckles. "I am stronger."

I shake my head as I try to fight off the memories bombarding me. He smirks, and I know it's him. He's in my head again, in my body, controlling me, and I cannot stop it. They consume me once more, flinging me into the past.

Screams echo in my head as flashes of death fill my mind. There is so much death—women, men, children, and the elderly. Their blood sprays across me until I swear I can taste it. The gods laugh as they fall.

So much death.

So much pain.

There's a sobbing teenage girl curled over her big brother. She lifts her head, meeting my gaze, and then a spear pierces her chest and is gone in the same instant. She falls, covering his body, her hand still in his as she dies. There's an old man holding his wife, tears silently streaming down his face as he watches me come for him. His eyes close as the blade strikes.

There are so many more, I start to scream as I am caught watching them die.

The grief and anger are overpowering.

The memories seek to drive me mad, trying to taint my soul and turn me into him.

No, I will not let him.

I cannot.

I am stronger than he thinks.

Phrixius's words come back to me—I am stronger than I know. Adder's voice fills my head, telling me I can do anything. Sha's warmth engulfs me, promising me protection.

I let the memories of our happiness and our love block the evil he is showing me, and it starts to wane, losing strength and power over me. I fill myself up so he cannot, allowing me to take myself back.

My fury and power slams through me until the remaining memories rip and fade, leaving me in darkness.

My eyes open, and I meet his shocked gaze. "I can fight this, and I will. You are not stronger." With a roar, I lift my hand and grab his arm, then I yank it from my chest. Gasping, I tumble forward, and I can't stop the laughter that falls from my lips.

Glancing down, I see my chest is still bleeding, so I wave my hand and let the darkness stitch it back together. It's still jagged and raw, but it's enough for me to get to my feet as he lies on his back, watching me.

"Let me show you how strong I am so you understand the enemy you made."

Turning, I hold out my arm, and with a bloodied grin, I release my magic.

Flames lick at buildings, turning into an inferno as they spread through the city, consuming the memories he tried to darken my soul with. I stand amidst the flames, the heat making sweat drip down my face.

"What have you done?" he roars.

I glance at him over my shoulder, my smile cruel. "Burn with your memories." Turning forward, I walk towards the flames.

"I will see you again!" he shouts.

"Not if I see you first," I respond as I wave my hand, calling a portal and stepping inside.

I shut it behind me, leaving him to burn in his flames, locked in the past where he belongs.

CHAPTER 39

Harnessing my power, I close my eyes and try to focus on the chains outside. I've been here too long, and what is worse, I cannot sense Freya anymore, which means he took her somewhere.

It was a calculated move. I knew he would not hurt her because he needs her, wants her alive, so I had to trust in that. If I did not, she would have gotten hurt, and I couldn't bear that—not as she stood there, so still and empty, her soul wherever he sent it. No, it was better to give in now and fight later. He cannot kill me, not easily, hence the reason he locked us up and we went without resistance.

Where is she? Is she okay?

I need to get out of here and save her. I know the others will be thinking the same, so I fling myself at the lid once more, thrusting my power into it to snap the chains. It doesn't work, but I keep trying. Suddenly, there's a crash, and I freeze, sensing magic.

I hear the chains rattle and slide away, and then the lid to the coffin is wrenched open. The light makes me blink and shield my eyes with my hand before I drop it, finding Freya. She runs her eyes over me, and I see something in them I can't read.

"Freya?"

She tilts her head as she stares at me. Something has changed.

She feels different. My eyes land on the bleeding wound in her chest, and I hurry over. Changed or not, she is my Freya. Wrapping her in my arms, I tug her closer before pulling away, running my hand across the wound. "Freya—"

"It will heal," she murmurs. "We need to free the others and go before he arrives. I don't think it will be long, and I am not strong enough right now to fight him again." She shivers in my arms, and I nod in understanding. Whatever happened, she drained herself.

I sit her on a pew and turn back to the coffins. Grabbing the chains, I yank while infusing my move with power, and the links snap and fall away. I throw the lid off, which flies through the open window, and then I do the same to the last. The demon and Sha rush out, both heading to Freya.

"You're welcome," I mutter sarcastically before crouching like they are. Her eyes are tight, and her skin is pale. My gaze lands on the wound once more. It looks deep and painful. She might have magic, but she is not invincible. "Let's get her home and regroup."

"No, I'm going to finish this fucking bastard. The only one who can use chains on me is my witch!" the demon yells. She laughs, but it turns into a groan, her head turning as she coughs up blood.

"I need to rest before we meet him again. If he tries to turn me again, I won't be strong enough to stop him," she whispers.

I don't know what she means, but we all share a look and nod. Whatever he did, it was bad and she's worried. Lifting her into my arms, I conjure a portal and shove us through, leaving before he comes back for her.

We underestimated him. He's strong, but he knows our weakness and used it.

We were fools, and now our girl is hurt.

I glance down at her in my arms, worried about the shadows I see dancing in her eyes.

They are the same shadows I saw in his.

ADDER

By the time we reappear in our witch's lair, she is paler than before and collapses into my arms. Lifting her up, I carefully place her on the bed before peering down at the wicked wound on her chest. It's partially healed, but it's still bleeding, and it's clear something inside is damaged.

We all share a look as she sighs and closes her eyes, looking drained and exhausted. Phrixius nods his head to the side, and we follow him to the entrance where she can't easily overhear us.

"I can heal her wounds outside, not inside. Whatever he did to her, it changed her," Phrixius murmurs. "I can sense it."

"As can I," I admit.

"Her magic seems . . . wilder," Sha comments. "I can taste the darkness on her now, whereas before it was buried deep."

"Hmm, it's like he has uncaged it. I guess only time will tell if she wakes up with her control. We will have to keep a close eye on her," Phrixius muses.

My eyes narrow, and my tail flicks in warning. "Do not tell me, god, that you are thinking of harming my witch for fear of what she may become."

"If I were going to kill her, I would have done it the moment she called me," he snaps, clearly offended. "Yet I have been here, fighting with you to keep her safe. Do not forget that. I am not giving up on her. I am simply worried."

"And the other gods? What will they do?" I murmur.

Sha frowns at Phrixius. "If you harm her, I will eat you alive, god or no god." He lumbers over to Freya, taking her hand. Who knew I'd be siding with an entity of evil?

"They will kill her, you know that." He lowers his voice. "I will not let that happen."

"Why?" I frown at him. "Why would you choose to protect her over your duty?"

It is all they have as gods, their righteous duty.

His brow furrows as he looks at her. "I can't do anything but." He glances at me. "Just as you can't. I am here with you and on your side. We may have been enemies before, but we aren't now." His gaze moves to Freya again. "Because of her. Now let's fix our girl." Ignoring my incredulous look, he moves back over to my witch, pressing his hands to her chest.

Making sure he doesn't do anything weird, I leap carefully onto the bed at her side and take her hand. Her eyes flutter open for a moment, and she offers me a soft smile—one that makes my heart slam inside my chest. Leaning down, I kiss her softly, unable to resist. "Rest now, little witch, we have you."

"I did something bad," she whispers into my lips.

"Hmm, I can assure you that whatever you did, I would do much worse to get back to you. Rest now." After kissing each eyelid, I lean back, ignoring Phrixius's searching look. I don't know if he heard her or not, but no matter what he says, I cannot trust he will choose her over his duty.

One is not created as a god because they have weak morals or duty. He cares for her, but if it comes down to choosing this path or her, which would he really pick?

CHAPTER 40

freya

I don't know how long I sleep for, but when I wake up, my home is dark aside from a few flickering candles. As I stare into the dancing flames, I'm reminded of what I did and what I was capable of.

The worst bit? I could have done so much more.

I felt it inside me, begging to be let out. It wanted more, so much more. Had it not been for the chest wound and my feelings pulling me back to the church, I worry about what I would have done. It chills me to my bones, yet I cannot speak it. Shame fills me as I turn my head to find my men sleeping around me. Even in their dreams, they look anxious.

I do not blame them. I can only imagine the sight I made when I appeared before them.

They worry I will fall into the darkness, and the truth is, so do I. It calls to me stronger than before, and after last night, something feels different in my chest.

Slipping from bed, I walk to the bathroom and shut the door, needing privacy to see.

Pressing my back to the wooden door, I take a deep breath to ease the panic inside me. I need to control my emotions to control my magic. Once I'm sure I'm not about to spiral, I pad across the heated floor to the floating sink and mirror above it. The claw-foot tub is framed by overflowing plants and flowers. I sigh in happiness, but I'm stalling. I force myself to look.

My dress is gaping, exposing my chest and the scar.

For a moment, I can almost feel the way he gripped my heart, and I clutch the sink as I push through it. I lift my hand and trace my fingers over it.

It's not as bad as I was expecting. I think Phrixius has something to do with that. It looks weeks old rather than fresh, and I have no doubt it will fade.

The scar is long and clean, but healing. My skin is forever marred, just like my soul is from the acts I committed, but it's more than that. Just like my skin has changed, so has my magic.

I meet my gaze in the mirror, searching for any signs of change. I'm terrified I will find the evil I saw in his eyes, but Freya is still staring back at me. That means I'm safe, right? I just . . . I just let go a little bit, letting my anger get the best of me.

I can't let it happen again.

I will not be like him, no matter what he does.

Turning away, I step into the huge glass shower and flick on the rainforest showerhead, letting the spray fall over me and wash away the lingering feelings of his touch, laughter, and the evil I feel like he placed inside me.

Tipping my head back, I close my eyes and let it cascade over me, warming my skin and soul. I startle when arms wrap around me, my eyes widening as I glance over my shoulder to see Sha.

His hand slides up my front, cupping my breast, as his lips ghost over my shoulder, making a sigh slip from me. "You are tense," he murmurs. "You are worried."

I don't know how he can tell, but I nod, turning in his arms and sliding my hands up his chest. I follow my movements with my gaze so I do not have to stare into his eyes.

Sha sees everything, though, and comments on it without bias or shame. There is no hiding from him, and I worry what he will see there. He's quiet for a moment before he starts to back me towards the stone walls of the shower. My eyes jerk up to his bright red ones as he seems to bulge and change, morphing between this form and his other one.

"I will kiss it all better," he growls.

I'm pushed onto the seat as Sha drops to his knees before me, the spray washing over him as his hands slide up my thighs and shove them open. His dark eyes lock on mine as his mouth presses against my pussy.

My head falls back on a deep sigh, and slow pleasure slides through me as he laps at my cunt. He slowly builds my pleasure, just kissing and licking me until I rock into his talented mouth.

The door swings inward, and my eyes snap open to see my demon framed there. "I didn't want to miss the party," he flirts. "I could smell your desire."

Licking my lips, I hold out my hand. He wanders into the shower and takes it, and Sha leans back, waiting, but I don't want to think right now. I don't want to be in charge.

Adder pulls me to my feet, and Sha stands too. I'm backed into him, trapped between them as Adder strokes my cheek softly, sensing my need without words. Years of understanding pass between us in one look.

He kisses me softly until I'm relaxed again, and when he pulls back, I wear a sad sort of smile.

"Make me forget," I murmur into his lips.

"I've got you, little witch," he promises.

I'm lifted, but Sha's hands on my ass hold me. I wrap my legs around Adder, and he rubs his cock across my pussy as he kisses me again. Adder turns my face, and then Sha kisses me. They take turns sharing me, pushing me between them until I roll into Adder. Taking the hint, he softly presses into me, slowly working deeper and then stilling.

I'm not wet enough, but I don't care, and neither do they.

Sha presses against my ass, and I prepare for it to hurt, but he goes so slowly, it's torturous. He pulls out and pushes back in, working back and forth until he's buried all the way inside me.

When I'm trapped between them, they start to move.

My head is turned so I'm kissing both of them. All three of us kiss as their hands glide all over me, making me forget.

My head swings up when there's an inhale. We all still for a moment, eyeing Phrixius as he blinks at us. "Is this what happens while I sleep?" he grumbles, his gaze heating. "I'm guessing you feel better."

Sex and magic have always gone side by side, especially for me, so I hold out my hand, offering myself to him. I will let them worship me as I heal and recover.

He doesn't hesitate as he heads towards me, not stopping until his lips meet mine. Despite Sha and Adder surrounding me, I only feel whole, safe, and strong enough to let go when Phrixius completes our group.

I let them carry me away on pleasure. All of their hands, mouths, and skin touch mine, and when I finally shatter, it's so freeing, I feel like I'm soaring.

We must all come back down, though, and when I do, I realise they are all still hard. They pull free of my body, and Phrixius gives me one last lingering kiss, ignoring his hard cock, before he grabs some soap and turns back to me.

As they pull away, I realise this wasn't about their pleasure, but mine, and as all three surround me and carefully wash every inch of my body, I let some tears slip free.

"It felt like he wanted it," I explain softly. "He wanted me to kill him." I don't know how to explain what I saw in his eyes other than that. "He won't stop. I saw it. It's only going to get worse. His trap was thwarted, so he's going to be mad, more so because we destroyed some of his army and I burnt his house."

"I wonder if it's time to ask the others for assistance before this gets out of hand," Phrixius murmurs. "If we are careful, we could ask Mors—"

"No, the less the gods know about my witch, the better," Adder snaps. "We can handle this alone. We simply underestimated him, and we won't let it happen again."

"I think the mask he stole is giving him more power," I say. "I think that's why he took it. Their souls and magic are trapped in there. It felt like he was . . . more than one person when he took control over me . . . like a million souls were slamming into mine and stealing who I was."

"Well, that's not fucking terrifying and creepy." Adder grins, making me smile, which is why he did it. "Okay, so we hunt down necro-boy again, kick his ass, and then spend the rest of the month humping like bunnies. Sound good?"

"You make it seem so easy," I mutter.

"Eh, let's not over plan it. Look where that got us last time. Plans are for pussies. We'll just rock up and knock his necro-socks off . . . . Wait, I don't think he wears socks. Oh, he really is evil. That's some nasty shit."

I laugh despite the situation, and he winks at me, letting me know he did it to cheer me up.

"He won't be waiting at the church this time. It felt like he was planning something bigger and that was only the beginning." It's just the feeling I got, but I have to be right.

"Phrixius, can you find him again?" Sha asks, being the calm one, as always.

"Hmm, I'll need to rest a little after last time and healing Freya, but yes."

"What kind of god are you? Do you have a battery we need to plug in?" Adder mutters. "Fine, we'll rest for the night, and tomorrow, we'll find him again."

"And if it goes like it did today?" I ask worriedly.

"It won't. We will all be ready this time, especially you, Freya. You need to block him. Now that you know he can do that, you need to ensure your wall is tight."

I nod, but it's easier said than done.

The rest of the night is quiet, all of us lost in our own thoughts, wondering what tomorrow will bring, and despite everything, I manage to fall asleep.

I awake at dawn with a thunderous roar in my chest. I gasp, gripping the splitting muscles where he tore into me.

"What is it?" Phrixius asks.

I swing my eyes to him, panicked. "He's calling . . . Not just me, he's calling everyone. Something is very wrong." Covering my chest, I curl forward with a cry as my heart rips in two, his roar filling my ears until they start to bleed.

I cannot see or hear.

"He's—oh god, I can see him."

"What is it?" Adder demands.

Part of me is here, and the other is with him, looking through his eyes once more.

"He's above the city. Oh gods, no, he's taking over the city. He's killing them all." My words end in a scream as he throws me from his body, his laughter following me.

He wanted me to see.

He wanted me to know where he is.

CHAPTER 41

freya

"It's a trap," Phrixius points out.

"Definitely." I nod. "But we have no choice. If we don't stop him now, he won't just end up claiming this city—he will devour everything until there is nothing left of the world." I blow back my hair in annoyance, and Adder is suddenly there, his deft fingers working on tying it back for me. "It's now or never."

"We're probably going to die," Adder comments conversationally.

"Maybe," I agree.

"Well, what are we waiting for?" Sha asks.

Laughing, I turn when Adder steps back, eyeing myself in the mirror. Today, I'm dressed for business. Gone is the flowy dress, and in its place are skin-tight, black trousers. My boots are to my knees, with a dagger in each, and my hair is plaited up in horns to match Adder's. When I look at my men, I see them nodding, also ready.

We know what awaits us and that we might not make it out alive, but it's a risk we have to take.

"We are like the A-Team." Adder grins. "Or Suicide Squad, just hotter."

Smirking, I hold out my hand. "Let's end this differently than they did. Either we all make it back or we die trying."

"I still think this is a bad idea." Phrixius sighs, but he lays his hand in mine. "But I'm with you."

"Until the end." Sha nods, placing his hand over ours, and Adder covers them all.

"Let's go kick some necro ass!"

Without another word, I conjure a portal and push us through since I was the one who saw him—we don't need Phrixius's magic this time. When we step from it, we stand in the middle of an empty, deserted street. The sun is high in the sky, the usually bustling cityscape around us devoid of life and sound. Cars lie on their sides or are smashed together, their doors open as if people just got out and walked away.

Lights flicker from green to red, sidewalks remain empty, and food, bags, and even coats just lie where they fell.

There isn't a body in sight.

"This is not creepy at all," Adder whispers. "I'm pretty sure this is how all horror games I play start."

"Where are all the bodies?" I murmur, and then realisation hits me. "He's gathering them."

Rolling my shoulders back, I search inside myself for the pull, my eyes turning upwards. There, in the heart of the city, I see a silhouette upon a roof.

He's tired of waiting. He wants to end this now.

"Welp, let's do it, I guess." Adder takes my hand and swings it back and forth as we start to walk towards the centre of the city. More signs of abandoned personal effects litter every street, and there still isn't a body in sight.

It sends a shiver down my spine, and trepidation washes down my body. Whatever he did will not be good.

When we turn the last corner, reaching the road leading right to the skyscraper he's on, we see them.

Like a blockade, facing every available street surrounding the building, are thousands of bodies.

The sun blazes down on them. Some are missing shoes and clothes, and others still have leashes and folders in their hands, as if they stopped in the middle of whatever they were doing and marched here.

We all stop, eyeing the massive crowd as a dog races past us, barking at a woman with a leash. It tugs at her, barking and nipping at her leg, but she completely ignores it, frozen bar his tugging.

"So creepy, yet I have the urge to run at them like a human bowling ball," Adder whispers, and then the air fills with magic.

Dark magic . . .

Every single eye turns to us, but this time, they are filled with life.

"We have a big fucking problem," I snap. "Those aren't just resurrected—"

"They are stolen." Phrixius glances at me. "This was his plan all along. He has broken the mask and freed the trapped souls of the necromancers within. They have taken over the bodies. He built an army of them and was waiting for us."

"Really?" Adder groans. "Like one wasn't bad enough, now there are hundreds of these fuckers?"

"You handle him while we handle those." Phrixius sighs. "If we stop him, then we might be able to stop everything. They have taken over, but without his powers keeping those bodies alive, they are nothing. They are wandering souls with nothing to inhabit."

"Easy-peasy," I whisper, my eyes turning up to the roof where he is waiting. "I guess I'll see you on the other side."

My gaze lands on all three of them, standing tall and strong at my side. They watch me back, and Adder grips me, kissing me hard. "We'll clear a path for you. Do not fucking die, do you hear me?"

"I won't," I promise.

"You better not, little witch. Your soul is mine, remember that," he says before letting me go, only for Sha to pull me into a sweeping kiss. No words are needed, as he gives me all of his emotions in that one move.

Nodding, I kiss his forehead and turn to Phrixius.

We should be enemies, but as he pulls me close, I know we are anything but. We are just two beings who never should have been on the same side but are. His big hand wraps around my neck, pulling me close until our foreheads touch.

"Remember who you are, Freya. Remember your differences, not your similarities. His war is fought with hate, yours with love . . . . We will see you when this is over." His lips touch mine in a scalding kiss, and then he steps back. A change comes over him, shifting from my soft, loving Phrixius to the god of magic.

His hair glows with his power, and his skin shines like the sun is trapped within. Golden armour grows upon his skin, shimmering with runes and magic, and two giant swords unfurl in each hand, moving like snakes until they snap into wicked points. Sometimes it is easy to forget he is a god, but not in this moment, especially as he takes a step forward and starts to levitate.

I glance at Sha as he groans, and I see the change coming over him as well as they prepare to battle. His skin turns the colour of coal, and shadows wrap around him as he triples in size. His bright red eyes move farther apart and higher, slanting and turning devilish.

"Show-offs," Adder mutters, drawing my gaze to him. He winks when he catches me staring, and despite knowing him all my life, he shows me the truth behind the demon who follows me around like a lost puppy.

Fire crawls along his skin and up his horns, blazing between them. His nails lengthen into claws as long as daggers, his tail transforms so barbs slide out, glistening at the points, and his body bulges with power.

I gulp as I glance between them. They are facing an army . . . . Can they do it?

I have to trust in them the way they are trusting in me.

If I want to save them, then I need to end this.

"Go." Adder winks. "Let's finish this, little witch. Let's be the heroes for once."

Nodding, I steal one last look at them before turning to the unmoving army. Their dark eyes track our movements, but there are no expressions on their faces. For some reason, that bothers me most.

There are no more words. My guys surge past me with silent calculation, forming a line and heading straight for the waiting bodies.

Phrixius uses the air to his advantage, hitting bodies in the front line and sending them flying back. All of us know these people are dead, there is no saving them, but watching them be tossed like bowling pins still makes me wince and beg for forgiveness for their souls.

There is so much death, it horrifies me.

I have no time to linger on the pain, though, as Sha leaps into the air and lands farther into the crush, where I can only see his shadows. Adder simply disappears before the front line and appears within them, all of them focusing on the middle as they tear through the black-eyed soldiers with precision until an opening forms.

They are clearing a path for me just like they promised, and when Phrixius's eyes meet mine, I nod and burst into a sprint. I hurry into the clearing they made, not wanting to use my magic and touch the bodies here to move them in case it consumes me like before. They are right, I have to trust them in this.

Phrixius flies above me, using his magic to clear away as many as he can, even with soldiers clinging to his legs, trying to climb him.

Sha roars and bulldozes through more, knocking them down like bowling pins, his shadows consuming them as he goes.

Adder laughs ahead, his fire burning bright and hot as bodies fly through the air.

I hurry through the bodies, ignoring the way the eyes track me despite my men tearing into them. They do not react. They simply stand there until I'm over halfway through them, then suddenly, the path closes before me. I turn to see those behind me marching straight at my men, their eyes glinting with determination and power.

I want to shout a warning, but it's clear they already know. Still, I hesitate as they converge on the men I love.

Gritting my teeth, I turn back to the wall of black-eyed soldiers standing between me and the wide glass doors of the skyscraper. I don't wish to expose myself to the magic again and risk becoming consumed by them, but I have to choose.

Conjuring my power, I let it fill my palms as I walk towards them, knowing my hair is darkening and my eyes shine with magic. They do not react, not until they step back as I come towards them. I draw closer to the door, confusion swirling through me as my magic crawls up my arms, begging to be used.

The whispers of death on the air call to me, and I ignore it as best as I can, unwilling to let even one of the faceless people touch me. Who knows what would happen?

As I reach the door, the black eyes follow me. I expect them to stop me, and I prepare my magic, but they incline their heads and step back, forming a passage between them. I hesitate at that. Why would they let me pass?

They have to know why I am here.

As I reach the door, darkness falls around us, and I raise my gaze to the once bright sky to see shadows reaching up into it, blotting out the light.

The shadows obscure the sun, plummeting the whole city into darkness.

Taking a deep breath, I turn back to the door and push inside, ready to face death.

CHAPTER 42

I spare Freya a look and see her stepping inside the building. Good, we bought her a chance. I wish we could be with her, but the army he created turns their eyes to us, and now that she is clear, their intention to destroy us fills the air.

She might be facing him, but we are with her in her heart and soul. He is assuming our deaths will make her weak, but I will not allow that. I will not allow him to hurt her like that. Her soul and heart are already ours, and he cannot have them.

This is not the first war I have fought, and it will not be the last, but it is the most important because it is for her. Freya called to me and gave me purpose, and she showed me love and kindness.

I have fallen madly and deeply in love with her, and despite my duty and station, I choose her. As I dive towards the undead soldiers filled with power of past necromancers, I let them see there is no one more determined than a god in love.

I bulldoze into the soldiers, feeling the touch of death wash over my skin as they try to claim my soul for the darkness.

If only they knew the darkness already claimed it—the darkness that lives in her.

SHA

They are strong. Before, it was like tearing through grass, easy and endless, but now they are fighting back. I feel Phrixius above me as his magic hits the crowd, melting them where they stand. They do not even scream, and even if they are missing limbs or dying, they continue to stumble towards him. He grabs them and lifts them into the air, dropping them from an incredible height before diving back down, cutting through their masses with his swords. Heads tumble to the ground, but their bodies carry on their assault.

Teeth dig into my side, and I snarl as I turn, focusing on those attacking me. My shadows swallow their silent screams, crawling along their skin and dragging them down to the ground, which opens. It swallows them whole, leaving no trace. My long arms swipe out, sending more flying. I hear bones break as I tear through the never-ending masses, refusing to give up or slow down.

Freya is counting on me. I will not let her down.

She is my reason for living. She is my master and my lover. I will decimate any army for her. I will bring their hearts to her as a trophy, and when this is over, I will show her what it means to be loved by a monster.

Snarling loudly, I bite the head of the next foe, spilling blood across me.

ADDER

We are spread out now and cut off from one another. They think that makes us weaker, but they are wrong. I am a demon born to do evil, and today, I let everything I keep inside out.

Fire scorches the earth as I step forward, the scent of sulphur filling the air, and those nearest to me catch fire. They still head my way, but as they bump into others, the fire spreads, moving across their masses.

Conjuring a portal, I shove a few through, knowing where they will end up. Sharks eat them as they drop into the water. Turning, I wave my hand, and a net comes down on more, acid burning through them as it captures them, pinning them to the ground.

I laugh and let all my wild, evil magic out, turning others to insects and stepping on them. I keep moving and killing. Their blood spills over me, only urging me on. My fires burn hotter until even the buildings around us scorch with the heat.

I will not stop, not until there are no more threats to her.

This battle is ours, just as the one up there is hers.

I will not let her down. I have spent the last twenty something years of my life protecting her, and I will continue to do so until the day she dies and I make a deal with another demon to kill me to join her.

Today is not our end—it's our beginning. I will ensure that.

Something slides through my side, and I turn, lava pouring from my hand and burning them to a crisp as the darkness seems to intensify. I can feel she's close to him, and he knows it.

He is waiting.

My eyes turn to the skyscraper, and I send up a prayer to the gods I never wanted to depend on, begging them to keep her safe.

We cannot help her now. It's all up to her.

CHAPTER 43

Freya

The lobby is empty, the marble floor shiny and polished. I pass the reception desk and walk through the open scanners to the elevator bank. They flash random numbers, and there are arrows drawn crudely on the silver fronts, pointing to a door farther down. I follow the banks, finding more arrows that point the way

The white door has its own message, written in blood.

Welcome home

"Not creepy at all," I mutter, then I grip the handle and twist. The door opens easily, and no alarm blares despite the emergency only sign. I step through then jump when it slams shut behind me. Swallowing hard, I glance up with a groan.

Floor after floor of stairs stretch above me, but when my eyes land on the bodies lining each step, I swallow. Okay, super creepy.

Pressed against the walls are zombies. They are all smiling, and when I place my foot on the first step with a creature, its voice reaches me.

"Welcome home."

Shaking my head, I start to climb, each zombie repeating the greeting until I'm practically running. Their voices fill the air like a promise, and there are so many of them, I want to cover my ears.

I grip the banister and run, sweat trickling down my temples by the time I'm ten floors up.

I was not made for this sort of exercise. I was made for naps, cocks, and magic.

Magic . . .

I hesitate, but honestly, I don't think I can climb these and stop him before the world ends. I mean, maybe that was his plan all along, make me late by forcing me to climb a billion stairs. Gripping the banister, I lean out and look up, seeing tons more.

I grip the railing as the building shakes with Sha's angry roar, and I send up a prayer, hoping he's okay.

Yeah, fuck climbing these stairs.

I'm not just a human, and despite the zombies here, I reach for my magic.

I'm a fucking necromancer, a goddamn witch, and it's about time I started acting like one.

I conjure a portal and step inside. I find myself at least ten floors up, so I do it again and again until I'm standing on the last landing. Looking down, I see how many floors I travelled and smirk. Turning back, I take a deep breath at the closed double doors. The keypad at the side is broken, the alarm cut at the top.

Refusing to hesitate, I open it and step out onto the roof. It shuts behind me, announcing my arrival, but he does not turn from where he stands in the middle, facing the city beyond. I see Phrixius fly past, and I hear them fighting below. I want to look, but I keep my eyes on his back, knowing he's the most dangerous thing here.

The mask he stole lies at his feet, broken into a million pieces.

Taking another step, I call out, "Stop this."

"It cannot be stopped." He turns to me, his face carved with a welcoming smile. "I have been waiting for you."

"I know." I take another step. "But it's never too late. Let them go, let's end this."

"You wish to end this? You know how." He tilts his head, watching me. "But you do not have it in you. Despite it all, you're not a killer. You are weak—not quite a witch, not quite a necromancer. You are caught in between, a child hiding from the dark. Can't you see the dark is not to be feared, but embraced? Without it, you are nothing. You are not fighting me, you are fighting yourself, and you will never win. You are weak!" he roars before he breathes out and glances around. "I did all of this without even feeling drained. Could you?"

"Why would I want to?" I ask. "Look at the destruction—"

"The beauty! This world needs to be destroyed. It needs to be rebuilt. It needs to be cleansed!"

Shaking my head, I stare into his eyes. He might have been a man once driven by grief, but he let it twist him into a monster. Does he not understand that the very reason they culled our kind is because of this?

This is not the way to change their minds, but it is too late for that now.

"Look." He gestures at the city beyond. "Look at what we are capable of." I hurry to the edge, peering down in horror. There are so many bodies, all because of him and what we are.

I glance back at him to see his proud grin. "It is not the darkness inside us they fear, but the power we hold. Even the gods fear us because they know we could be even more powerful than them, and they hate that. They kill us not just because they are afraid, but also because of jealousy. The gods wish they could be as strong as us."

"They killed us because of this! You conquered an entire city to make a point. You killed thousands, and you wonder why they killed our people. One person did this. No wonder they feared what more of us would do. You are not helping us. You are just confirming everything they think is true. Everyone else forgot, thinking we are just nightmares whispered in the dark to scare kids, but now, we will be the horror in their past, a constant reminder of the abuse of magic necromancers are capable of. This isn't making us a future. It's damning us once more." The words tumble from my lips as I step closer. "What they did to your family was wrong, but how many families have you killed today? How many children have you taken? How many parents' souls have you slaughtered? You are no better than them—no, you are worse because you know the pain it causes and you still did it anyway. You let revenge blind you and called it change. We can be better than this. We have to be, or we don't deserve to live."

"We are what we are made into," he tells me. "We are born to be this. You cannot fight fate no matter how hard you try. Death is all they understand, and I am willing to be the evil covered in blood if it changes the future. Are you? Will you do what it takes for your ideals?"

As I stare into his eyes, I understand what he means. Am I willing to sacrifice everything to stop this?

To fight the devil, you must be the devil.

You cannot win against evil without being evil yourself.

I will never win against him like this. He has no weakness or reservations, but I do.

I hold back the darkness with firm control, and that makes me weaker than he is. I will not win, and my men will die.

What is one life, one soul, against all of that?

Everything I have fought for, everything I have tried so hard not to be fills me, and I know I must become like him to end this. I must become what everyone said we are—evil.

I must embrace who I was born to be or I will die here like everyone else.

My soul is a small price to pay, even though I know it will destroy my men to kill me after.

It will be worth it to keep them and everyone safe.

"Yes," I tell him. "I am willing to become whatever it takes to end this."

I let go.

I release the darkness inside me, letting the shadows leak through me. I demolish all that careful control born from fear. I tear down the wall Phrixius taught me and let it out.

I feel it fill me, darkness crawling under my skin, and when I lift my hands, I see it moving. My eyes and face feel different, and my hair flows around me, lifted by power.

"There you are." He grins. "Magnificent. Let's see, shall we?" He turns to the city. "Kill them."

"No!" My hands lift, and shadows pour from them, wrapping around him. They cover his mouth and hands, sinking into his skin as one of my men roars in agony. "No!"

The darkness explodes, the thorns ripping into the necromancer as fury fills me.

He dares to hurt what is mine?

His eyes are wide as my darkness tightens around him, ripping him to pieces. Power flows from me as I begin to rise into the air, and with a yell, I send it out to the city.

I steal all the souls filling those bodies, my command clear.

Die, die, die, die, die, die, die, die, die, die.

I feel them fall, one by one, their screaming, fighting souls rushing back to me, and then I fling them into the mask. It flows through and around me. There is so much raw magic, the earth trembles with it.

I could not stop this now even if I wanted to, but he's right . . . . I don't.

I want his death for daring to touch what is mine.

I let it fuel me, and I consume it. I feed on the death I control, on his pain and power, until I'm full enough to burst. The entire city dies below me, and I become what I never wanted to be—evil.

I become like him and our ancestors.

I become a true necromancer.

A noise from one of my men brings me back. Releasing my hold on him, I drop him to the ground. His powers are stolen, and now he is nothing but a weak, dying mortal. Ignoring him, I step to the roof edge to check on my men. I see them below, climbing to their feet, alive and well, and relief pulses through me alongside the mocking darkness covering my soul.

It's begging for me to kill them and taste their power, telling me how wonderful it would be.

I turn away from them before I do just that, unsure how much control I truly have right now. I became this to keep them safe, and I know how this ends—with my death. I will not take them with me. It is my sacrifice . . . my choice.

The necromancer kneels before me, blood pouring from his eyes and lips, yet they tilt up in a smile that should make me feel cold all over, but I already am.

"There it is, our greatest weapon—you. This was all for you. Go, Freya, and be our vengeance. Be the evil they called us. Ruin them for what they did to us. This was always my destiny, and this was always yours."

I frown, not understanding until it dawns on me.

He wanted it to end this way.

He planned all of this so I would embrace the darkness inside and become what he needed—a weapon against the gods.

He was willing to die for his ideals like he demanded of me, and as I stare into his eyes, his smile only grows. He gave it all so I would become this, and I played right into his plan. This was never about ending it . . . . It was about starting it.

This was just the beginning. There is no going back now, and we both know it.

"What have I done?" I whisper, and I stumble back in horror.

"What none of us could do. You have become our future." He grins, blood still pouring down his face.

There is so much power inside me, there will never be any going back.

"Freya!" is shouted from below.

I hesitate to turn and face them and let them see what I have become. Suddenly, something echoes through the air like a horn—a warning.

A sense of an ancient rivalry and anger demands I kill them before they kill me.

I turn in horror, racing to the edge of the building and leaping onto the lip as the heavens open and bright sunlight cuts through the darkness.

The gods arrive in a halo of righteous fury.

They pour into the air, all dressed in armour, and they have so much power, it thickens the air.

For a moment, I meet Phrixius's eyes, which are filled with fear as he stares at me like I'm a stranger as the gods descend around us, taking in the scene.

I feel their eyes on me.

"Abomination!" one roars.

It is not me they are speaking to, though, and I follow their power breathlessly, watching as it arcs through the air, aimed like a spear at the ground below, where Adder and Sha stand, staring up at me.

My scream of horror rips through the air as magic closes around Sha. He turns, reaching for me, and then suddenly, he is ripped away from this world. My soul shatters when I cannot feel him anymore.

Phrixius heads my way, but more magic slams down into the earth, glowing brightly like a circular prison, surrounding Adder. He glances from the gods to me, his mouth tilting in a smile. "I love you, little witch," he calls as chains slither around his body and drag him to his knees. They start to glow, and his jaw clenches, but he never once cries out or looks away.

"No!" I fling my magic, but it's too late. The prison glows brighter, and suddenly, he's gone as well.

Something inside me cracks and breaks, and my eyes turn to the gods.

With a roar, I fling my magic at them. "No!" Phrixius screams, and he appears before me, taking the blow. My eyes widen as he flies through the air, a million cuts appearing all over him.

The last shard of my soul breaks as I stare into his hard eyes as he accepts the hatred meant for the other gods. Even now, he's protecting me, knowing what I have become.

Everything else is gone.

I feel nothing but hate.

"Freya," Phrixius whispers. "Come back to me."

"Too late, god." The necromancer behind me coughs. "It was always going to be this way." His laughter reaches me once more as I turn to see him lying on his side, his lips tilted up. "This was always how it was supposed to end, Freya. Now do it. Do what we could not. Destroy them. This world is yours, light eater. Embrace it. It is too late to fight now. The gods have taken what was left of your soul and those who helped control it. All that is left is evil, just like me. Welcome home, necromancer. Welcome to your future, our queen."

I look at the gods for a moment, and with a snap of my fingers, I rip apart his body without even looking. "You have taken what is mine!" I call. "Return them or end up like him."

"Freya, please," Phrixius says, heading my way, panting and still bleeding. His glow lessens, as if I stole his magic.

"Necromancer, you are to be sentenced for your crimes." Their voices come as one as they turn their attention to me.

My eyes go back to the earth and the scarred marks where my demon and creature were. Without them, I am nothing. My soul is gone.

Without even meaning to, the gods just stole the last of my humanity.

I laugh. All this resistance, and this is how it ends. Gods, I was a fool. My laughter tumbles out, louder and louder, until power flows into me, trying to force me to submit to their wills.

He was right. I understand his willingness to give up this world for the one you love.

Fuck this world and fuck the gods.

They will all pay.

I lift my hands, ready to do just that, when their combined magic hits me. I scream in agony as it tears through me, ripping me to shreds. Their power floods me, obscuring my own and stealing my control over it. I'm surprised I'm not dead as I fall to my knees on the edge of the roof.

"Stop this!" Phrixius calls to them. "Stop it!"

Golden shackles appear around my wrists. They glow and start to burn, and I scream as they block everything, making me numb and weak.

I meet his panicked gaze as he stops before me, turning to face them. "Give me time to explain. Just stop."

"Phrixius," I murmur, and he glances at me over his shoulder.

"Shh, I've got this, Freya. I will keep you safe, just hold on." I search his desperate eyes, and I realise he will. He'll stand against the gods for me.

I cannot let that happen. They will kill him too.

The necromancer was wrong.

This is not destined. We make our destiny, and I choose him. I choose to save him. I choose to save whatever is left of the Freya he fell in love with.

"I love you," I tell him as I throw myself forward.

I do not scream as I fall. The wind roars around me as I plummet towards the ground to stop this once and for all. My death will accomplish that. This is the only way.

I turn with the force of the wind, my hands chained in front of me as Phrixius dives towards me, his mouth open in a scream of denial, but we both know he will not be fast enough.

Surprisingly, peace fills me. I have been fighting for so long, and I am ready to rest.

I do not close my eyes as I hit, ensuring he is the last thing I see in this world.

CHAPTER 44

freya

Death is not what greets me when my eyes flutter open. Instead, I see the gods sitting on thrones, eyeing me with disgust.

I look down, realising I'm alive.

My hands are still shackled with glowing chains, but I am whole.

How am I alive?

Phrixius turns to me, and I blink, not realising he was there. He seems to slump when he notices I'm awake. Relief fills his eyes before he turns them back to the gods.

"If you will let me explain—"

"Silence!" one of them roars, but my eyes are only for him, memorising the way he stands against his own people for me. "You may have forsaken your duty, but we have not, Phrixius."

"She is capable of control. The fact that she has lived this long proves it," he argues.

"Or that she is good at hiding, the vile creature," one hisses.

"Hmm, it is interesting." I know that voice. I glance at Mors to find him looking at me with interest.

"Please, give her a chance," Phrixius begs.

"You should be ashamed of yourself," one sneers. "You have

forsaken everything we are. Do you feel no obligation or shame for your actions?"

"No, not if it keeps her alive. I will forsake all dignity." He drops to his knees, and I freeze as the god of magic kneels to save me. "Give her one chance to regain control."

I can't. They stole my control.

It is only now that I see my life was all about balance. Sha and Adder helped without realising it. The gods stole them and it away. My soul is torn into pieces, scattered to the winds, and it leaves me unbalanced and alone, but they do not care. Whatever control I could have had before is now gone. I am only able to hold my power back because of the shackles, but even as I think that, I feel my shadows wind around them, working through the locks.

Anger fuels me, but there has been too much death, and I am so tired.

"Enough!" one barks. "This is not a negotiation. You will destroy the necromancer and atone for your lapse in judgement."

Oh gods, they are going to make him kill me.

I know that will destroy something in him. Whether they want to know it or not, Phrixius loves me, and asking him to kill the one he loves, even if it's to save the world, would fracture him.

I stare at his back as he shakes, and I realise he's crying. When his face turns to me, it's pale and glowing tears track down his cheeks. "Do not ask this of me, please. Let me save her. I can save her."

"No. End her now. Do your duty to this world and the magic that created us. These are our laws. This is our duty. This is our purpose."

They repeat it, all apart from Mors, but I stare at Phrixius as his eyes close, his duty warring with his love. Phrixius is a good man and a lawful god. He believes in his duty and the laws to keep this world safe, and I ruined that. I have made him falter. I have made him question his morals, and if I didn't already hate what I am right now, then that would do it.

I caused the god of magic to falter in his duty, and now he's fighting a battle I cannot help with.

Or can I?

I made the choice before, so I can make it again.

I cannot let Phrixius do this. I can't let him destroy himself. He deserves better. It is my fault he is here, and it's time I took the blame.

I should have died many years ago. I'm only alive because of Adder, and now he's gone.

Death and I are old friends, and when I look at Mors, I see the knowledge there—I am living on borrowed time, and he knows.

He knows what I will do.

I don't know how I know I can do it, but I send my next thought to him.

Protect him, please.

He inclines his head, letting me know he will, and I let my shoulders droop in relief as I glance at Phrixius. Swallowing, I climb to my feet, and every eye swings to me.

"I cannot apologise for what I am," I tell them, "but know I never wanted this. I just wanted a quiet life. I just wanted to make my spells and maybe be happy, but I know that was never my fate. I wish I could say I was strong enough to resist what I am, and maybe I could have with their help, but it does not matter now." I sweep my gaze over the gods. "There has been enough death. You destroyed my kind, and we try to destroy you. It's just an endless cycle of rebirth and death, and it's time it stopped. It's time to move on. I hope, in the future, there will be a person, one born into this magic like me, who will change this world for the better and give people hope, not hate, because I will take it with me now. I will take it all so that when that person is born, they stand a chance, hopeful for the future. I hope, one day, you're able to accept we are not born evil—we are made evil."

I look at Phrixius as he climbs to his feet and faces me, my smile soft as I memorise his handsome face. I would have been happy making spells at his side, watching those rubbish movies he likes, and playing for an eternity, but it was never our destiny.

This love was never meant to be. We had some stolen moments together, and it's all we'll get. I just hope he finds happiness again in the future because no one deserves it more.

"Thank you, Phrixius, for trying to save me and being with me despite the paths we both knew we would have to take. Thank you for giving me something good to hold onto and something to love. I'm beginning to understand that the meaning of love isn't just a feeling, it's hope, and it's those you would willingly sacrifice yourself for. Even if it means unhappiness for you, you do it anyway because you love them and you want them to be happy."

Stepping forward, I release the chains the god placed around me. It's effortless, just another sign of how strong my powers truly are. When I meet Phrixius's tear-stained face, I see hopelessness in his eyes.

"It's going to be okay," I promise him with a soft smile. I feel the darkness swirl around my feet, and the gods panic, stepping back. Seeing the gods' terror only hammers home that what I am doing is right. "I do not want to be this world's destruction, but the bitter truth is, I would if it would save you. I should care more about it, but I don't. All I care about is you three. I would swallow it whole and fill it with death if it meant keeping you safe, but I cannot save you if I am alive."

"Freya—" He stumbles to me, but I hold him back with a flick of my finger. Watching our magic meet for the last time gives me a sad sort of nostalgia for simpler times, when I didn't know the true depth of my love for this man.

"This world needs you, Phrixius." It's one of the only times I've ever used his full name, and I see the moment it registers. "It needs you, but it does not need me. I was supposed to die all those years ago. I was never supposed to live past my birth. I will rectify that wrong now. I'll go out on my own terms for you," I say with a tearful grin. "I love you so much that I will not let you live with this on your soul for the rest of your life, even though you know it's the right thing to do." I see his soul being torn apart. Duty and honour fight with his love for me. It's not his fault he fell in love with someone so evil, but it's also not my fault I became this way.

We are just two storms destined to meet, but I will not let him die out.

Moving across the floor, I ignore everyone else, placing my hand on his cheek for one more stolen moment. His eyes close in bliss as I lean in. "I love you, remember that, and live for me. Find your happiness once more and live every day like it's your last life." I step back, and before he can stop me, I wave my hand across my body, directing all the evil and death towards myself.

I implode into a million tiny pieces and take the legacy and vengeance of our people with me.

I seal our past with my death, and I free his future.

CHAPTER 45

I stare at the place she was.

Glittering ashes of her body and soul swirl around me, whispering across my skin in one last, stolen touch.

Her smile, laughter, kindness, and love are gone.

Everything that made her Freya is just . . . gone, blowing away with the wind.

"Well, she was not as foolish as she looked," someone jokes behind me.

They joke.

About her death.

As if I was not just forced to watch the only person I have ever loved kill herself to protect me.

She ended her own life simply for being born the way she was.

She was right.

We made her evil.

She was not born like that. Freya was kind and filled with laughter, but we stole that from her. She never would have been here if not for that necromancer and the gods. She would be in her coven, never knowing, happy with her demon.

Now she is gone like she never existed, a bad memory for them, but for me, my whole world was destroyed with her.

What is the point of going on?

Adder accused me of not being able to keep her safe, saying I would be unable to choose between her and my duty, and he was right. When it counted, I failed her. I hesitated, and she knew it. She saw it, and she saved me one last time when I couldn't save her.

I did not deserve her, and neither did this world.

They always told us the lives of many were more important than the lives of a few, but I do not care. I would give anything for her to be before me, and it's then I realise I do not care anymore about this duty, my purpose, and this world.

I care nothing for it without her.

"I had given up on this world and our duty before her. Did you know that?" I snap at them, anger filling the pavilion as I face them. Magic pounds through me, demanding their heads for what they made her do, but I would have to take my own as well. I am no better than they are. "What is the point in doing our duty if we cannot protect those we love?" I shake my head, a bitter laugh escaping me. "We are pointless figureheads. We do nothing, yet we judge everything. It is not the world that doesn't deserve us. It is us who don't deserve it. We know nothing of the way they love. They live such short lives, but they live more freely than any of us, while we are an archaic, useless body." I stare at them, knowing they will never change. "I was happy," I whisper. "You stole that from me. I would have given all my lives for just one with her. I pray you never know this feeling inside me now. I pray for all of this to end," I admit. "All of us . . . It's pointless. We are pointless."

I fall forward, my bellow of agony filling the world as my back bows. I feel so much pain, I choke on it as grief consumes me.

I now understand why they did what they did and why they were willing to burn the world for losing those they loved.

I let the pain wash through me and fill my soul. I deserve for it to hurt.

Find her, a voice says in my mind, and I lift my head to see Mors staring at me. *What is gone is never truly gone. Her power lives on. Find her and bring her back before it's too late.*

I frown, unsure what he means. *She is dead.*

Death is never truly the end. It is just another rebirth, he tells me. *She lives on in what she loved.*

My eyes widen as I realise what he's saying, and a spark of hope fills me.

You will have to give up everything. He leans forward. *A warning, my friend. You will have to embrace what she did to bring her back.*

I do not care, I tell him. *I will do anything.* I clamber to my feet, watching him, and then I nod my head in thanks.

He gets to his feet, standing away from the others, and we stare at each other for a moment before I turn and walk to the edge of the pavilion.

"Phrixius, if you take another step, you are forsaking your duty . . . your godhood."

"Then I forsake it," I snarl, my lip curled in disgust and anger. "As my woman would say, fuck my duty and fuck you. It means nothing without her. I am done. I am done with it all. I do not wish to be a god anymore, not without her. Take your duty and your laws, I will not live without her."

As I walk away, I swear I feel the god of death's approval wash over me, but it's snatched away, stolen by my pain and anger as I take a step off the pavilion and fall.

I am coming, Freya. Hold on.

CHAPTER 46

I hiss as the chains continue to wrap tighter around me, burning through my skin to the bone underneath, only for my skin to regrow before the process restarts. It's a constant agony, the godly magic within them containing my own so I am unable to free myself.

Wherever they sent me, it's dark and humid. I can barely see around me, but what I do see are sharp, jagged rocks surrounding me as I swing from the chain. With nothing else to do, my mind wanders to my little witch.

Is she okay? The gods . . . They wouldn't hurt her, right? Phrixius wouldn't let them. I have to believe that. I have to trust that. I would know if something was wrong. I would feel it, but that doesn't mean my heart doesn't ache at her memory.

The last sight of her haunts me—her devastated eyes as she reaches for me. It's all I see in the dark as I struggle to get back to her side.

We have not been apart this long since she was born, and I hate it.

I will get free and find her again, and if they laid a single finger on her, then I will destroy them, gods or no gods. Nobody fucks with my little witch. I just need to get free.

Agony rips through me, tearing me to pieces as something within my soul snaps and crumbles.

The deal, the bond . . .

"No!" My roar fills the cavernous space as pure grief rolls through me.

No, no, no, no.

It cannot be.

She cannot be gone.

I felt it though. It was the deal breaking, which only means one thing.

Freya is dead.

I fall into a pit of despair and fury, letting it burn through me as I bellow my agony to the world with a promise to make every single person burn.

SHA

I do not know where I am. All I know is that she is not here. I cannot sense her, and my body vibrates with anger at being torn from her.

She is mine. I need to get back to her.

I turn my head as much as I can, fighting the encroaching black dirt trying to reclaim me as vines crawl along my body, tugging me deeper. The sky or air around me is black, like my shadows, stealing my vision. I hate it, but I fight to get back to her.

She needs me, I remind myself as I tear through the vines and kick off the dirt, continuing to fight, my entire focus on getting back to her.

The tether that links me to her and this world . . . it snaps, ripping up my insides as pure terror and pain pump through me.

No, no.

Freya!

My roar can be heard across the world as the ground swallows me once more.

Freya, my mistress.
She's gone.
Without her, the world claims me as its own.

CHAPTER 47

I suppose I should feel something. I have spent millennia serving these worlds as a god, but I walked away, and the only thing I feel is freedom.

Have I given enough for my duty? Yes is the simple answer.

I have given enough, but I would give more to bring her back. Mors said there is hope, and I have to believe it. Nobody understands death more than he does. I never thought he would be on my side, but as he watched me go, I saw the truth he hides from them.

He stands with us, with the humans and this world, not the gods.

He might do his duty, but it's for us, not them.

I do not know where to begin, but I have a vague feeling I must find Adder and Sha. If we are to bring our girl back, then we need all her pieces and bonds. One had a deal with her, and the other was created by her. We are tied to her.

Finding them is easier said than done, though, because the gods took them and didn't tell me where they hid them. I know they are alive. I can sense their magic in the world. We were around each other enough to create our own bonds as well, and it is that which I follow as I wander aimlessly through the world.

I follow the tug deep into the Earth's crust until my feet are ripped open from the rock and I am spent and exhausted. I wander for days in the wilderness not even the humans dare explore. Deep in the earth, the air becomes hard to breathe and my lungs beg for oxygen. I become lightheaded, but I do not stop, and when I stumble around a corner, I still.

There, hanging from chains, snarling and biting like a wild animal, is Adder . . . but not as I remember.

Half of his body is melted, and he's almost feral, fighting to free himself.

"Demon," I murmur, stumbling over to him. I watch his muscles grow around the spelled chains. Snarling, I fling my magic at them and they snap, falling to the ground and hissing with the fire that flows from him.

He falls to his knees, his body shuddering and trying to heal, but he claws at the ground, a whine leaving his lips. When I fall to my knees before him, I realise it's not a sound, but a name.

Her name.

He once told me breaking the deal would kill her, but if anything, I think it has killed him.

"Demon, pull it together," I order.

"Freya is gone." He looks at me, his eyes burning with hatred and vengeance, and I am reminded just what he is capable of. Things could end badly for this world. "You let them kill her."

"She killed herself," I snarl as his hand wraps around my throat, and I show him. He must know, he has to know, and I can't bear to speak it. When it's over, he slumps, all of his energy gone.

"My little witch." It's a sorrowful cry.

"I know." I lay my arm across his back, tugging him close even as he pushes at me before he slumps and begins to cry.

I know he loves her, but seeing the proof brings tears to my eyes. If she were here, she'd want me to help him. She'd want me to look after him. I failed her, but I won't fail her again. I can do this. I can bring us back together.

It's the only shot we have.

Cupping his half-burnt face, I peer into his eyes. "Shh, I have you. We can bring her back, brother. I know we can, but I need your help."

"She's gone." His voice is sadder than I have ever heard it. Everything the little witch instilled in him, all that love and laughter, is gone, and in its place is the supernatural creature made for death and murder.

"Not forever, I know it. If you look past your pain, you will feel it too. There is a chance, but I cannot do this alone." I press my forehead to his, searching his eyes. "She needs us. Will you help me bring her back?"

"You think you can?" he asks, hope blooming in his eyes as his skin starts to heal.

"I have to try." Standing, I offer him my hand.

He looks up at my face, swallowing hard before he gives me his taloned hand—a demon and a god making a pact.

"I will do anything to bring her back. Let's do it."

"As would I." I clench his hand tightly. "Now let's make our family whole again."

CHAPTER 48

The burns across my body slowly start to heal. I almost wish they wouldn't. I wish I had a physical scar to make sense of the pain running through me like a current. I simply become a machine, a living live wire of pain wandering at Phrixius's side. Both of us cling to a tiny shard of hope that her soul exists somewhere in this world and we can bring her back.

I know death is not set in stone, but part of me is screaming inside that she's gone.

I cannot feel her.

That's what it is. For as long as I can remember, I have felt her at my side, heard her voice, and even bathed in her warmth, and now it's just gone, taken from me like she never existed. I made a deal to save a necromancer, but she was the one who saved me. I am nothing without my little witch.

If she cannot be brought back, then I will join her in death so we can be together again.

I would do anything for one more quiet morning at her side, just sitting in silence and watching her brew. I'd give anything to see her aim an exasperated smile at me or sigh and curl into my arms. It's not the mayhem we caused, nor the big, exciting days I wish for . . . . It's the little things that made up our lives together, that made me love her. Love is a human emotion, but it's so potent that I understand it now. It's memories, tiny snips of almost unimportant time, yet they change you in a fundamental way. Every smile, kiss, touch, and moment make up a life we shared and a bond that I will simply cease to exist without.

I formed myself around Freya, and without my anchor, I am nothing, just an empty shell of a demon thrown into the pits, denied warmth and love.

If I knew how important she would be to me the moment I made that deal all those years ago, I'd still make the same choice because it gave me her. It gave me more happiness than a vile, evil creature like me deserves.

I am lost in my thoughts when Phrixius grabs my hand. Usually, I would hate the physical contact, but I find myself clinging to it, needing something to hold me to this world when I feel like I am sinking into the ground. "We will bring her back." He sounds so sure, but I see worry in his eyes.

He is lost just like me and holding on to the hope he can bring her back. Edging it all is a madness I understand. It seems losing Freya has corrupted the once moral god.

"What would you do to achieve that?" I ask.

"Anything," he replies, and my eyebrow rises. "I mean it, anything. I do not care what it takes or how long. I will bring her back."

I meet his eyes, seeing how determined and serious he is. "Even if it means losing your soul along the way?"

"I have already lost it. She took it with her."

Maybe that should worry me, but if anything, it only makes me feel relieved. We will have to pervert nature to bring her back, probably damning ourselves, and I need to know I can trust him with this. It seems losing her has altered Phrixius irrevocably.

Gone is the god of magic, and in his place is a fallen, bitter man searching for his lost love.

Why does it feel like we are repeating history?

Finding Sha is not as easy as we thought. Although we have a connection to him, it's nowhere as strong as the bond is to each other or Freya. He is a creature born of intention and magic and only exists for her, so it makes me wonder if he has been reclaimed by the earth now that she is gone, but Phrixius is determined to find him.

We do not sleep, eat, or rest as we walk, searching for signs of him. Phrixius's magic is draining as he scours the world.

"We are wandering without direction, focus," I snap.

"I am trying," he retorts as he glares at me.

Leaning down where he's sitting cross-legged near the lake, I narrow my gaze. "Try harder," I demand, my voice deadly. "We are running out of time. Every moment we waste, the further she is from us. You are a god, find him now."

I don't know whether it's my pushing, his anger, or the reminder we could lose her, but he snaps. With a roar, he tackles me to the ground. We roll over the hard dirt, clawing and yelling at each other, expressing our anger and grief. I land below him, his hands pinning me down. He slams my hands down into the earth, and I feel his magic pour through me and below.

"I am trying. What are you doing?" he yells. "How are you helping, you useless fucking demon?"

Something rolls in the ground beneath me, and I freeze. He must sense it because his brows draw together in confusion, and he removes his hands from mine as my body jerks again, something big rising below me in the dirt.

The ground under us continues to move, and we both sit up, our eyes wide as we stare at the rolling, upturning earth.

Please don't be a zombie or some fucked-up creature. Please don't be a zombie—

It breaks apart with a roar, dirt flying across us.

Yelping, I clutch onto Phrixius, who grips me too, as we blink at the creature in the hole.

Sha.

Clearing his throat, Phrixius shakes me off and brightens at the sight of Sha. "My magic must have summoned him," he explains.

Sha's eyes are closed, and he's unmoving. We share a look. "You check him."

"No, you." I push him, and he shoots me a glare before crawling over and kneeling before Sha.

"Sha?" he murmurs, and when there's no response, he clears his throat. "Sha?" he prompts louder.

"Touch him or something," I snap, and he throws another dirty look my way before gently laying his hand on Sha's chest.

"Sha, it's us. Are you in there?" he murmurs.

Sha jerks, his eyes snapping open and mouth parting in a vicious grin, and Phrixius jerks back as Sha leaps and pins him.

I sit back, my head tilted as Sha snarls in the god's face. "Help!" Phrixius yells to me.

Sighing, I clamber to my feet and stop at their side. "Sha, if you eat Phrixius, we cannot save Freya." His head snaps up, and his bright red eyes land on me. He appears more like a monster than the man she made. "Freya, you remember her?" He blinks, shutting his mouth. "I know you do. She's not gone. We are bringing her back." Crouching at his side, I smile softly. "I know you're in there, and she needs you, so don't eat the god. He's probably our only chance to get our girl back."

"Mistress," he hisses.

I nod. "Yes, your mistress, Freya."

He blinks again, and some humanity comes back into his eyes as he swings his gaze to Phrixius. "Bring her back."

"That's what we are going to do," he says, his hands still pressed to Sha's chest in case he tries to eat him again. "But for that, you need to not kill us first."

He watches us both for a moment before sitting back. It seems when Freya died, it took whatever made him human, but at the mention of her name, he is able to hold the animal back. I don't know how long it will last, so we need to act quickly.

"Bring her back." He nods. "Now."

"Yup, now seems like a good plan." I help Phrixius slide out from under him, and we share a tight look. "You heard the man—erm, monster," I mutter. "Bring her back now."

"Then there is one place we need to go," he says, dusting off his back and glaring at Sha.

"Where's that, oh mighty god?" I smirk as Sha snaps his teeth at him again. He really doesn't like the god right now.

"The pool of souls."

It's my turn to gape at him. "The pool of souls is a myth, a story for children—"

"It exists. The gods have protected it since the beginning of time. If we are to bring her back, then we need to find her soul there." He stands and offers me one hand and the other to Sha. "Let's go get our girl."

"Fucking gods," I mutter, but I take it and so does Sha, and within seconds, we are gone from the lake and transported across the world.

CHAPTER 49

The pool of souls is not a place I have ever been to, but I have heard of it many times. It's one of the most sacred secrets in this world, protected by the gods since the beginning of the universe. It holds ancient magic connected to death and rebirth, but it has no master. Not even Mors can control the pool, nor can he step foot here because something about his death magic messes with it.

It is our only hope.

We have to capture her soul before she passes on.

Standing before us is a snow-capped mountain, with clouds obscuring everything around us since we are so high up. All we can see is a narrow path leading to a black, yawning entrance carved into the side of the mountain. Power pulses from it, warning us away.

The language of the gods is carved above the entrance, cautioning those who would dare defile this holy place.

HERE, THE DEAD REST TO PASS—BEWARE, CORRUPTERS

"This is where the pool of souls is?" Adder teases, but I sense his discomfort. This is ancient holy ground, and he is a creature of sin, so it must weigh on him.

Sparing him a look, I nod. "Let's go." I head up the path. Either they will follow or won't, but I am not turning back. Her soul is in there, it has to be, and I will bring her back. At the entrance, I do not hesitate before I plunge into the darkness, feeling the magic pass across us.

It will either kill us or allow us entry if our hearts are pure.

I emerge into a stone cave with bioluminescent, glass-like stones. There are many levels to it, but down a set of carved steps is a deep, glowing pool. The water shines like a trapped gem, whirling with its own magic and motion. I expected more protection, but then I spy an ancient one lurking above us, and then another. They do not stop us, however, and I realise they are not here to protect the pool, but to help us.

Mors must have sent them, or more accurately, his mate, Avea.

I nod my gratitude and turn back as Adder and Sha stumble through. I breathe a sigh of relief because it let them pass. I know to bring her back, it will take all of us.

"What now?" Adder asks softly, no doubt sensing the importance of this place so he's serious for once.

"I am not sure."

He whirls to me, his eyes wide, and I rub at my head.

"It's not like I have done this before. I just knew there was a chance, and if there was, then she would be here."

"He's right. There's a chance," a deep, powerful voice calls, filling the space.

Whirling, I meet dark eyes as the person—no, the god steps from the shadows and faces me.

Not a god, I correct, a fallen god.

This must be the father of demons.

"You are seeking the soul of your love, no?" he asks, leaning against the rock as he watches us. "You would not be here if not."

"You said there was a chance." Adder steps closer. "Tell us how." Despite this being his creator, he does not seem bothered, demanding his assistance.

Luckily, he is not offended and bows his head. "I sense you are one of mine. I am sorry for your loss, though it is interesting. You love the one you have lost."

Adder's nostrils flare. "Yes. I know I am not capable of love—"

"Everybody is capable of love," he murmurs while watching Adder. "I was, and so are you. The fact that you are here only proves it. Us creatures of evil tend to love deeper than most others. We cling to the light and hope that love offers us, banishing the darkness from our souls. How long ago did you lose her? That will make a difference."

"Recently," Adder replies, relaxing slightly. "We are here to bring her back. If you try to stop us—"

"I am not here to stop you, blood of mine. I am here to help you." He pushes from the rock. "Is she capable of surviving death?"

"No grave can hold our witch," I tell him. "She is here, I know it."

"Why would you help us?" Adder asks. "You do not know us."

"No, but I know the agony in your eyes. I know the pain of losing the one you love. If I can help, I will."

"You are here for what you lost, your love," I murmur.

"Mine is no longer in there," he murmurs, "yet I always find myself here to check. There is not much time, as souls do not stay here forever. You will only get one chance to bring her back, and you must be strong enough to do so."

"Tell us how," I plead, bowing my head in respect. "I will give anything. My strength knows no bounds when it comes to her."

"Good, you'll need that determination." He looks at the pool once more. "To bring back what is lost, you will have to give a piece of yourself. A piece nobody should be able to live without. A soul must be taken and given, and it must have a host. However, if she is reborn from your sacrifice, it will live within her, and you will only be whole when you are together. You must make that decision—to live without your heart or your soul."

"She can have it. She can have it all," I say without hesitation.

Adder and Sha agree instantly, and he smiles. "You will lose your godhood."

"I do not care. None of that matters, only her."

"A god in love is dangerous indeed. That's what they told me at least. Personally, I always found we were more powerful." He glances at the pool. "Go, before it is too late. I wish you well. I hope you find your love and will be whole again."

Nodding my thanks, I share a look with the others. "You do not have to do this. I can go alone."

"No, it is not just you who loves her, god," Adder snaps. "Besides, she's had my soul since the day she was born." He smiles softly and heads down the steps as I glance at Sha.

"She is mine," is all he says before he follows Adder.

Taking a deep breath, I turn and pass them, marching down the steps to the glowing water. As my feet touch the edge of the swirling liquid, power washes over me, making me gasp. It feels wrong to touch it, as if I'm defiling life itself, but I ignore it as I step deeper.

Despite its appearance, the water only goes to our knees, and we sink into its glowing depths. Kneeling there, we face each other. I hold out my hand, and Adder takes it, nodding at me, then I offer my other one to Sha. He places his in mine before taking Adder's. We are connected, and as one, we bow our heads above the flowing water.

We do not speak as we wait, our hearts open as we pour our agony and grief into the waters, asking for her return. We beg this pure power to give her to us, and in offering, we give up our souls.

It hears us. The water rises around us to create a glowing, circular wall of water, spinning until it shoots into our chests like spears. I jerk from the force, my mouth opening on a silent scream as it reaches deep inside me, carving out my soul.

I do not fight it. I give it up, even as pure pain pours through me. I am dying, I am being torn apart, but I still do not ask it to stop. I allow it to take what it wants. I feel every molecule being torn from me, as if I am bleeding from a thousand cuts. I keep my eyes locked on Adder and Sha, who do the same.

The spears of water glow where they pierce our chests, and then our skin begins to shine with power. As I watch, those spears grow down like roots, hitting the water and sinking deep into the pool.

The water starts to rise like a cradle, cupping a bright orb that I know is my Freya.

It's her soul, and it is beautiful.

It rises through the water towards us, our souls flowing down in its place. We are just balls of agony, lost, empty shells of what we were.

I glance up and see the fallen god step back into the shadows, his eyes glistening with tears.

She will be reborn, and we will have her back, while he is doomed to watch.

The glowing orb continues to rise until it glistens in the light between us, and I stare at it in awe. "Freya." I do not know if I speak or think it, but I put my love into that one word. "Come back to us."

The spears pull from our chests, and the last thing I see as I plunge face-first into the water is her glowing soul beginning to expand, joining ours.

CHAPTER 50

freya

I do not remember where I am or what happened.

One moment, everything is dark, and the next, my eyes are snapping open, my chest expanding with a deep gasp as if I haven't breathed in a very long time.

I blink as I stare at a glowing ceiling, trying to remember where I am. Did I fall asleep? This isn't my home. What happened?

My brain is slow, but my body buzzes with strength and power I didn't know I possessed. Turning my head, I frown, not understanding what I'm seeing for a moment. My arm is stretched out, dipping into some glowing water, and there are shapes in it.

I sit upright, gaping in horror as I take in the scene.

My men are floating in the pool.

Adder is the closest to me. His face is turned away from me and his tail is limp. Sha is next to him, his eyes open but unseeing, and beyond them is Phrixius.

My god is face down, his blond hair spread around him like a halo.

"No!" My scream echoes through the cavern, and I throw myself into the water.

I scramble into the pool. I don't know what I'm doing, but I thrust my hands into the water and reach for them. I grasp Adder's arm first, tugging him up. I lay him down on the rock. He is motionless and his eyes are closed, but I do not have time to worry. I turn and grip Sha, pulling him out and laying him next to Adder, and then I wade into the pool and grab Phrixius, flipping him over. His eyes are closed as I pull him out with a grunt and lay him beside Adder and Sha. Their feet dangle into the water as I scramble up, first heading to Adder. I press my head to his chest and listen, but there's no heartbeat.

"No, you don't get to leave me." Guided by something beyond my knowledge, I cup his cheeks and press my lips to his. Something passes between us, and I swear I feel something click, tethering us together like a rope.

He gasps, his eyes snapping open and clashing with mine. I pull back as he breathes. "Little witch," he whispers.

Grinning, I kiss him before turning and kissing Sha. Once more, I feel that click, and another rope pulls taut. His eyes open with shocking brightness, his lips moving against mine until I pull away. He shudders, breathing rapidly.

"Mistress," he murmurs as he tries to pull me closer, but I climb over him with another swift kiss before leaning over Phrixius and pressing my lips to his.

Once more, something passes from me to him, and another thread snaps into place until it feels like I am whole once more. A sense of rightness fills me as memories bombard my brain, including things I did not experience, but I push them away to sort through later.

I collapse on top of Phrixius, feeling him take a deep inhale before his eyes open.

"Freya," he whispers.

"I'm here," I murmur.

"You're alive." He tugs me over him and kisses me again.

Pulling back to breathe, I grin at him as I feel the others move closer. Adder's hands slide down me possessively, while Sha's lips find my shoulders. All of them touch me, and when they do, something pulses happily inside me.

As I lean over Phrixius, movement draws my gaze up, and I find a man watching us with an expression of pure longing on his face before he blinks it away and smiles at me.

"I am glad you're whole."

I know instantly who he is and why he is in pain. It's not knowledge I possessed before, but Phrixius did, and it came into my mind as if I were born with it.

He starts to back into the darkness, and somehow, I know if he leaves now, he will be lost to this world. He is tired and hurting, but the world needs him, so I plunge myself back into the pool, my eyes on him.

"I have only used my powers for evil so far, but let me help you." I reach deep within the pool. I know no living being should be able to do this, but somehow, I know I can.

Our powers mix inside me.

The combined magic of a necromancer, a god, a demon, and a creature fills me, making me stronger than any being on Earth, and as I plunge my hand into the water, I demand it return what it stole. I demand it listen to me as I reach into the place of the dead beyond and call to the one he lost.

I feel her on the other side, lingering like he is. Closing my eyes, I push my intention into the water and force the pool to open in her world, then I yank her through. Two hands slap into mine, and I grip them, yanking her up and out.

My eyes open, and I meet the bright orbs of a woman as she gasps.

Smiling, I look at the fallen god, who gapes. "My love," he croaks.

Her head turns, and she cries out, releasing me and throwing herself towards him, screaming his name.

He stumbles over and drops to his knees, and they crash together in an embrace, laughing and crying. I fall back, but as usual, my men are there to catch me, holding me up.

I lean back into my men, exhausted and hurting, but I can't help smiling as we watch them kiss like they will never let each other go again.

I'm beginning to understand myself more as I watch them.

Being a necromancer isn't about being evil. Like with all magic, it's about intention. We are not born evil, we are made evil, and although this thing inside me craves death and destruction, it also craves life and laughter, and I will feed it both.

There is no right or wrong, no good or evil, just the grey area we all live in, and if we're lucky enough, the grey will sparkle with the colours of those around us.

I glance at my colours and smile. "Take me home."

CHAPTER 51

freya

I wish I could say it was not weird being dead, but I can't remember it. However, from the pain in my guys' eyes as we appear in my house, I know they have not forgotten, nor will they anytime soon.

"I am sorry—" I start, but my words are cut off as Adder closes the distance between us and crushes me in his arms. When he pulls back, he kisses me deeply.

"If you ever try to leave this world without me again, I'll bring you back once more and kill you myself, you hear me, little witch?" he warns, but despite his words, his tail wraps around my thigh, tugging me closer.

"Okay." I grin as I lean into his warmth. I feel his pounding heart, and when we are connected, something just feels right, like puzzle pieces sliding together.

More arms wrap around me, and I lean into Sha. He kisses my cheek, and I turn my head to kiss him deeper. "I cannot exist without you, nor do I want to," he murmurs. "Death cannot have you."

"I'll tell it." I grin and turn my head, meeting Phrixius's gaze. He swallows, and I hold out my hand. I know he's struggling. He watched me die, and I know him well enough to understand he's blaming himself. Guilt eats away at him, even though he's happy.

"Phrixius," I call. "I need you."

That does it. He's unable to deny me anything, so he takes my hand and wraps his arms around me, holding us all as our lips come together. When he pulls back, I kiss across him softly. "I am sorry you had to see that, and I am sorry it hurt you. I just wanted to protect you."

"I know," he murmurs. "Nothing else matters now. You are back, and at this moment, that is all I care about. Everything else can fuck off."

"Did you just curse? It seems I've corrupted you." I giggle, and his wide smile lets me know he will be okay.

"You have," he murmurs, gripping my cheeks and bowing his head. "Corrupt me again, right now. Reclaim me, my necromancer, and bring me back to life."

"Bring us all back," Sha requests, licking my neck. "Remind us you are here, and wipe away the memories of losing you."

My gasp is swallowed by them as their hands slide over me, and something about this new bond between us awakens with their touch, increasing the pleasure of each stroke.

My head is turned, and a forked tongue sweeps across my lips. "Let us make another deal—my soul for your heart and body for eternity."

"Deal," I croak, and he groans, kissing me deeply as I lose myself in them.

They are right. Everything else can wait as I hand myself over to them.

They lay me down on the floor of my home, their hands sliding across me. Lips kiss every inch of me. We are one, all connected, so my pleasure is theirs and theirs is mine. It rolls through us, bringing us back to life.

A mouth meets my cunt, and the other two wrap around my nipples. I cry out, reaching down to cradle their heads. I see horns pressed to my stomach, and Adder's eyes are locked on me as he licks my cunt. Throwing my legs over his shoulders, I press harder against his face, riding him as Sha and Phrixius bite my nipples.

Their magic and shadows slide across me like a caress, and I swear we glow, but all I care about is that they keep touching me.

I cry out Adder's name as he nips my clit, and when his tail pushes inside me, I crumble, tipping over the edge. My pleasure explodes through us, and I'm ripped from Adder and rolled so I sit astride Sha. He slams me down on his cock, making us both groan. It hurts so fucking good, and I can feel his pleasure.

My nails seem to lengthen, and I stab them into his chest like blades, using them as leverage as I ride him. My darkness seeps into every bit of him. It's only then I realise his power, his life, is flowing into me from my nails in his chest.

I'm feeding on him.

I try to pull back, but he covers my hand. "It's an honour to feed you, mistress. Feed, use me . . . I'm yours."

I can't hold back. I ride him harder, feeding until I feel like I'll explode.

I feel Sha's heart stop as I drain him. He dies with a smile on his face, trusting me, and within two heartbeats, I bring him back, our soul link and my magic working in tandem. He groans, fucking deeper inside me like nothing happened. One of his tentacles slides into my ass, claiming it.

I'm bent forward by Phrixius, and he presses inside my ass alongside Sha's tentacle, filling me to bursting, but I know I can take it.

I was made for them.

That's why no one else ever satisfied me.

My head is jerked up, and I reach out blindly, touching horns. Adder groans and kisses me, swallowing my cries while Phrixius and Sha fuck me. Finally, he pulls away, and I open my mouth, waiting. His eyes glow with fire when he sees that, and he slides a hand through my hair as he presses inside my mouth.

Pleasure and power explode between us as we connect, and we all bellow.

The world darkens, the earth shakes, and we shatter.

Pleasure rolls through us until it finally frees us, leaving us all sweating and panting.

My lips taste of cum, and I feel it in both my holes. I can't help but laugh. They join in, and I hold them tighter, knowing that whatever happens next, no one can ever take this away from us.

We will always have each other.

CHAPTER 52

Our little paradise cannot last forever. Despite being locked in my home for two days straight, where they showed me how much they missed me, I know we have other things to deal with. The gods will not give up if they know I am alive.

They will hunt me forever, and moreover, I am a danger to my coven.

As I look over my sleeping men, I realise one thing—this place is not my home anymore—they are.

If I remain here, I could put everyone in danger, not to mention I do not wish to hide anymore and the coven will never accept who or what I am. I also can't be away from my men, which means I will have to leave. It makes me sad because this place has been my shelter, my protection, and my home for so long, but I know it's time to move on. It's time to find out who I really am and enjoy my life.

For now, though, I soak in the morning light and quiet happiness we have fought hard for, and I let them rest, knowing they will need it.

I do not know where we will go. I suppose it depends on if we survive the gods' wrath or not, but as long as we are together, it does not matter.

I was right. Our peace could not last forever. Word has spread of my return, and the coven has amassed outside my home. I dress and pack up the last of my things, boxing them in case we have time to come back, and then I step out to face them.

Agatha stands there, but she looks worried, not hostile. Stepping closer, I take her hands and kiss the backs of them. "Thank you for everything you've done for me. You sheltered me and took me in despite knowing what I was. I will forever owe you my life for that."

"You owe me nothing. You were an innocent child, one of us, I simply did what was right. I owed your mother—" She swallows, and tears well in her eyes. "I see it in you now, that power."

"I am okay," I promise. "I will not harm anyone." I glance back at my men. "They are here to make sure of it."

"They will never allow you to live." She squeezes my hands. "You must hide."

"No, I am done hiding." After kissing her hands once more, I step back. "I will leave, and I will not be back. I will not endanger anyone here, and I know despite you all thinking I'm odd and strange, you have loved me, protected me, and lived with me. I will miss this place, but if you ever need me, I will be here. I will always answer your call." I look back at Agatha. "It's time I found my own home, though, and time I found a future rather than living in the present."

"I wish you all the luck in the world," she calls brightly. "Word has spread about what happened in the city. The threat is gone, and we are all safe once more thanks to you. Remind them of that if they come for you. Remind them what you sacrificed, and tell them evil is not born, it's created. You, my child, are not evil. You never were and never will be, not with a heart so full. Whenever you need a reminder, come back here. There will always be a home for you," she promises.

Taking Phrixius's hand, I nod and smile, looking over the coven that I realise did not come out of fear, but out of concern, to say goodbye.

I spare a glance at Phrixius. "Take us to the gods. Let us end this so we can move on." I glance back at my coven and smile. No words can express how thankful I am for this life. They will always be part of it, but I'm excited for what's to come.

We fade and appear on the dais, the one I died upon not too long ago.

There are no chains on my wrists this time, and my men stand at my side as the gods appear, called by the disturbance.

"How?" they ask as they all speak as one.

I hold up my hands. "I will stop the abomination, pervert of nature talk right here," I warn them, arching my eyebrow. "We are here to make a deal and finish this so we can move on with our lives."

"There is no moving on. Your death is demanded."

I roll my eyes, and Phrixius steps forward. "And her death was given," he retorts. "You will not get it again. She is linked to us now. Our souls reside in her. If you kill her, you will kill us all. You might be okay with killing a necromancer or a demon or even a creature of the night, but can you kill one of your own? Fallen or not, I am tied to this world, and killing me would alter it. You know that."

They look unsettled, all except Mors, who grins, winking at me when I catch his eye.

"Freya has already died, so she has paid her price. She will not commit any crimes. Our magic helps her control who and what she is. She is not evil. She is simply asking for a chance at life. We cannot keep repeating history. It is time for a new future. The world is changing, and so must we. I ask you to spare us. I ask you to make a deal with us. In return, I will leave this place with her and be at her side forever, protecting her and keeping an eye on her. All I ask is that you allow us to leave and do not follow us."

"You would give up everything for her?"

"I already have," he says proudly. "And I have never been happier."

"I see no issue," Mors remarks. "Technically, the necromancer died, and what is standing there is a mix of a god, a creature, a demon, and a witch."

"If we allow her to live, then we are announcing that we condone necromancers being born and living," someone else says.

"Is that such a bad thing?" Mors retorts. "The dark wars are over, so leave them in the past. I say let's give necromancers another chance. They might just surprise you. Plus, this world needs a bit more dark magic to fight true evil out there."

"Blasphemy!"

"Oh, shut up, Vanessa," Mors snaps. "You're boring me. We'll kill the evil ones, like always, but we'll let the innocent live. It seems like a fair deal to me." Mors stands. "Now hurry up and make the deal. I wish to get back to my mate. I left her in bed, and she will be angry when I return." He looks far too happy about that.

The gods share a look, and I hold my breath. Can they truly embrace the chance, or will this all be for nothing?

"If—and that is a big if—we allow this deal, then you cannot go back to your coven. You are too much of a risk."

"I don't plan to," I reply, "nor do I wish to harm anyone. I just want to be given the same opportunity as anyone else to have a life, free from looking over my shoulder."

"I suppose we have no choice," Vanessa murmurs. "We cannot kill Phrixius, he is right, so we'll make a deal. This will not change overnight because there is too much history with the necromancers, but maybe we should give them a chance—one chance. If they prove they cannot live amongst us again, then we will not hesitate to end their kind, you included."

I smile brightly. "You won't need to." I truly believe that because it's all about how you are shaped a person. We are not inherently evil, and we will show them that. We will be reborn.

"Then leave this place and do not return. We will not follow, but we will be watching all you heathens."

I grin and glance at my men. "Heathens, I like it."

"Go now, before we change our minds," one calls.

"You don't have to tell me twice," Adder mutters, making me grin.

Turning away, we head to the end of the pavilion as I take Phrixius's hand once more. Adder holds my free one, and Sha holds Adder's.

"Where do we go now?" Sha asks, glancing at us.

"Not back," I murmur, staring at our joined hands and smiling at them. "We'll go forward and find somewhere new to be our home."

CHAPTER 53

freya

"Well?" Adder asks nervously from my side. Phrixius stands behind us, and Sha is to my left. We are on a small hill, overlooking the empty land before us. There is a lake to the right, which shines brightly under the sun, and a forest in the back leading to a red-tipped mountain. There's an old church to the left, forgotten and abandoned, and so much sprawling green land that I cannot help but grin. The arched welcome sign from before stands down the path from us.

Something about it calls to me. It's the perfect mix of life and death, a place that's been forgotten and abused, just like us.

"It's perfect," I murmur, shooting him a wide grin to see his own relieved smile. Sha and Phrixius sigh in relief. I don't blame them. I have been searching for weeks for the perfect place. Every time we have come up empty, I know they have taken it hard, since I left everything else behind. What they don't understand is that I have everything I need right here at my side, and now it's time to start fresh.

This will be a new home for all of us, but also others like me who are born with my gifts and shunned. This will be a home of learning, laughter, love, and death.

It's time to bring the necromancers into the light and give them a court like everyone else has.

A court of heathens.

This time, it will be above ground because we are not hiding anymore.

Taking the first step, I head down the hill, my hands held out on either side as I go. Magic flows from my fingertips, merging life and death, and something new blooms into existence. Black flowers slither from the grass, mixed with purple and red, and they spring up on either side of me as I walk. A path forms under my feet, leading into the heart of the land, where I stop and sink to my knees, thrust my hands into the earth, and close my eyes.

I pour my intention into it, and when I straighten and step back, roots dig deep into the land before bursting from the earth, and as we watch, a great tree grows. It reaches far into the sky to offer shelter and remembrance. Once it's finished, I fashion a blade in my hand and step towards the street. Silently, I begin to carve before I step back. Three names are now etched there forever.

William Great—the necromancer.

Serenity Great—his wife.

Ryan Great—their child.

No matter what, they need to be remembered. That is what this place will be—a memorial for those who were lost and a place to grieve without guilt.

"What do you think?" I ask as I reach back blindly for them.

Hands take mine, and more press to my shoulders as they surround me and peer at the tree. "It's perfect." Adder kisses my neck.

"I like it," Phrixius adds.

"Now to build a home," Sha says.

Smiling, I close my eyes and send my power out into our land. I feel it take root and change. I know when I open my eyes, a new home for us will have grown, where we can love and laugh and be together.

When I glance at it, I want to cry. It's not a cave anymore, it's a grand cottage, and I know this is where I will live until the earth finally calls me home. When my time comes, this is where I will lie to rest with my men at my side.

I turn to my men and grin. "Spread the word to all four corners of the world. Welcome those like me. It's time for them to come home."

Three Months Later

Our home has expanded over the last few months. There are so many new houses on this land, I have lost count. Word spread quickly, but it was weeks until the first person stepped foot here. I saw fear in their eyes, but there was also hope. We welcomed them, and ever since, someone else arrives every day.

Life is beginning here again. Each person who comes has their own story of survival. Some are young, and some are old, but we all have one thing in common—what we are and what we have lost.

The tree's bark now holds so many names, I ache when I see them, each person that comes adding more, adding their losses and their lessons. Like that tree, we will stand tall, creating new roots and offering shelter.

As I watch our land bustle and grow, I cannot help thinking about how hard it was to get here and how much was lost, but everything I have gained has made it that much more worth it.

I lost myself along the way, but they found me again, and I know they always will.

I hear a grumble and smile, knowing Teddy will be playing with the kids again. I returned to my cave and brought him back—he's ours, after all. He makes a good pet. Our pet zombie . . . I even let Adder keep the hand, Bobby, and it's currently cooking in the kitchen.

Flicking my fingers, I watch the water balloon soar through the air and hit Phrixius in the back of the head. He whirls to me, his eyes widening in shock since Adder had been chasing him with them.

He gives me the tiniest shake of his head, but his smile is wide as I grin at him. "Don't you join in, that's cheating!" he calls, even as he laughs and ducks under Adder's reach.

Sha suddenly appears before them and dumps a full bucket of water over my god before racing towards me and hiding behind me. Laughing loudly, I lean back into his arms as Phrixius storms over.

"Is that how it is?" he grouses, blowing wet hair from his mouth. He grabs me, and I squeal as he tugs me closer, soaking me through, but it soon turns into a moan as he kisses me. When he pulls back, I'm smiling for a whole other reason.

I was worried he would regret losing his godhood, but I have seen him embrace this life and become so happy that I know he doesn't. He found his purpose with us.

Adder suddenly appears and presses his lips to Phrixius's cheek before dancing back. Phrixius groans and wipes it away. "Demon," he warns.

"Catch me if you can, god," he taunts, and then he winks at me before he races away, a fallen god and a monster chasing after him.

"Are you coming?" Adder calls. As I look at all three of their grinning faces, I can't help but overflow with love.

"I'm coming," I reply as I hurry after them.

I might have been born a necromancer, but I chose to be something more important—theirs.

EPILOGUE

Lifting my head groggily, I feel blood drip from my parted lips along with my breath. My ribs are definitely broken—at least two, or maybe more. Betrayal sits thickly on my tongue as I stare at the men I trusted with my life, my soul, and my future.

We are family. We have been together for years. I might not have always agreed with their methods, but I agreed with the end result—until now . . . until this.

As the very elite of our kind, we have survived things no others have by trusting in one another and fighting side by side, but as I stare at them now, all I see are strangers willing to hurt innocents—strangers willing to torture and imprison me, one of their own, to get what they want.

They are corrupt. It has taken me too long to see it, and now I am left without any options or freedom. Everything we have built lies in tatters, and my belief in our kind, in what we do, is gone.

My dreams and hopes were all broken along with my body.

"I am sorry, Tate," Eric, one of our youngest and newest recruits, says as he walks to the cell door.

"You will be," I spit.

"You won't make it out of here alive to make us," Sergeant Black says as he wipes his blade clean of my blood and grins at me. I knew the first time I met him, he was capable of evil, but it was aimed in the right direction until it wasn't anymore.

"We'll see about that." I smirk, even as it causes agony to ripple through me.

He simply spares me a disgusted look. "We could have been great together, Tate, an unstoppable unit. Such a waste. Now, if you'll excuse us, we have some hunting to do." I watch him walk away, and I feel hatred so strong, I'm surprised he cannot feel it licking at his skin like a flame.

The outer door slams shut with Black's mocking laughter, and I let my fury fill me.

They won't get away with this.

I will hunt down every ounce of evil within our house and destroy them all.

It's time I become a monster rather than just hunting them.

Sometimes, it takes evil to fight evil, and before this ends, my soul will be as black as theirs.

ABOUT K.A. KNIGHT

K.A Knight is an USA Today bestselling indie author trying to get all of the stories and characters out of her head, writing the monsters that you love to hate. She loves reading and devours every book she can get her hands on, and she also has a worrying caffeine addiction.

She leads her double life in a sleepy English town, where she spends her days writing like a crazy person.

Read more at K.A Knight's website or join her Facebook Reader Group.
Sign up for exclusive content and my newsletter here
http://eepurl.com/drLLoj

OTHER BOOKS BY K.A. KNIGHT

CONTEMPORARY

LEGENDS AND LOVE *CONTEMPORARY RH*

Revolt

Rebel

Riot

PRETTY LIARS *CONTEMPORARY RH*

Unstoppable

Unbreakable

PINE VALLEY COLLEGE *CONTEMPORARY*

Racing Hearts

DEN OF VIPERS UNIVERSE STANDALONES

Scarlett Limerence *CONTEMPORARY*

Nadia's Salvation *CONTEMPORARY*

Alena's Revenge *CONTEMPORARY*

Den of Vipers *CONTEMPORARY RH*

Gangsters and Guns (Co-Write with Loxley Savage) *CONTEMPORARY RH*

FORBIDDEN READS *(STANDALONES)*

Daddy's Angel *CONTEMPORARY*

Stepbrothers' Darling *CONTEMPORARY RH*

STANDALONES

The Standby *CONTEMPORARY*

Diver's Heart *CONTEMPORARY RH*

DYSTOPIAN

THEIR CHAMPION SERIES *Dystopian RH*

The Wasteland

The Summit

The Cities

The Nations

Their Champion Coloring Book

Their Champion - the omnibus

The Forgotten

The Lost

The Damned

Their Champion Companion - the omnibus

PARANORMAL

THE LOST COVEN SERIES *PNR RH*

Aurora's Coven

Aurora's Betrayal

Book 3 - *coming soon..*

HER MONSTERS SERIES *PNR RH*

Rage

Hate

Book 3 - *coming soon..*

COURTS AND KINGS *PNR RH*

Court of Nightmares

Court of Death

Court of Beasts

Court of Heathens

Court of Evil - coming soon…

THE FALLEN GODS SERIES *PNR*

Pretty Painful

Pretty Bloody

Pretty Stormy

Pretty Wild

Pretty Hot

Pretty Faces

Pretty Spelled

Fallen Gods - the omnibus 1

Fallen Gods - the omnibus 2

FORGOTTEN CITY *PNR*

Monstrous Lies

Monstrous Truths

Monstrous Ends

SCIENCE FICTION

DAWNBREAKER SERIES *SCI FI RH*

Voyage to Ayama

Dreaming of Ayama

STANDALONES

Crown of Stars *SCI FI RH*

SHARED WORLD PROJECTS

Blade of Iris - Mafia Wars *CONTEMPORARY RH*

CO-WRITES

CO-AUTHOR PROJECTS - *Erin O'Kane*

HER FREAKS SERIES *PNR Dystopian RH*

Circus Save Me

Taming The Ringmaster

Walking the Tightrope

Her Freaks Series - the omnibus

STANDALONES

Kingdom of Crowns and Daggers *DARK FANTSY RH*

The Hero Complex *PNR RH*

Dark Temptations *Collection of Short Stories, ft. One Night Only & Circus Saves Christmas*

THE WILD BOYS SERIES *CONTEMPORARY RH*

The Wild Interview

The Wild Tour

The Wild Finale

The Wild Boys - the omnibus

CO-AUTHOR PROJECTS - *Ivy Fox*

Deadly Love Series *CONTEMPORARY*

Deadly Affair

Deadly Match

Deadly Encounter

CO-AUTHOR PROJECTS - *Kendra Moreno*

STANDALONES

Stolen Trophy *CONTEMPORARY RH*

Fractured Shadows *PNR RH*

Shadowed Heart

Burn Me *PNR*

Cirque Obscurum *PNR RH*

CO-AUTHOR PROJECTS - *Loxley Savage*

THE FORSAKEN SERIES *SCI FI RH*

Capturing Carmen

Stealing Shiloh

Harboring Harlow

STANDALONES

Gangsters and Guns *CONTEMPORARY*, IN DEN OF VIPERS' UNIVERSE

OTHER CO-WRITES

Shipwreck Souls *(with Kendra Moreno & Poppy Woods)*

The Horror Emporium *(with Kendra Moreno & Poppy Woods)*

AUDIOBOOKS

The Wasteland

The Summit

The Cities

The Nations - *coming soon*

Rage

Hate

Den of Vipers *(From Podium Audio)*

Gangsters and Guns *(From Podium Audio)*

Daddy's Angel *(From Podium Audio)*

Stepbrothers' Darling *(From Podium Audio)*

Blade of Iris *(From Podium Audio)*

Deadly Affair *(From Podium Audio)*

Deadly Match *(From Podium Audio)*

Deadly Encounter *(From Podium Audio)*

Stolen Trophy *(From Podium Audio)*

Crown of Stars *(From Podium Audio)*

Monstrous Lies *(From Podium Audio)*

Monstrous Truth *(From Podium Audio)*

Monstrous Ends *(From Podium Audio)*

Court of Nightmares *(From Podium Audio)*

Court of Death *(From Podium Audio)*

Unstoppable *(From Podium Audio)*

Unbreakable *(From Podium Audio)*

Fractured Shadows *(From Podium Audio)*

Shadowed Heart *(From Podium Audio)*

Revolt *(From Podium Audio)*

Rebel *(From Podium Audio) - coming soon*

FIND AN ERROR?

Please email this information to thenuttyformatter1@gmail.com:

- *the author name*
- *title of the book*
- *screenshot of the error*
- *suggested correction*